# THE BLADE IN THE ANGEL'S SHADOW

# THE BLADE IN THE ANGEL'S SHADOW

## ANDY DARBY

Tiny Blue Alien Press

First published by Tiny Blue Alien Press 2024



First edition



First Printing, 2024

For Jane and Emily

# Prologue

Black as the wings of the ravens that legend has it will roost at the Tower until doomsday, the robes of the slender figure blow in the sudden wind. He gathers them to him and glances up at the lead-coloured clouds piling up along the skyline. A slight shiver as his eyes pass over the corpses hanging from gibbets on Tower Hill and the misplaced shadows that seem to hover there; then he ducks his head down as a faint drizzle sweeps across the open ground.

His robes mark him as a man of learning, but the quality of the cloth gives away his position. Not a threadbare lawyer this one. The skull cap above his long, pale face accentuates the features of a man used to working late into the night. Bright, mirthless eyes that miss nothing. He has a long, greying beard that flows over the unfashionably restrained ruff around his slender neck. This is a man who knows things.

Beauchamp Tower looms above him, and the warders at the dark wood and iron-studded door usher him inside as the lack-lustre drizzle finds its venom and becomes a squall that sweeps across the flagstones.

"Good evening to you, Dr Dee." He is a large man this warder, made larger by the cuirass of polished steel wrapping around his not inconsiderable belly. A dense, straw-coloured beard bristles above the metal plate, and although he looks like he could be formidable, he has a friendly enough smile.

"You have brought the weather with you. There was no sign of this a while ago." He waves a large hand to indicate the now violent downpour.

"Aye, Sergeant Hobert, you are not wrong there. When I boarded the wherry at Bridewell, we were in the midst of God's glorious autumn, and now we appear to be in January!"

The second warder, whom Dr Dee does not know, closes the wicket gate behind him, shutting out the spiteful, stinging rain. Dee studies the lean fellow with a practised eye and decides that this one is here because he has no squeamishness when it comes to inflicting pain upon his fellow man.

"This is your last visit then, doctor?" Sergeant Hobert leads the way into the dark interior of the tower.

"I fear so. Your charge has her appointment with the scaffold in two days, and that cannot be changed except by Her Majesty, which I am certain will not happen." Dee follows the Sergeant's bulk to a narrow stairway, and they begin to ascend.

In the shadowy glow of the candles, Dr Dee notices, not for the first time, the stains on the narrow stair walls. Grubby, sweating palms have left their ghostly marks as their owners have braced against the stone as they made their way to their appointment with the rack or the executioner. The good doctor can almost feel the dread leaking from the ancient walls.

"Will it be a late one again, doctor?" they make a right turn at the first landing as the Sergeant glances over his shoulder to make sure that Dee has heard his question.

"I fear, good master Hobert, that it will be tomorrow before I have finished with Lament Evyngar. She has sent a message that her confession is finished, but I must hear it from her lips. There can be no ambiguity in the meaning. When a woman is accused of attempting to kill the Queen, it must be clear that no others are waiting to take up her failed task." *And,* he thinks, *when the sort of heresy that he has heard come from Evyngar's lips since her return from the Low Countries is linked to his name, he must be ahead of any possible repercussions.* After all, he may be the Queen's pet astrologer, as some contemptuously call him, but she has a nasty habit of dropping favourites, even valuable ones as if they have the plague.

"Well, I will have a chair brought in for you and some supper later. Beel will attend in the corridor should you require anything else." Dee raises a quizzical eyebrow, and the sergeant responds.

"The other man at the gate. He was sent over from Newgate the day before yesterday. Odd sort, but I takes who I'm given." And Dee gets the feeling that this *Beel* may be in the pay of certain members of the Privy Council.

Sergeant Hobert leans in and adds in a low voice, "The prisoner has been talking to herself again, often in different voices. I think she may have lost her reason." But Dee raises an eyebrow and says nothing, holding his judgement.

They come to a halt before a low door. The iron grill set into it reveals not much more than shadows, but as it swings open and the lantern light spills into the cell, there is one shadow that refuses to scuttle into the corners. Sitting on the edge of the cot bed, a figure hunches, clutching a sheaf of papers to her chest. She wears a dirty white shift, not her usual attire, at least before her incarceration. Her left hand is bound in filthy rags, her posture giving mute evidence of a woman who has been put to the hard press, a woman who has been physically broken over many months. She rocks a little as they enter the room before coming to a sudden stop that makes Dee think that the scene before him has been transformed into a grim painting.

The woman's eyes look up at Dee; her face is returning to its normal proportions as the swelling from expert beatings recedes, but purple and green bruises are still a stain that is gradually turning yellow across a once handsome face usually marred only by a narrow diagonal scar.

"Ah, Lament, you have been ill-used." Crossing the small room quickly, he places a hand on the seated woman's unusually broad shoulders, and Lament flinches at the touch. The rack is no friend to the shoulder joints.

Sergeant Hobert frowns a little at the intimacy shown to a traitor by one of the Queen's trusted councillors, but his is not to question, just to make sure that the prisoner is fit and well enough to greet the executioner at the allotted time.

"I will have Beel bring in a chair and a jug of wine. Would you like him to set a fire?"

"No, no, if he brings in some kindling and a taper, I can manage that. I fear it is going to be a long night, and I would soonest get it started." Dee has no wish for Beel to be in the room any longer than he must be. The more he thinks of the man, the more he smells the machinations of the Privy Council.

"As you wish, doctor. If you need anything, you have only to ask." Dipping his large head slightly, Hobert leaves them to it, and Dee can hear him giving instructions to the waiting Beel as he moves down the passage.

A chair has been brought, and as the hard-faced warder, his greasy hair constantly falling over one eye, brings in a tray with a jug of wine and two cups, Dee busies himself with lighting a fire in the small, cold fireplace. His influence and the once-good family name of Lament Evyngar have conspired to procure her a cell of moderate comfort. And, of course, having access to a relatively large supply of coin has meant that the prisoner has been reasonably well fed, at least with pottage.

As the fire catches and Beel departs to his station in the passageway, Dr Dee settles himself into the chair and pours two cups of the watered-down wine. He holds one out to the woman opposite, who for a moment just stares at it, and then as if remembering what should happen in ordinary life, she puts the sheaf of papers down on the cot and reaches out painfully to take the proffered cup. Her blue-grey eyes, still a little bloodshot from the violence of torture, stare into the wine with a faraway intensity, and then she slowly brings it to her damaged lips and takes a long gulp.

Dee allows her to settle herself, gazing at a woman who seems to have aged immeasurably during her months of incarceration. She is obviously in pain, but there is more to it than that. It is as if some part of her has been lost, and Dee realises that it was noticeable when Lament returned from the Low Countries this last time before her attempt on the Queen's life.

"Did you know when you recruited me into your service that

it would end like this?" There is no accusation in Lament's voice, just a weary resignation.

"No, Lament. There are always risks involved in magic, but much of this you have brought upon yourself." Dee puts down his cup and leans forward, steepling his fingers as he stares at the young woman opposite him.

A hard look enters Lament's eyes, "But you are the Queen's astrologer, are you not? You saw nothing in the cold stars?"

The irony is not lost on Dee, and he shakes his head sadly. "Mere mortals can only glimpse the possible future. Once the dice are cast, we must all take our chances..." The look on Lament's face stops the platitudes that would have sought to make an excuse.

"What is it that you saw, Lament? When you returned, you would not speak of what occurred during your commission, and we never had a chance to fully discuss events which I suspect may have unhinged you. And then things became... a little problematic."

Lament holds the cup to her lips again, but she does not drink. It is as if the act gives her some sort of comfort. Instead, she speaks across the rim of the cup.

"It is all written down here, doctor. I have left nothing out. They may take my breath, but they will not take my deeds." There is anger in these last words.

"I know, and I thank you. But I would hear it from your lips, and there will be time to read what you have written later..." Dee inwardly curses himself for his callousness, but it is done now, and time is running away from them.

Lament gives a harsh laugh, which turns into a cough, and

she drinks more wine to calm it. "Where shall we begin then, doctor? I have a fancy that we should begin at the beginning, as maybe that will cast light on later events in a way that I have not yet seen. Or maybe it may give you pause when you are reading my confession... later."

Dee holds up his hands, but before he can begin to make an apology, Lament continues. "No matter, I think we are beyond that now, you and I. Let us start where this ill-fated venture began, and may whatever gods there be have mercy upon us."

# Chapter 1

The door of the tavern swings open, and for a moment, a gust of differently stinking air clears the stench of ale fumes, sweat, and meat searing in the kitchen. The group of revellers who enter are already the worst for drink, and it is clear to all that they are actors from one of the nearby theatres. They have a reputation for drunken squabbling these thespians, one that can often lead to drawn blades. They commandeer a table near the fire and shout for ale.

Captain Lament Evyngar pushes back a stray lock of dark hair from her forehead and grins at the look on her vast companion's face. Lament is not a small woman at an inch below six feet and broad of shoulder as befits a swordswoman, but her companion towers over her by more than half a foot. Lament has always imagined the man next to her as more bear than human and frequently taunts him that they need to steer clear of the baiting pits lest he be mistaken for an escapee unless, of course, they need the extra coin. Sergeant Pieter Hertgers, her massive friend, does not take offence at these jokes. He is rather pleased at being considered so great and fierce. But he has no love of actors.

"Come now, Pieter, take that scowl off your face. You will sour the ale!" Lament slaps the giant upper arm propped up by an elbow on the table boards.

"Strutting, miserable, painted bastards." Pieter manages to growl between gulps of knockdown. His Dutch accent gets stronger the more he drinks, and he has consumed quite a lot. His large head is shaved down to a scar crisscrossed red stubble on top, while the bristling beard of the same colour mostly obscures his lower face. It is not the face of a man that you would willingly want to upset.

Lament knows what Pieter thinks of actors. That they are jumped-up fools who believe that just because they enjoy a little notoriety, they can behave how they please, mainly because they have never been tested. Maybe, but it would not be such a happy result to end up attracting the attention of the Watch because his massive paws have crushed a few heads. So, Lament steers the conversation back to the topic they had been discussing before the arrival of the players.

"What think you then? Shall we throw in our lot with the wine merchant and become vintners?" They have considered many options for a life beyond that of a soldier; they both have more than a passing interest in wine. Pieter's family have dabbled in the sale of wine and ale in his hometown of Hamburg, where they fled to escape the Spanish, so he believes there would seem to be some merit in this career move.

"Aye, it makes more than a little sense. We can use my paters contacts to bring in good Rhenish, and we should turn a handsome profit if we keep a close eye on the merchant. I still think we will miss the ring of steel, though, and we have made good coin these last few years." He gives his coin purse a fond pat and grins wide, showing off broad, white teeth.

"We have discussed this my friend. We need a new venture, something that is not tainted by the stench of the charnel house. Besides, there are always rich men who are willing to pay handsomely for the services of good bodyguards when they travel. At least we would not be fighting off hordes of Spanish intent on putting us to the torch as heretics!"

Pieter nods his great head, but the look in his eyes says that he is not entirely convinced. Coming as he does from a family of Calvinists, he has more zeal for fighting the Catholic armies in the Spanish Netherlands. Lament is far more pragmatic.

As the youngest daughter of a minor knight of the realm, Lady Lament Evyngar learned quickly to adapt her religious alliances. Born into a Catholic family, it had become a death sentence not to renounce the faith after the death of Mary and the ascension of Elizabeth, and although her parents and older sisters are recusants, she sees little distinction in the chanting of one priest or another.

Only the symbology and ornateness of the setting seem to make a difference despite the arguments of theologians as to whether you can talk directly to God or not without the intermediary of a priest. The fact that she has personally sent more than a few Catholics to their afterlife while not being struck down by a bolt from above adds to her conviction that, in the end, there is little to separate them.

"My friend, we can always try our hands as merchants for twelve months, and if it doesn't suit or is not profitable, then we can easily re-enlist with one of the companies heading off to the Low Countries and go back to our old trade." She raises the mug of ale, drains it and then wipes the back of her hand across her lips. She is considered not uncomely in a handsome sort of way, this soldier of fortune. Not perhaps the charming, good looks of the ladies of the court, especially with the fine scar that bisects her face from left eyebrow to right cheek, more the roguish charms of a woman who has lived a life of adventure. That's fine by her.

Pieter rises off the low bench; he cannot stand up straight as the ceiling of the Bull Tavern is several inches too low for most men, and a colossus like the Dutchman stands no chance. The group of players by the fire go quiet as he eclipses the room. They nudge each other, but fortunately, this evening, none are drunk or foolhardy enough to make the sort of comment that might cause Pieter to break someone.

Lament passes coin to the tavern keeper, a pot-bellied man with the sort of bulbous nose and broken veined skin that speaks of a fondness for his wares.

"Thank you, Captain. God give you good rest." He drops the coins into a large pocket on the front of his leather apron and clears the empty ale jug and mugs off the table.

"You too, Arthur," smiles Lament as she settles the wide-brimmed black hat with its single red feather upon her dark hair and follows the bulk of her companion out through the doorway and into the early evening light of Southwark.

"Shall we away and see this merchant then? He said he would be free to talk after his last delivery of the day." Lament watches as Pieter dons his barett, the wide slouch hat with the hidden steel cap from his days as a Landsknecht and wanders over to an alley between two rows of buildings that look like they might just fall against each other for moral support. The brickwork is crooked, and the timbers sag, but like most of the buildings that have been around since at least the time of the last King Edward, they will most likely last another hundred years. Although the way Pieter is pissing against that one may undermine its foundations. The thought makes Lament laugh.

Pieter grins as he laces up his breeches, the coloured ostrich feathers adorning his barett bobbing in time to his movements. "Needed that! Yes, let's go and talk to your merchant. If nothing else, we may be able to sample his stock."

* * *

London Bridge stretches out before them. The severed heads of traitors glare impotent and eyeless from above the south gateway as they pass. Lament grips the finely wrought hilt of her sword just a little tighter. It is not as if she is unaccustomed to death, but the heads above the gate always leave her with a sense of unease each time she passes. Pieter seems oblivious, humming a tune that Lament does not recognise but can guess is from his homeland. He, too, wears a sword, although not the slimmer-bladed type of Lament's sword; no Pieter carries a falchion, a long butcher's blade, in the baldric slung across his vast frame. But even this is delicate when compared to the zweihander sword, which is his favoured weapon on the battlefield. The falchion is a compromise so that he does not draw even more attention to himself by parading the streets of London with nearly seven feet of steel.

Pieter had learned his trade as a Landsknecht fighting alongside the Germans and then taking the coin of William of Orange after a series of ill-fated adventures had left his regiment decimated. So, back to the Netherlands and latching onto an English mercenary force where he met and immediately befriended Captain Lament Evyngar. Immediately meaning amid a pitched battle and befriended meaning back-to-back fighting for their lives. Pieter had thought Lament a little too skinny, but he could not deny her skill with sword and pistol. Lament had been more concerned that the giant behind her might accidentally cut her in half with an ill-timed swing of his two-hander or take a ball and fall upon her, crushing her to death. They have been inseparable friends ever since.

They enter the already twilight world of the bridge. The dwellings, shops, and warehouses that line the sides of the bridge cut out much of the evening light, and there are lanterns placed at regular intervals. Now and then, they pass through a bright window of light formed by narrow gaps between the structures. Here, there are precipitous views down to the river and the fiercely turbulent current that roars against the starlings and drives around the water mills set between the arches.

A multitude jostles their way across the bridge. Horses and carts force their way through pedestrians who wander in and out of the shops or stop to buy pies and baked eels from the women who carry them in baskets on their heads. The usual collection of purse-divers and ne'er-do-wells are on the lookout for the naïve to swindle or rob outright. There will be more than one fellow the worse from drink who wakes in a doorway to find he is missing his coin purse and possibly most of his clothes. The cutpurse's eye Lament and Pieter from a distance. This pair promise nothing but hard knocks and sharp steel, and there is far easier prey to be had in this twilight arcade of noise and smells.

Towards the northern end of the bridge, Lament turns to the open half of a large gate leading into the courtyard of a warehouse. The hanging wooden signs above the gate advertise the goods on offer, and one of the signs is three barrels.

A short flight of stairs leads up to a loading dock and a series of winches, and there, half in shadow, is the stocky frame of the merchant they have come to meet talking to another man.

"Ah, Captain! May God give you good ease." The merchant turns away from his warehouseman, dismissing him by the mere act of giving him no further attention. The lean figure slinks away deeper into the shadows and pools of black that chequer the cavernous storeroom. As he goes, he casts a furtive look over his shoulder at his master's guests. Lament catches the glance and unconsciously notes the direction the man goes in.

"Useless addle pate that one." The merchant sighs. "I took on him and his cousin after my two lads went down with the sweating sickness these six months gone. God rest 'em." He scratches the thick, greying beard that grows like a spear point from his jutting chin. He is broad around but not fat. Years of manhandling his stock have given him a strong body and kept him from getting too portly, despite the best efforts of his new wife to fatten him up.

"Yes, Master Thomas, we will have to recruit better help for you if we are to have a successful enterprise. It wouldn't do to let incompetent buffoons ruin business now, would it?" Lament grins and claps Thomas on the back as they make their way up to the locked office where he plots his business ventures. A quick search through the keys on the brass ring attached by a chain to his belt, the door creaks open, and they enter a low-ceilinged room. A small window that overlooks the Thames lets in the last of the daylight through open shutters, and Thomas augments it with candles lit from the lantern by the door. Flickering yellow light reveals the shelves around the walls with their casks, bags of spice, and bolts of cloth, all samples from the storehouse below them.

He gestures for his potential business collaborators to sit in the chairs placed around a table spread with parchment and maps as he collects three glasses and a couple of bottles from one of the shelves. As he uncorks the bottles, Lament sifts through the pile of gilded trinkets strewn across one of the maps. They are covered in intricate geometric designs, and the artistry fascinates her.

"From the land of the Moors", says Thomas, pouring wine into the drinking vessels. "Fine workmanship even if it is done by heathen barbarians." He laughs with the pragmatic humour of the trader and hands the drinks to Lament and Pieter.

"This is a Flemish wine. It is sweet and heady. It is a favourite of many at court, and I have managed to secure all of the current stock." He smiles, very pleased with himself and the knowledge that he can dictate the price.

"With your connections," he nods at Pieter, who downs the wine with an appreciative grunt, "we can bring it in via the Netherlands and avoid the Spanish. The captain tells me that your father deals with the Sea Beggars." He refills the glass enveloped in Pieter's massive fist. Thomas is more than a little intimidated by the huge, grinning Dutchman.

"Aye, he does. He has aided them with supplies and safe anchorage against the Dons. In return, they run trade goods through the blockades. A mutual benefit to all." He smiles and takes another large gulp of the newly refilled wine, smacking his lips with relish.

"Well, with all of the stock of this wine, plus a large quantity of brandy I have secured and a consignment of nutmeg and cinnamon captured from a Spanish ship, we will be sitting pretty on the profits of our first venture." He raises his glass to toast their anticipated good fortune, and Lament and Pieter join him.

"Are you happy, Pieter? I told you this would mark a change in our fortunes." Lament gives the big man a good-natured nudge with her foot, and Pieter turns his glass upside down to show it is empty.

"I would be even more content with a further sample of the goods."

* * *

It is dark when Thomas shows them out of the warehouse, and they bid him God's ease. They walk further north along the bridge. Pieter has heard tales of a particular stew, and the wine has his blood up. When they reach the door, the bawd sizes them up and recognises them as adventurers who still have full purses.

"Friends, welcome." She smiles a most welcoming smile and gives an arch wink. Placing her small hand on Pieter's massive chest, she lets her eyes travel up and down his colossal frame.

"I am not sure we have enough girls to satisfy you, sir. But we can try our best!" She lets out a shrieking laugh and turns to lead them inside.

Lament puts her hand on her comrade's arm.

"I am going back to the merchant. I have a desire for more of that Flemish wine; I will procure a cask and come back. Try to leave something for me." She slaps the laughing Pieter on the back and heads off south again along the bridge.

As she approaches the gate to the darkened warehouse, there is a muffled crash, and the sound pottery makes when it is broken with some force. *Thomas must have had more of his wares than usual*, thinks Lament as she reaches up to pull the chain that rings the bell within the storerooms. She stops. The gate is slightly ajar. She knows that Thomas closed it behind them.

Pushing gently against the gate, she slips through and lets her eyes become accustomed to the deeper gloom within. When she is sure of her surroundings, Lament quickly mounts the stairs to the loading dock, keeping to the sides to avoid any unnecessary squeaking. The door to the store is open, and she can make out the office door at the far end, the glow of lantern light bleeding out around its frame.

She halts when she hears raised voices, trying to discern how many and the possible reason for the increasingly angry tones. There is a choked scream followed by an agonised groan that trails into a whimper. A voice laughs cruelly, and there is another strangled moan.

Drawing her sword, Lament advances silently between the stacks of crates, bulging sacks, and barrels that form low walls on either side of her. She flings the office door open, and there before her is the scene of a butcher's shop.

Thomas is face down over the table. Most of his clothes have been torn away, and long iron nails have fixed his hands to the wood with brutal efficiency. A bunched-up rag is stuffed into his mouth, and his eyes bulge with fear and pain.

The two other occupants of the room stare open-mouthed at the intruder. Lament recognises the lean figure holding the bloody awl which he has been twisting into the merchant's thigh. The warehouseman pulls the awl free of the quivering flesh, causing Thomas to shriek through the gag and brandishes it at the woman who has surprised them. Lament's sword takes him through his still gaping mouth and exits the back of his skull and out of his felt cap.

His accomplice, who Lament guesses to be the cousin, grabs for the hand axe lying on the table. The fingers missing from both of the merchant's hands would indicate that it has already seen action. As Lament withdraws her blade from the first man's head and lets him fall to the boards, the second gives an enraged cry and lunges forward. The axe describes an arc that Lament easily avoids, and before her assailant can return with a back-hand stroke, the sword darts out and enters him through the armpit. He staggers backwards into the racks holding the wine casks and drags them down on top of him as he falls.

The merchant is dying. The wound to his thigh has severed the artery, and despite the pressure that Lament puts on the wound, the blood flows without stopping. It is impossible to free his ruined hands from the table without causing further agony, and all Lament can do is stay with him as his life flees.

"Bastards wanted money. They… they thought we had done a deal and that you… and that you had left me with a heavy purse." A cough rakes through him, causing a spasm that twists the iron in his hands and makes him cry out.

"Fuck them! May they burn in hell!" There are several diminishing sobs and then another spasm and stillness.

Lament releases the pressure on the wound and sits on the table next to the red ruin of the man who was to be their business partner. She wipes her blade clean on the warehouseman's shirt and slides it back into the scabbard. But before it finds its home, she hears another sound. Movement in the storeroom, and once again, the sword is in her hand.

The Watch dislike open doors at night. They have been tasked to be especially vigilant as papist spies and assassins have been reported to be increasingly active. So, seeing the open gate to the warehouse, they take it upon themselves to investigate.

Not that they are overly worried. They are two large men wearing cheap but effective breastplates; both wear kettle helmets, and they carry swords and cudgels. The taller of the two also carries a pike, although in the confines of the warehouse, it might not be of much use. But the main cause of their confidence is the huge mastiff that accompanies them, drooling jowls barely hiding teeth that can crush a man's bones.

The lantern they bring with them illuminates the stairs and the loading dock. The door into the store is wide open, and they glance at each other as if to confirm their suspicions.

As they enter the storehouse, the mastiff begins a low growl in his thick throat. The watchman holding him allows the chain to run out through calloused fingers so that the beast is a good two yards ahead. It gives a bark that is more like the sound of a saw blade ripping through timber, and it strains against the chain as a figure appears silhouetted against the open door and lantern light at the far end of the rows of trade goods.

The figure is holding a sword, but she quickly places it on the floorboards as her eyes take in the great, snarling dog and the armed men sheltering behind it.

"Good sirs, there has been foul murder. Master Thomas has been put to the hard press by villains who were in his employ, and he has died of the injuries." Lament makes the quick decision to tell her side of the story with all speed before the mastiff is released upon her. She knows she could best the watchmen in a fight, but the dog changes the odds considerably, which is, after all, why they have it with them.

"I have slain the murderers. I came upon them in the act of torture, and when they attacked me, I delivered them to God's justice." She opens her hands out at her sides to show she means no threat.

The watchman holding the dog gestures for her to go back into the office.

"Master Thomas is dead, you say. Back into the room then and show us what has occurred." He nods to his companion, who scoops up the sword as they pass, noting the well-worn black hilt of a sword that is meant for warfare, not gentlemanly duels.

Back in the merchant's office, it is a scene from hell. The stench of blood and emptied bowels fills the room. The watchmen visibly pale.

"It's like the fucking shambles in here! What in Christ's

name has occurred?" The watchman with the pike finds his voice breaking, gagging on the stench.

"I was here earlier conducting some business with Master Thomas. I came back to procure a cask of his wine and found the gate open, and these two..." Lament indicates the body on the floor by the table and the other partially buried by the tumbled contents of the storage rack.

"They worked for Thomas, and before he died, he vouched safe to me that they believed I had paid him a large amount of coin, and they were pressing him to ascertain its location. I defended myself, and they died, as I told you in the storeroom."

The watchman with the dog pulls the chain with a violent jerk to stop the mastiff from lapping up the rapidly congealing blood on the floor. He seems to be senior in rank and puffs out his iron-cased chest.

"That's as well, but we will have to summon the justice."

There is a groan from the corner of the room, and he swings the lantern in his free hand to illuminate the wreckage.

"This one's not dead! George, drag him out from under there." He keeps his eyes on Lament as the watchman called George leans his pike against the wall along with Lament's sword, and kicking casks, boxes, and bottles out of the way, he grabs the groaning form by the ankles and drags him out into the light.

As soon as he is out into the room, the man looks around at the scene. The dead merchant, his dead cousin, the woman that the merchant called *Captain*, and the two watchmen with their massive blood-stained dog. He clutches the wound in his side, and a feral light, a desperate light, comes into his eyes.

"God save me from this traitorous heretic! She was in league with Thomas, the merchant. They planned to smuggle Jesuit agents into the realm from the Spanish Netherlands hidden in the shipment of wine. My poor cousin Ralph," he points at the body on the floor, "and myself overheard them plotting. Them and a big foreign sort, Ralph said he sounded Dutch. When this one and the foreigner had left, Ralph said that we should do our loyal duty to Her Majesty and find out the details of their plan. So, we put Thomas to the hard press, and he had just confessed that they was in league with the agents of the Anti-Christ to bring murder and mayhem into our fair land, even to the body of the Queen herself, when that bitch comes back and runs through poor Ralph! I do believe she has done for me also..." He falls back against the sideboard, coughing and wheezing. Pink bubbles form in the corner of his mouth, and it is obvious that his lung has been pierced.

Lament stands there, her jaw dropped. She gives a harsh laugh and is just about to ridicule the man when she sees the looks on the faces of the watchmen. To them, this is the most serious of accusations. A papist plot to destabilise England and imperil Her Majesty. This will not be the first or last heretic they will bring to justice, and their eyes fix upon Lament with a steely resolve.

"Come now, good fellows. You cannot believe this nonsense! He and his cousin must have dreamt up this rouse in case they were caught in the act. Why would they take it upon themselves to try to extract a confession instead of bringing their suspicions to the authorities?" She looks down at her accuser, but there is no response. The man has passed out or worse.

"You will get your say in good time, but now you will

accompany us to Bridewell and wait for the magistrates' ruling on all this. I dare say that officers of the Privy Council will need to question you as well."

Captain Lament Evyngar wishes now that she had stayed in the bawdy house with Pieter or maybe not given up her sword. She feels an impending sense of doom as only a woman who comes from a family of recusants can when she is accused of heresy and plotting regicide.

* * *

It has taken Pieter two days to track Lament down. Two days in which Lament has sat in a dirty cell on a straw pallet in Newgate.

Her full purse has brought her these meagre comforts, but she is getting increasingly bored and likely to cause a riot. Pieter gives her an all-encompassing hug, lifting her off the ground and laughing at her protestations. But he knows that it is a serious charge that has been brought against the captain, one in which he could be implicated.

Lament relates the events that occurred at the merchants, and Pieter nods, a black scowl on his scarred face.

"The only saving grace seems to be that the local constable knows the Hooper family, of whom the cousins were members. They are well known for their larceny and for running gangs of cutpurses on this side of the river. There is not much belief in the confession that the scum gave before he drowned in his blood, but it is a serious accusation and, therefore, will come before a magistrate. I also killed two men under unclear circumstances.

With any luck, I will be able to pay the blood price to their family, and that will be the end of it, but I have a fear that the stain of being accused of heresy may not be so easily wiped away." Lament takes a welcome sup from the wineskin that the big Dutchman has brought with him.

Pieter stares at her and shakes his head, a grin splitting his wide face.

"You should have stayed at the stew, my friend. Far less trouble when you are tupping wenches; you just have to dodge the French pox." Then his face clouds over.

"They know about your families' beliefs?"

Lament nods and takes another swig of the wine.

"Yes, unfortunately, they do. It seems that my reputation precedes me."

"Then they should know that you have killed your fair share of Catholics. They should know that you serve the Protestant cause." He reaches out a huge paw of a hand and takes the skin.

"Will they be looking for me?" He asks between gulps.

"You were mentioned in the accusation, but the fact that you were not there and that this seems to have become just a question of the killings... I think you will be ignored if you refrain from trouble." They both grin at that, and then Lament's narrow face becomes serious, and she strokes stray hair from her face as she stares at her friend. "Seriously, Pieter. Keep your head down, and do not attract any more attention than you need to. There is a zeal to seek out the heretics, an obsession, and I wouldst not have us swept into oblivion by it."

Pieter takes his leave, saying that he will enquire as to when the magistrate will sit and decide Lament's case, but for the present, he leaves some more coin to make the captain's stay more comfortable.

* * *

They come for Lament in the dead of night. Four large men clad in padded leather and steel, wearing helmets. They manacle her wrists and ankles and then lead her out to the water stairs leading down to the lead-coloured surface of the Thames.

There is no moon, and the sparse cloud is blown in ribbons across the vault of the sky. Before she can protest, a heavy hood is dragged over her head, and she is manhandled down the stairs and out onto the waiting wherry that is invisible in the shadows.

Her thoughts turn immediately to escape, and just as quickly, those thoughts are disregarded. Manacled, on a wherry casting off onto the Thames at night... Even without the four guards, that would be a recipe for drowning. So, Lament calms the rising voices clamouring in her head and runs through the possible reasons why she might be moved under guard at night. Another gaol? There is no good reason to transport her at this hour. Unless they have decided that the accusations of heresy and plotting assassination have merits, then they could be taking her to a very different location, one where she might expect to be put to questioning. She knows what to expect if that is the case; she has seen it often enough in the Low Countries, administered by both sides.

That is the only explanation for this journey that her mind can conjure, and suddenly, the night has grown very cold.

# Chapter 2

The wherry bumps against the jetty, and as it is tied off, Lament is hauled off the bench and onto her feet. One of the men-at-arms guarding her speaks to another armed figure waiting behind an iron gate set into the high wall. There is a rattling of keys, and a heavy bolt slides across, and then the gate swings open silently on well-greased hinges.

Lament is well aware that the journey has been a short one and, as far as she can ascertain, upriver. There is a sinking feeling in the pit of her stomach. They could well be at Somerset House or possibly even Northumberland House, but either one bodes ill. They both have something of a reputation for having deep cellars in which confessions are extracted by less than delicate means.

A man stands on either side of her and takes an arm, and she is marched as best her manacled ankles will manage through the gate and into a passageway lit by guttering torches. Not that she can tell as the hood is still firmly pulled down around her neck.

There are several right and left turns and two more heavy doors before they climb a short flight of steps, and the air becomes less damp and musty. Even through the hood, Lament can smell the difference.

They stop at another heavy wooden door bound with iron straps. But this time, her guards stand and fidget as if they are on uncertain ground. There is a brief nod from one to the other, and after wiping his hand nervously on his padded arming jacket, he knocks on the door, pulling his hand away quickly as if he is afraid of being burnt.

When there is no response, the other guard nudges him. "Go on, knock again. This time louder." He looks around nervously at the shadows as he eggs his comrade on. His comrade scowls and wishes he had stayed back at the wherry, but all the same, he lifts his fist and bangs with a little more vigour on the dark surface of the door.

There is nothing for a moment, and then the door creaks inwards, and Lament suddenly smells strange exotic aromas that work their way beneath the hood. She is shocked for an instant as some of them remind her of the incense burnt during Catholic mass. Smells that unwillingly take her back to her childhood in a vivid rush.

*Instructed by the family chaplain, the young Lament reads her catechism and primer. She recites the paternoster and the Ave Maria. She observes the fasts and celebrates the feasts. She prays for her family and the souls of her dead ancestors and goes to confession. She receives instruction for her first communion, the consecrated wafer, the transubstantiation.*

With a jolt, she comes back to the present. A deep, low voice bids them enter, and she shuffles through the doorway with her escort in front and behind. The voice commands that the hood be removed, and as it is pulled none too gently from her head, Lament blinks hard at the sudden brightness of the many candles arranged around the room.

There before Lament stands a tall, lean figure in the black robes of a scholar; a black skull cap hugs his long, narrow head, and a long, greying beard falls over the modest ruff that circles his narrow throat. There is a calculating look in the intelligent eyes, and for a brief moment, Lament believes she catches a glimpse of something else – perhaps pity.

"Remove her manacles and return to your duties. I have no further need of you this night." The manacles are rapidly undone, and the black-robed figure ushers the guards from the chamber with more than a little impatience. When the door is closed, he turns to Lament, and the shadow of a smile crosses the saturnine features.

"Sit you down, good Captain. We have much to discuss, you and I." He motions Lament to one of a pair of finely carved chairs. "Sit, sit."

Lament obliges. As her eyes become accustomed to the light, she takes in the strange paraphernalia around the room. Braziers, copper flasks perched on trivets, glass orbs and peculiar black mirrors. There is a waist-high rectangle standing on one of its ends in the centre of the chamber. Geometric grids in which oddly unnerving figures that look like some sort of writing are painted upon its dark sides. On its top is a disk that could be wax, which has been etched with concentric circles and stars and more of the strange writing.

Censors hang from the beams of the low ceiling, and Lament

is aware once again of the heavy scent of frankincense and something else that she cannot identify.

"Why have you had me brought here, sir, in the dead of night and with such covert drama?" As she speaks, Lament ties her hair back once again. The bag placed over her head had been no respecter of any attempt to keep the hair from her face.

"All in good time, Captain, although I must offer my apologies for the clandestine nature of our meeting and the unnecessary roughness of your escort. They have their uses, but they are not subtle instruments." He sits in the other chair, taking a goblet from a small table beside him and passes it to Lament, and with only a moment's hesitation, she takes a thirsty swig of the sack it contains.

Her black-clad host nods and smiles. "You are not afraid that I might poison you?"

"If you wanted me dead, sir, it was in your gift to have me done away with long before you had me sit in this chair. The river could have claimed my body without the necessity of having to meet me in person. You look like a man who can afford a decent vintage, so why waste a drink?" Lament takes another sup as her host appraises her.

"My name, Captain, is Dr John Dee. Have you heard of me?"

Lament lowers the goblet and raises one eyebrow. "I know of you, sir. I know that you are Her Majesty's astrologer. I believe that it was you who provided the Queen with the most auspicious date for her coronation."

"Oh, to be remembered for something greater!" Dr Dee laughs, but it is a mirthless laugh, as if at a joke that is no longer funny.

"I have dreams, Captain Evyngar, dreams that will outlast the reign of even so great a queen." He gazes off into a distance that only he can see, lost for a moment in a vision that encompasses millennia, and then his eyes snap back onto Lament.

"So, good Captain, you will aid me in making those dreams a reality. And in return, the charges that stand against you will be dropped."

Lament gives an amused grunt and places the goblet on the oriental pattern rug that separates her chair from Dee's.

"Come now, sir! I defended myself from the foul brigands who tortured and murdered my business partner. When I get to court, I may be asked for the blood price, but that I can discharge, and then I will be on my way. So, pray tell, why should I aid you in your scheming?"

Dee steeples his long fingers, and his gaze is once again calculating when he responds. "But you have been declared a heretic, an enemy of the state. In the current climate, the Privy Council does not play Hazard without holding all the cards. Even a small possibility that a Jesuit assassin may be on the loose is enough for them to call for Richard Topcliffe."

The mention of the infamous interrogator causes Lament to narrow her eyes. There are serious forces in motion, and in times such as these, it is not enough to know that you are innocent when an accusation has been made against you.

"What if I would take my chances? After all, I served with honour in the Low Countries, and many would vouch for my loyalty and my faith." She sits back in the chair and wonders how far she would get if she throttled the life from this gaunt mage and made her escape.

"You may have converted to the true faith, but we know that your family are recusants. They could be brought to account. Lands and titles are no longer protection for those who follow the blasphemous teachings of Rome. It would be a shameful thing to see your father, mother, and sisters on the rack. If they were convicted of aiding a popish plot, then the women may even face the stake and your father the scaffold. It only takes a word in the right ear to set tragedies in motion..." Dee's eyes stare into Lament's over the tips of his fingers, still pressed together. Perhaps he senses just how close to death he is in that moment, but he is a man who is used to staring into the void.

"And there is the matter of your large comrade. A Dutchman, is he not? It would be an easy thing to have him taken into custody and charged with being a papist sympathiser. I believe he served with a regiment in the Spanish Netherlands under the Dons. Perhaps his allegiances have never altered?"

"You clearly know little of my sergeant if you think it an easy task to take him. However, you do seem well acquainted with his soldiering. You must know then that he served with the Landsknecht as a mercenary, and as with all mercenaries, you go where the coin is plentiful regardless of the paymaster." It is obvious to Lament that even should she brain this court magician and make her escape, her family and those she values would be forfeit. She is not so worried about Pieter; after all, he is not a man who has ever let long odds concern him. But...

"What do you want from me, Master Dee? What is it that draws me to your attention above all others?"

The doctor stands and goes over to a desk set against the wall. Its surface is littered with apparatus of exotic description. He reaches out both long-fingered hands, the rings glinting in the candlelight, and rests them on a large globe of the world that sits at its centre. Slowly, the fingers turn the globe on its pivot, the shapes of land masses coming into and going out of view.

Without turning, he begins to speak. "You are unique, Captain Lament Evyngar. Oh, I do not mean just as a swordswoman and adventurer; they are indeed uncommon in this realm. You, Captain, have the skill of moving effortlessly through difficult waters. Born a Catholic, yet you adopt the Protestant faith without the slightest hesitation. Your ability with a blade has become somewhat legendary, yet so has your ability to talk your way out of trouble. Simply put, Captain, you have a combination of malleable moral and ethical boundaries and the physical and mental capacities to make the best of any situation. This is not something that is common amongst the gentlemen who fight and swagger and preen like peacocks. Mayhap it is your female humours that give you an *edge.*"

The globe stops turning. Britain is set between the doctor's long fingers like a fly caught by a spider. *No, Lament decides, it is more like a jewel being caressed.*

"I have seen a future, a future told to me by the angels. We will have an empire, a British Empire, ruled by our most noble Queen, who is the descendant of Arthur." Lament observes the sudden tension that comes into this tall, lean figure as he speaks. There is undisguised zeal in the voice, and the fingers grip the surface of the globe, the tips turning white as if to drag the future from this inanimate object.

"There will be a time soon when Britain will rule over these other petty, squabbling nations." He spins the globe to indicate the rest of the world. "When our ships will command the oceans, and the trade routes will be ours. There is a start in the New World, but other lands will come under our dominion until we have created the greatest empire the world has ever known! When this is done, we will have brought all peoples to the true word of God and begun the work of Revelation. The Kingdom of Heaven will once more reign on Earth, and man will return to his natural place in the Garden." He raises his head and stares at Lament. There is an intensity in the cold eyes that verges on madness.

Lament does not pretend to understand these ravings and instead decides to question the practicality of Dee's plans. "Do you not imagine that Phillip of Spain might have ambitions that will conflict with yours? Or the Ottomans? There are other players in this game of conquest..." Lament raises her goblet again and drains the last of the sack, but her throat is still dry. The incense that is heavy in the air sucks the moisture from her mouth.

"Tell me, good Captain. Why did you return to England? You were riding high on the victories of which you were no small part. There would have been no shortage of plunder, no shortage of glory to be had, and it is not so frowned upon by our continental cousins for a woman to wield a sword. So why return when you did and decide that the life of a wine merchant was more to your liking?" Dee lifts the wine jug from the side table and refills Lament's goblet. Lament stares at the swirling contents as if hoping it might give her the words to explain. There have been many, many times when it took the thoughts away, and perhaps maybe it will return a few of them now.

"It was Bartholomew's Day. We received word that the French

had slaughtered the Huguenots, and there was a frenzy amongst the men. The stories were bad, but it was nothing we hadn't seen before, even been part of. But something was set afire in the men and fanned by the Calvinist preachers, and there was havoc. Catholic villages and towns were laid waste. None were spared as if it could balance out one wrong by exacting another. I stood and watched as soldiers I had known for many months on campaign became beasts, using religion as an excuse to torture and kill..." Lament drinks again.

"I was sick of it. We had stopped fighting the armies of the Dons, and we had begun to make war on civilians. It was the thing that we had always decried the Duke of Alba for – murdering women and children – and now we had become him."

Dee leans forward, his hands gripping the back of his chair, eyes piercing.

"There, Captain, there it is! You asked me why I want your help in my enterprise, well there is your answer. You are not like the men of this age. You are not driven by the words of preachers and the threat of hell or the promise of heaven. You are beyond that. You are already lost!"

Lament has the feeling that the floor has fallen away beneath her.

"I know about the preacher you murdered. There are eyes everywhere, and a good many of them belong to me. When I received the news that a captain serving with the English forces had wilfully assassinated a prominent Calvinist, seemingly because that Calvinist was inciting the slaughter of innocents, then I knew I had found my means. It would appear that the shadows in the church were dark enough to hide another on that night.

Oh, do not fret; it is not common knowledge. And in truth, it is no crime on these shores to have murdered a foreign preacher. Although there are those who would say that it pointed towards certain sympathies."

Jaw muscles clench, and eyes narrow at the memory. Lament doesn't feel she needs to justify her action, but she does so anyway, just to make sure that this Dr Dee understands what type of woman she is.

"The preacher was a bastard of the first order. When we arrived, he had already sanctioned the pressing of a dozen women for the purpose, he claimed, of establishing the guilt of their men folk. Whether they had taken up arms against Protestants, whether they had rejoiced at the actions of the French, they could not ask the men as they were already hanging from anything that would take a rope. So, in absentia, they crushed their women folk slowly to death. We rode into the town square as they were burning the children. They were herded into wooden animal cages, screaming for their mothers as they were roasted to death. And that fucking priest chanting as to their destination in the everlasting fires of hell while the men at arms cheered and drank their stolen wine."

A savage smile twists Lament's face into a demon mask in the candlelight. "I followed him into the church later that night. All the popish trappings had already been smashed or looted, and he was standing by the altar with an ecstatic smile upon his face, exhilarated by the death he had caused in the name of the same god as the murdering lunatics who had run amok in Paris. I knew then, as I cut his throat that I wanted no more to do with these wars of faith. He had to die to stop him from initiating more of what I had witnessed!" Lament slumps back in her chair. Her hand trembles slightly, and she grips the goblet with both hands to prevent from spilling its contents.

Dee smiles a not-unkind smile and sits down opposite Lament. He leans forward, and there is excitement mingled with intensity as he speaks again.

"I would change all this, Captain. I would put an end to this killing over whose image of the Almighty is correct. We can take the world into a new age, but we can only do it if we are strong enough to be the power that leads. The power that sets the rules by which this great game is played." His hands reach out and grip Lament's, who does not seem to possess the strength to pull away.

"You will aid me, Lament Evyngar. You will aid me because you want change in this world, or you will aid me to save your family from the rack. I would wish it to be the former, but in the end, it matters not which it is because you will be my instrument."

The room seems to grow darker, and suddenly, Lament wonders if she has been drugged. She watches Dr Dee rise and go to the door from where he calls for a guard. Then, Lament is partly carried to a chamber a little further down the corridor. She slumps onto the cot bed and tries to make her vision focus on the tall, black-robed figure in the doorway.

"Rest Captain. On the morrow, I will explain your mission, and we will do what is necessary for you to be successful in its completion."

And not for the first time does Lament wish she had stayed at the stew with Pieter instead of going back to the merchants.

Dr Dee returns to the candle-lit chamber, a look of satisfaction on his vulture-like features. There is much to prepare for tomorrow, and so he begins to collect the ancient grimoires and the trappings of his art.

# Chapter 3

The plague has returned, and on top of that, Pieter has become aware that he is being followed.

Bidding farewell to the wenches of the Bankside bawdy house where he passed last night, Pieter makes his way down through Southwark towards the Bull. He stops to buy a coney pie for his breakfast from a comely young woman with a basket of savouries balanced on her ample hip. As he flirts with her, he spies the figure in the short grey cloak and hood standing by the corner of the square. As soon as the man realises he has attracted the big Dutchman's attention, he moves quickly off into a side street.

Pieter watches the man scuttle away, but his thoughts are drawn back to the pretty young pie seller who is telling him that there has been an outbreak of the plague north of the river.

As he continues to the Bull, it is evident that folk are concerned about the news of the pestilence. They avoid walking too close to strangers, and he sees a stream of people coming from the direction of the apothecary with packages and bottles that he knows will be used to ward off the plague. Having seen its effects in the Netherlands, he also knows that these packages and bottles probably contain nothing but false confidence. When it comes a calling, there is nothing to be done. Death can't be bargained with, nor can it be diverted with a few bags of herbs. It would be best if Lament gets out of gaol, and they put some leagues between themselves and the contagion before it takes hold of the city.

As he enters the Bull, he catches a movement out of the corner of his eye, and he is sure it is the man in grey again. He stoops through the doorway and, once inside the dimly lit tavern, takes a seat in the corner along from the door. From here, he can see dimly through the tiny polished horn panes into the street beyond. The taproom boy brings him a jug of ale without being prompted, and he nods his thanks to Arthur, the tavern keeper and returns to his watch.

*There!* The grey figure sidles out of a side alley and leans casually against the wooden corner beam of a house. He shifts his weight to make himself more comfortable, the sagging brick-work providing a better resting place, and the shadows from the overhanging second floor give more cover. But Pieter knows he is there, and it doesn't take much to pick out his shape if you know what you are looking for.

The morning wears on, and a second jug of ale follows the first. The Dutchman's capacity for drink is enormous, but he avoids the knock-down, sticking to a weaker beer so that he has all his faculties about him. The watcher may be a fraction of his size and not a particularly able spy, but the fact that he is relaxed in an area known for cutpurses and villains gives Pieter cause to think that he is armed and capable. He has learnt over his years of soldiering that to underestimate an opponent can get you bloody or dead.

The watcher folds his arms beneath his short cloak. It is cooler in the shadows, and Pieter smiles at the man's discomfort as he calls for a bowl of pottage.

It is around a half hour after the ringing of the noon bell has sounded, and Pieter decides that enough is enough. This grey man owes him some answers.

He drops coin onto the bar top and nods to Arthur, who, like all good tavern keepers, has realised that something is afoot and today has resisted asking after Captain Evyngar's health to allow the big Dutch soldier to concentrate on whatever has grabbed his attention through the windowpanes.

*It must be at least three hours*, thinks Garrat Blexham as he pulls the short grey cloak tighter around his shoulders. The shadows of the overhang seemed God sent to keep him hidden from the tavern, but the weather had been unusually inclement of late, and today, the cold had started to gnaw at his bones.

The big Dutch bastard seems to do nothing but drink, eat, and whore, and all the while, he must lurk in some dark alley just in case anything of interest may occur. He is cursing his luck at being chosen for this task when a vast paw of a hand closes on his shoulder, and he is pushed violently back against the sagging brickwork.

Garrat's instinct is to go for the dagger at his hip, but another hand with fingers as thick as mooring rope closes around his wrist with a crushing force that draws a groan from his thin lips.

Pieter had left the Bull through a small courtyard at its rear, climbed a low wall and dropped into the alleyway that ran behind. Then, it was just a matter of following the alley to the next street and cutting around to the far side of the watching man so that he could step around the corner and be upon him before he was aware. For a big man, Pieter can move with great speed and delicacy when needed, something he attributes to the compulsory dancing that he and his fellow Landsknechts had to perform. It had greatly increased their fighting footwork and stamina and had proved to be popular amongst the men. He prides himself on his dancing skill, which is always a winner with the wenches, and smiles brightly at his talent as he crushes the grey-clad figure against the wall.

He lifts the struggling man bodily and drags him along the length of the wall to the alley where he had stopped for a piss before he and Lament had set off to see the wine merchant on that fateful evening. Skilfully, he disarms the man before throwing him into the dirt of the alley. Pieter kneels over him, his left knee pressing down on the narrow chest, and he pulls back the grey hood.

The face, gone deathly pale, is marked by the ravages of the pox. A hole has been burnt through an ear, marking him out as a criminal. Greasy, tawny hair falls across a low brow, and pale eyes dart frantically back and forth, searching for some escape.

"Now, little rabbit, prithee, explain why you are keeping watch on me?" The massive fingers close around the pockmarked face and turn the head so that they are eye to eye, and in Pieter's blue eyes, there is no mirth even though his lips are smiling.

Garrat stares up into those cold eyes and the broad, scarred face into which they are set. The red beard seems to be so many spear points, all aiming menacingly at him. He squirms ineffectually and then goes limp as the pressure on his chest increases.

"I... I can't breathe..." he gasps out.

"That is sort of the point." The Dutchman is almost cheerful.

"Please... Please master... let me have breath!" It feels as if his ribs are about to give way, and he knows he will tell this man anything just to be able to breathe again.

The pressure continues for a few moments longer, and Garrat's eyes are beginning to bulge when the knee stops its downward journey and eases back enough for him to drag in a desperate gulp of air.

The Dutchman tilts his head to one side quizzically, looking for a moment like a curious bear, and waits for an answer to his question. When the answer is not immediate, he lowers his knee again.

"No, no! Let me get a breath. Please master, I will tell you!" Garrat is panicking. He has performed many dubious acts for his employer, but he has never had to face a creature such as this.

Pieter nods and releases the crushing weight again, waiting patiently for the grey man to speak. But that patience will not last too much longer.

"My master charged me with following you. I was to keep an eye and report to him your movements." Garrat manages to gasp this out, aware that to try to delay, even for another breath, will result in that giant weight crushing his ribs flat to his spine.

"And who is this master of yours that has such a keen interest in my affairs?"

"It is Dr Dee." He says this as if Pieter should know of this doctor and be amazed, but the Dutchman just stares blankly.

"He has your friend, the captain. I was to make sure you didn't leave the city. I know not why."

Pieter stares down into the disease-ruined visage and narrows his eyes. The fingers that grip the man's face tighten, adding a new level of discomfort.

"He has Captain Evyngar? Where is he holding her?"

"She has been taken to Somerset House, where the doctor has apartments!" Garrat is terrified by this man's brute strength, but he thinks he may be able to buy his life as he gathers his wits.

"I can take you there. I can help you get to the captain." *And into a trap that even this behemoth will not be able to escape*, thinks Garrat Blexham.

* * *

Goosebumps. That is the first thing that comes to the exceedingly groggy mind of Captain Lament Evyngar. She attempts to raise a hand to her face, but her arm will not move. She tries the other, but it is the same sorry story. She can't feel fetters on her limbs, and as she regains her senses, she realises that she can feel nothing on her limbs, nothing whatsoever. Her limbs just feel... *heavy*. Yes, heavy. Not the sensation of having lain on an arm and waiting for the blood to flow back and the painful tingling to start. She can feel her arms. They just appear to be made of lead.

With a colossal effort, she manages to open her eyes and stare at the dark, candle-smoked ceiling above. Slowly, shapes form in the periphery of her vision, and with another supreme effort, she rolls her head to one side and squints at the shapes that gradually come into focus.

The rectangular block with its strange symbols. A lectern holding a large book bound in some dark, polished hide. Candles, a great many of them, and a brazier from which issues a cloud of bluish smoke. And there, moving purposefully around the space, is the tall, saturnine figure of Dr Dee.

Lament glances down at her shoulder and realises that she is naked. *That would explain the cold*, she thinks, and as she ponders this, she realises that there are designs drawn upon her skin. She fights to raise her head for a better look, and for a moment, she sees that she is indeed naked and spread-eagled upon the floor and that the marks drawn upon her appear to cover much of her body, at least that part which is visible. Her head bumps back against the cold stone of the floor, and she suddenly feels very exposed.

Her throat is parched, and she sucks on her tongue to try and gain enough moisture to be able to talk. Her eyes follow the black-robed figure as it moves in and out of her field of vision, collecting items from shelves and distributing them with seeming method around the space that Lament occupies. Then the doctor halts in his tracks and looks down at Lament, a beaming smile cracking the long beard. There is no lust in his gaze as she might have imagined in the eyes of other men who had her at this disadvantage. Instead, Dee's gaze is businesslike, and he seems focused on less worldly things.

"Ah, God give you good morrow, Captain. I was wondering when you would awake. It would have been a shame to start without you, so to speak." Dee laughs at his jest and leans over to gaze into Lament's eyes, moving her head from side to side with those long, bony fingers.

"What is happening here?" Lament manages to croak out at last.

"Why, Captain, we are preparing you for your mission. You

will need more than mortal aid if you are to locate and retrieve the things I require." Dee holds a cup of wine to Lament's lips, and she greedily sups upon it as the doctor holds up her head. When the cup is removed, Lament glares at Dee.

"You drugged me, sir! I never agreed to help you in your madcap enterprise, and now I find myself in the midst of some blasphemous sorcery. Let me up, damn you! I have had enough of your addle patted nonsense!"

But Dee simply moves out of eye line to the cabinet along the far wall and returns with a parchment, which he unrolls before holding it out to Lament.

"Do you not recall signing this confession, Captain? This singular confession that implicates you, your family, and your Dutch comrade in a plot to assassinate Her Majesty. A plot to bring down fire and slaughter upon the realm. A plot linking you to Phillip of Spain and the heresy of the antichrist himself. You signed it freely enough last night, good Captain, with no need for any persuasion." Dee smiles, pleased with his deviousness as Lament lies helplessly, seething, staring at her signature.

"Bastard!"

"Very witty. I'm sure Master Shakespeare would benefit from your input into his plays." Dee rolls the parchment and ties it before moving back out of Lament's eye line and depositing it safely in the cabinet.

Lament's head is whirling. The *confession* was obviously written out in advance, and all that was needed was for her to sign it when she was drugged. This whole connivance has been planned for some time, and she is beginning to wonder if the murder of the merchant wasn't indeed part of the plan to ensnare her. No, that can't be true. There was no way they could guess that she would return to the warehouse. It seems a collection of unhappy coincidences has furnished Dee with the opportunity he needed. Lament fumes, grinding her teeth in impotent rage. This is not something that she can solve with a blade, at least not yet...

"I believe we are ready to begin." Dr Dee has been moving around the room, placing more things taken from cabinets onto the floor in strategic locations. He steps behind the lectern, holding a short staff in one hand. Lament can just make out symbols marked upon it that look like those on the rectangular block. The doctor scoops something up with his left hand and throws it onto the brazier beside him. With a hiss and a great whoosh of flames, the brazier begins to emit clouds of dark purple smoke. Bright golden sparks appear, rising amongst it like stars glimpsed through storm clouds.

Dr Dee begins to make sounds. He talks in a whisper as if to someone in another room, but the language he speaks is not one that Lament understands or recognises.

The candles in the chamber seem to dim, although that could just be the smoke that is billowing up to the ceiling and spreading outwards. From her position on the floor, Lament watches as the short staff begins to move in time to what is rapidly becoming a chant as the volume increases.

Lament blinks hard several times. And again. But the impression that shapes are forming in the poisonous-looking vapour does not go away. She turns her head as best she can, and in the corners of her vision, she sees figures standing around her. Tall, ghostly forms that stoop beneath the ceiling, large heads that seem to have more than one face and too many eyes. They stare down upon her, these things from nightmares, and she can hear a rustling as of wings.

As the chanting becomes more frantic, more desperate, the smoke engulfs the chamber like a spreading bruise. Lament can hear a drumbeat that she swiftly realises is the blood pounding in her head as she fights the panic rising in her. She has faced death many times, but *this* this is something altogether worse, and she still has no use of her limbs.

Suddenly, the wild cacophony of gibberish stops. In the silence, following it, there are creaks and groans and strange tittering laughs that cause the skin to crawl.

Dee is speaking again, but this time, the words are almost conversational, if still unintelligible. He is addressing the figures that have coalesced from the smoke, and he gestures towards the prostrate form of the captain in the centre of the room. A multitude of eyes, far too many eyes that blaze like miniature suns, lock their stare upon her. But there is no heat in their gaze. Instead, it feels cold, as if all the warmth has been sucked from the chamber. Perhaps this is what the void between the stars feels like.

Lament wants to scream. She can hear babbling and is horrified by the realisation that it is coming from her own lips. She tries to stop the noises, but they just turn into an extended groan as she forces her lips to stay clamped shut. Her eyes dart around the chamber as much as her frozen state will allow, and she tries desperately not to meet the gaze of any of these entities from the smoke.

A sound, like the screeching of metal against metal, has begun, and somehow, it forms a version of the language that Dee is speaking. The things are conversing with the doctor, who has bowed his head in deference. Lament is at the far edge of her reason, and she feels blackness beginning, gratefully, to take her.

Dr Dee opens his arms wide and then thrusts the short staff that acts as his wand towards the now unconscious spread-eagled captain. As if awaiting this signal, the figures, which seem to extend in some such way beyond the bonds of the chamber, surge forward. There is terror in the doctor. He has the power to summon these angels from their realm, but they still fill him with fear and dread. As they move, they rend the fabric of space, and he glimpses the endless void and a vision of the boundless firmament that threatens his sanity. Man was never meant to gaze upon the eternal.

They are upon the captain now. Strange whisp-like tendrils that pretend to be limbs snake out and wrap around the naked body. There is a glow like that from a blacksmith's furnace, and it is as if stars from the heavens themselves circle her form like a cosmic whirlpool. The geometric symbols which Dee has painstakingly inked over most of Lament's flesh begin to glow like molten iron. There is a flapping of colossal, unseen wings that brings a freezing chill from the void, and the symbols no longer glow with red heat. Now, they seem to flow like quicksilver.

Dee's eyes are fever-bright as he stares with wonder and delight at what he has wrought. The figures drift back to the edges of the seven-pointed star in its circle of arcane symbols in which Lament lies mercifully unconscious. The symbols on her flesh dull to a lattice of faint grey lines that Dee is sure writhe with alien life before they are still.

* * *

The wait has been frustrating, but even Sergeant Pieter Hertgers can't alter the flow of the tide with threats. They disembark the wherry at the water stairs at Bridewell along the river east of Somerset House in the early evening. Garrat has informed the big man that the stairs at Somerset House are closely guarded and that there is no way past, at least not for someone of his size. It is not as if Pieter can easily disguise himself. He is almost of a mind to go in sword swinging and fight his way through the guards, but getting shot with a crossbow bolt or a ball from a wheellock pistol might just ruin his rescue attempt. So, they climb the stairs at Bridewell and make their way past the scurrying, black-robed lawyers at Temple Bar and then out onto Milford Lane.

Pieter's giant fingers are curled into the grey hood hanging down his captives back. It would not do for him to make a break for freedom so close to their goal, and chasing him down through the busy lane would be somewhat bothersome, even though most of the folk are keeping to themselves and moving quickly to avoid contact. The plague does have its uses, after all.

Pieter pushes Garrat up against the wall that surrounds the grounds of the house and growls, "So, how do we get in there then?"

"There is a hidden gate just above the river. If we can get through that, we will be in the gardens, and I can show you the way into the cellars and tunnels that run beneath the house and grounds. That is where the doctor has his working chambers. It is where he spends most of his time when he is not at his library in

Mortlake, and I would wager that is where you will find the captain." Garrat has become generous with his information, mainly because the Dutchman informed in lurid details what he would do to him if he did not comply, but also because he believes that there is no way that even this behemoth can best all the guards that Dr Dee employs. So, for now, he is content to keep his skin whole while he leads this Netherlands pig fucker to his fate.

The gate above the river is unguarded save by a carved stone gryphon that squats, moss-covered, amongst the bushes. It has possibly been left without a guard because it is partially overgrown with ivy and rusted shut. Pieter scowls at the gate and then at Garrat. He can certainly open the gate, but it won't be quiet.

Garrat stands and stares innocently at the gate as if he sees no problem in alerting all of Somerset House. Pieter gives serious thought as to whether to use his captive's head as a battering ram to breach the gate, but his eye catches something further along the wall to their left. He drags Garrat away from the overgrown entrance and further into the gloom, where he has spotted a darker shape amongst the shadows.

It is a pile of broken masonry. Left by the builders and never cleared away, it has remained unnoticed by anyone – until now.

Keeping hold of Garrat's grey cloak, Pieter clambers up the heap of stone, dragging his struggling prisoner with him. The masonry comes to an end about halfway up the wall, leaving about five feet to be negotiated. The Dutchman grins; that will not be a problem. Keeping hold of his prisoner, on the other hand, could present a challenge. In the pouch at his belt, he remembers there is a length of hemp cord, not much, but enough to bind Garrat. He quickly and expertly trusses the man's hands to one of his ankles and then bodily heaves him up to the top of the wall.

"Do not attempt anything foolhardy. You have served me well so far. It would be a shame to spoil our relationship by giving me cause to crush your skull." The smile on Pieter's lips is not mirrored in his eyes.

Garrat is too shocked to make any bold moves. Once again, he is awed by the sheer physical power of this brute. He feels like he did as a child when his father would swing him up into the air. He didn't like him either. So, he stays lying flat on the coping stones as the Dutchman effortlessly heaves his bulk to the top, then, spotting some dense, manicured bushes close to the wall, pushes Garrat from his perch and follows suit.

The well-clipped hedging does not fare well, but it does break their fall and provides instant cover. Pieter keeps a large hand on the back of Garrat's neck to prevent him from either rolling out of cover or, in some way, alerting any watchmen who may be patrolling the grounds. Crouching in the wreckage of the shrubbery, he surveys the gardens and the house, but although there are lights in some of the windows, everything seems peaceful.

"Well, my friend. We are in the grounds, so it is time to make good on your promise and show me these tunnels and rooms of your master, Dr Dee." Pieter releases the cord from around his ankle and then hoists Garrat to his feet. The man is a mass of scratches from landing face-first in the bushes, and he silently curses the Dutchman, wishing plagues of boils upon him.

A watery sun is sinking as they come to the centre of a

lawned area with a raised iron grating that sits incongruously amongst the grass.

"That is one of the main tunnels down there." Garrat nods his head towards the gloom that can be seen through the bars of the grating.

Pieter wraps his thick fingers around the bars and gives an exploratory tug. The grating gives a little. He takes his dagger and works it around the edge to help free it. With another couple of heaves, the heavy iron is free of its mooring and lying next to a gaping hole in the lawn. There is dim light below, and Pieter can just make out the edge of a pool of yellow light from a lantern or candle.

"Are these tunnels guarded?" He cranes his neck to see what he can in the passageway below.

"No. There are guards at the entrance by the water stairs. Sometimes, there are guards escorting prisoners, but there are no men stationed in the passageways as a rule. The doctor likes to conduct his experiments and meetings in private, and he has other means to keep his guests amiable." Garrat shudders at his own words; he has heard stories and once a series of unearthly sounds. He also knows that he hasn't spoken true. *There will be guards in the tunnels.*

"Will you fit through *there,* big man?" Garrat nods again at the hole where the grating used to be.

"Just." Pieter grabs Garrat and lowers his writhing form down into the hole, and then he lowers himself down and drops to the floor of the passage in time to grab the grey hood and prevent Garrat from disappearing into the shadows.

Garrat's shoulders slump despondently. He would never have

believed that a man this large could move so fast. Once again, he silently wishes all manner of pestilence upon him.

"Which way, my little sewer rat?" Pieter pulls the hood a little tighter around Garrat's neck.

Garrat thinks for a moment, remembering where the house was and the pattern of the gravel paths in the garden above. "This way." And he leads the giant off between pools of flickering candlelight.

# Chapter 4

Dr Dee jerks his head around at the sudden noise in the passageway. His eyes narrow, and then they become very wide as the door bursts inwards. An unconscious form is flung over the threshold, armour and weapons clattering on the stone floor, and then a second figure is thrust forward, tripping over the first. This second one lies on his side where he has fallen and looks up apologetically at the doctor.

"I am sorry, Master Dee. He forced me to lead him here. I had no choice..." Garrat's words stammer to a halt as Dee turns a withering gaze upon him. But before he can respond, a third intruder enters the room. Or perhaps fills it would be a better description.

"Is this the fucker?" A question growled at the sprawled Garrat—a question spoken with a strong Dutch accent.

Dee tries quickly to regain his composure, although he finds himself rapidly stepping backwards to avoid ridiculously large hands that reach out towards him. He goes on the verbal offensive as he puts a long workbench loaded with the trappings of his alchemical workings between them.

"Ah, good Sergeant Hertgers. I was going to send for you in the morning. It would have saved the necessity of this escapade."

Pieter is still advancing, getting ready to throw the heavy workbench onto the scrawny doctor and squash him like a bug, when he spies another in the room. Sitting off to one side in a highbacked chair and wrapped in a heavy cloak is a rather pale Captain Lament Evyngar. The Dutchman stops in his tracks, and Lament raises a hand in salute, a weak but grateful smile on her lips.

"You took your time."

"By all the hells Lament! What has been done to you?" The cloak has fallen from Lament's naked shoulder in the act of saluting her friend, and Pieter can see the grey markings that crisscross the visible skin. Pieter goes to Lament and opens the cloak, staring at the patterns that now cover her torso. Lament is still too feeble from the drugs that Dee has plied her with to resist. *At least*, she thinks, *I am now wearing hose.*

Pieter begins to turn again towards the black-robed man who has caused this, but Lament places a hand on a massive forearm and shakes her head. "No, my friend. He is a spider, and we are caught in his web. He has documents that incriminate you and me and members of my family in a popish plot to assassinate the Queen. For the present, at least, I fear we must dance to his tune."

"Let us burn these documents and this doctor and have done with it." Pieter has rage in his eyes at the treatment of Lament and the unjustness of the blackmail that they find themselves victims of. He reaches for the falchion hanging in its scabbard, fully intent on prizing the location of the documents from this Dr Dee one way or another.

"Come now, sir! Do you truly believe that I would have only one copy of the signed confession of Captain Evyngar? That I wouldn't have already sent a copy into safekeeping with members of the Privy Council?" Dee tries to exude a confidence he barely feels. He is aware of how close to death he stands. But a man who consorts with angels must have steel in his spine.

"Pieter, we can't fight our way out of this one. The doctor requires us to find some objects for him, and when we have fulfilled that part of the bargain, then we will be free again. Let us make the best hand of it that we can."

His shoulders slump in defeat, and the Dutch giant pushes his blade back into the scabbard. Dr Dee breathes a sigh of relief and a silent prayer of thanks.

"Get up, you addle pate!" You are less than useless." Dee turns his attention to Garrat, who is now sitting cross-legged on the floor. Garrat indicates that his hands are still tied and then drops his gaze as Dee strides over and cuts the hemp cord with a small pair of shears from the bench.

"Escort the captain and sergeant to the captain's chamber along the corridor, and then fetch someone to take that away." He indicates the unconscious guard with a nod of his head. "And have another cot brought for the sergeant."

"You will find your clothes and other possessions in your chamber, Captain, including your sword. I had it collected from the watchmen who arrested you. I will have food and wine sent to you. I think you will have some catching up to do, and we can reconvene in the morning and discuss what will happen next."

Over roasted capon and a very good Rhenish wine, Lament has related the whole story. The description of the ritual has been disjointed at best, and Lament would like to believe that the things she saw were the product of some drugged infusion given to her by Dee. Pieter seems happy to agree that it must have been a hallucination. The possibility that it was some sort of supernatural manifestation would be the only thing that could make his blood run cold.

"You should have killed those two watchmen and their dog at the merchant's. We always get into trouble when you want to be reasonable." Pieter waves a chicken leg in the air as if to make a point.

"Respectable wine importers do not, as a rule, go around slaughtering the night watch or their hounds. I think I was still harbouring the belief that what had occurred was perfectly reasonable and that they would just send me on my way. It is the fault of that bastard accusing me, with his dying breath, of smuggling Jesuits that did for me. Ah, big man, life was simpler in the Low Countries. We could kill who we fancied and not be brought to book for it."

The bitterness in his friend's voice is not lost on Pieter. They left the regiments fighting against the Spanish specifically because there was no mediator to prevent atrocity. They had crossed lines several times that both of them suspected would see them ending in some purgatory when their time came. It had become hard enough to reconcile deed and motive when the nights drew in, and many a time, sleep had been delayed until enough ale and wine had been imbibed to make dreaming an impossibility.

"So, we are going back then?" Pieter tears a mouthful of flesh from the bird's thigh. He is less bothered by the wanton excesses of war. If he can find food, drink, and warm thighs to lie between, he can force the demons from his mind. He is aware that Lament sometimes struggles with the morality of what they are part of and blames it upon the captain's Catholic upbringing. All that guilt must sit somewhere.

"Yes, we are going back. I think we have a choice of that or the scaffold, and I may have taken that choice if you and my family were not part of the bargain."

Pieter laughs through the grease and wipes his mouth and beard on the back of his broadcloth sleeve. "You need not concern yourself about my health, Lam. When I go out of this life, I will be swinging steel, and it will be with no regrets."

"Aye, my friend. Let us hope that will be a while longer in coming." Lament raises her wine in a toast to her massive companion at arms, the only man she allows to call her *Lam* as if she were some defenceless creature - she enjoys the irony. But somewhere deep inside her is the dread feeling that they are about to be plunged into something that is not of this world.

* * *

In his chamber lit by a multitude of candles, Dr Dee breaths in the acrid incense drifting from the braziers. He hunches over a black disk that sits on a bronze stand on the small table in front of him.

He mutters to himself in a language revealed to him by the angels, and he gazes with bloodshot eyes into the inky swirling depths. Something in there gazes unblinkingly back at him, and he shudders.

# Chapter 5

A watery, grey light filters through the leaded diamonds of the windowpanes. There is a thick morning mist rising from the Thames and drifting through the grounds of Somerset House, obscuring much of the view from those leaded panes.

This morning, Lament and Pieter have been escorted along a different underground passage to find themselves eventually in a large reception room inside the house. Now, they stand in front of the windows, gazing out at the formless grey as they await the arrival of Dr Dee and the briefing for their reluctant mission.

Lament has already given Pieter the information that the doctor disclosed during their initial meeting. At least as much of it as she can remember. So, they know that they will be returning to the Netherlands and that they will be searching for certain objects that the doctor needs to complete his plans for empire.

"No offence, my friend, but if Dee thinks that he is going to turn your little island into a world power, then he is even more moonstruck than you think he is!" Pieter laughs, not for the first time, at the absurdity of the megalomania of the court conjurer's plans. He rubs his thick fingers across the stubble growing from his even thicker skull and stretches, yawning loudly.

"No offence taken, you big ox." Lament smiles at her lounging companion, nodding in agreement. "It would seem that the doctor is under some delusion. I think it is likely just a ploy to get us into a position to collect intelligence. They appear to have a passion for the espionage game these courtiers, as long as it is another putting their head in the noose." However, the memory of those alien things gives her cause to wonder.

A cough alerts them that they are no longer alone. Dr Dee stands in an alcove across the room. He has entered through another of the house's secret doors and has been there long enough to hear Lament's appraisal of the situation.

"Good morrow to you. I trust you slept well?" He doesn't wait for an answer. "It matters little what you believe the purpose of your mission to be as long as you complete it. If you can gather intelligence useful to the Crown, then all well and good. It helps to keep the Privy Council from prying into my affairs. But your primary mission, the thing that must take precedence over everything else and the thing that will guarantee the burning of your confession, is the collection of two objects." He sweeps out of the alcove, his black robes billowing around him, for a moment making him seem much larger than he is. Lament notices the dark rings around his eyes and the greyness of his complexion. Dee, quite obviously, did not enjoy a restful sleep.

"So, sir, what are these fantastic things you can't do without?" Lament perches on the window seat, and her hand drops automatically to the black hilt of her sword. There is a familiarity and comfort there. Dee comes to a halt on the far side of the low, ornate table that separates them. He has not missed the position of Lament's hand.

"In Naarden, you will find a map. It is a thing of great antiquity created by the ancient Sea Kings who navigated this globe before the great flood. It is amongst other relics that are being assembled on behalf of a famous collector, and you must get to it before it can be transported to him. I can't see its location or design; there is another that obscures my vision, but I believe it may be part of a consignment that will soon be shipped beyond my reach. There will be many curiosities amongst this collection of relics, but you will know the right one." The doctor gazes hard into Lament's blue eyes.

"How will we know it if it is amongst other relics?" Pieter leans forward, elbows on his knees, challenging.

"I have given the captain the gift of witch-sight. Did she not tell you that? Maybe she is not aware herself of what has been bestowed." Dee has not broken eye contact with Lament, and Lament is beginning to feel a growing unease.

"What is it that you imply, doctor?"

"The ritual that I performed yesterday was not merely meant to decorate your skin. It has given you the ability to see things as they truly are. To see things that others can't see. And to recognise objects of power. It will take a little time for it to come into effect, but soon, you will see the world through different eyes." Dee finally breaks his gaze with a seemingly innocent smile while Lament feels the hairs on the nape of her neck rise.

"You mean those things in the smoke were real? Come now! You drugged me, sir, and I had strange, hellish hallucinations, but that is all they were!" But Lament has a sense deep inside herself that what had driven her into blackness had more substance than she would want to admit, especially to herself.

"Are you moon touched?" Pieter growls low in his throat. He does not understand what has passed between Lament and this scrawny figure in black, but he knows that whatever it is, it has put fear into his fearless friend. There is a moment when the future of them all teeters upon the knife edge that is Pieter's temper, but Lament places a hand upon the giant shoulder, and the moment passes. Pieter looks across at Lament, and Lament just shakes her head and turns back to Dee.

"And the second object?"

"That is a jewelled necklace. It will be found in the city of Haarlem and, from what I can deduce, may prove to be the more difficult of the two to attain..." Dee looks at them as they sit in the pale light. He knows that this is his best chance, but he is not a man given to games involving luck. He sighs, knowing that the dice are already cast. "You must leave London as soon as possible. The plague is spreading through the poorer districts, and soon, it will be difficult to leave the city. The Queen has already departed to her country estates, taking much of the court and Privy Council with her. I will go to join her when our business here is concluded." He takes a letter from a pocket in his robes.

"You are to take passage on a ship at Tilbury. It is carrying a company of light cavalry to join Sir Humphrey Gilbert's force. This is a letter for Sir Humphrey from the Queen, and delivering it should give you ample enough reason to be there." He leans forward and hands the letter to Lament.

"I understand Sir Humphrey never turns away a good sword. We should be welcomed without this deception." Lament waves the letter as emphasis.

Dee's voice takes on a steely tone as his eyes follow the letter.

"Understand me, Captain, there can be no confusion in this. Whether Sir Humphrey greets you with open arms can't be left to chance. Delivery of that letter will guarantee you a place in his company, and the rest is down to you. My shew stone will allow me to keep an eye on your progress, so do not seek to dally or avoid your commission. There is a wherry awaiting you at the water stairs. It will take you to Bankside, where you can collect your possessions from your lodgings. My man Blexham will escort you, and while you retrieve your belongings, he will make sure that another wherry is ready to take you to the docks." As he speaks, the grey-clad figure of Garrat Blexham emerges from the shadows of the alcove. He looks more composed now that he is not tied at the wrists, and his clothing has had the dust and debris brushed from it. Pieter grins at him, and if Garrat was thinking of making some retort, he wisely does not, but his eyes are far from friendly.

"When will this sorcery that you have worked upon me begin to show its worth? And when it does, how will I know? Lament looks sceptically at the doctor as she puts the letter into the pouch at her belt.

"Oh, my dear Captain, you will know soon enough. These things can take a little while to manifest, and then there will be no doubt. After all, this is not some *court conjurer's* sleight of hand." He gives Pieter an arch look. "The consequences of this great work will change history. What you see and do from this moment on, just by your mere presence, will create different futures, and what you bring back to me will mark the beginning of the greatest future of all! Now go. You must not miss the tide."

Dee waves them away, and they follow Garrat as he turns and walks back into the shadows.

# Chapter 6

Five ships slip free of the river's mouth and out into the Narrow Sea. The wind is fair, and although there is a swell, they ride confidently.

Lament and Pieter sit upon the steps of the forecastle of the second ship, the White Bear, and watch as those unaccustomed to the sea lose their breakfast over the side. They had collected their possessions from the rooms they rented on Bankside, mainly spare clothing, a few pieces of armour, and, of course, Pieter's great zweihander sword, wrapped in its oiled leather bag. Then another wherry had taken them to Tilbury, where they had boarded the White Bear.

The ship's captain had given them the once over and accepted a purse of coin from Garrat before finally motioning them onto the deck. They were obviously soldiers, and the other men on board barely gave them a second glance except to comment on the gigantic size of the Dutchman and to ask if he was the White Bear that the ship was named after. They had stowed their gear and then watched as the dock and London receded from view.

On the jetty, Garrat had stood and stared until the current had taken the ships, and they had passed out of sight. He had been instructed to make sure that his two charges did not some-how abandon their ship. Satisfied that his task was completed, he pulled his hood around his head against the still-present mist and faded amongst the crowd on the docks.

*  *  *

The wind has dropped, and the seemingly omnipresent mist has thickened into a dense fog that has enveloped the other ships until they can't be seen by those onboard. Bells are rung at regular intervals, and halloos are shouted from mastheads. The horses tethered below deck are skittish, and the cavalrymen spend most of their time grooming them to help keep them calm.

It would be barely half a day's ride on a fast horse over land, but sometimes it happens that the elements conspire, and then it can take days to reach the other shore. Sometimes, it is never reached at all...

Lament and Pieter, cloaks wrapped around them against the chill damp, lounge on a heap of rope up on the forecastle. They managed to acquire a ham, cheese, and bread on Bankside before they were rushed to the wherry. Plus, a couple of bottles of a decent Rhenish, and now they pick at the food and pass a bottle between them.

"Tell me the truth, Lam, are we fucked? Are we ever going to get out from under the debt that we now owe this caster of spells?" The chunk of cheese that Pieter examines as he asks the question has a thick rind, and he eats what he can before tossing the rest overboard for the fish. The questions are asked without resentment, just a desire to know how deep this obligation runs.

After all, they have faced dire situations before and undoubtedly will again.

Lament sighs and leans her head back on a coil of rope before answering. The murk above is darkening as the night draws in, and she wishes that they could get lost in it, gone from Dee's scheming clutches.

"I have no reason to suspect that Dr Dee will cross us. He appears to have gone to extreme lengths to secure our services at no little cost to himself if he is to be believed. You and I know what slippery bastards those in high circles can be. So, let us just say that when we have secured his baubles and returned to him, I will get back my signed confession, both copies and then when they are ashes, I will look to a reckoning with the good doctor." Lament takes a drink of wine as Pieter grunts his agreement.

"Do you believe that he can spy upon us from afar with this *shew stone*?" Pieter looks suspiciously at another piece of cheese that seems to have a greenish patina.

"I believe he has some unnatural abilities, so let us imagine that he can see us from afar and proceed accordingly." Lament closes her eyes for a moment, feeling a drowsiness from the wine and the rocking of the ship, and then she hears the big Dutchman gasp. Opening her eyes, she sees that the fog has begun to thin, but the darkening sky above is stained with undulating streaks of colour. Greens and pinks twist in the sky, and a stiff breeze begins to shred the mist and fill out the sagging sailcloth.

They stand at the rail and stare out at the emerging horizon. The streaks of colour disappear down beyond view, and to Lament, it looks as if a careless painter has dragged his colours from the earth into the sky. She almost crosses herself, a reflex action from her childhood. Something that she had not even thought about doing since she was ten years old and something that now would get her thrown overboard.

Awed whispers sound around the ship, and prayers are said. Even Pieter is caught in superstitious awe. The ship's captain appears beside them and rubs at his straggling grey beard.

"Tis the Northern Lights. We don't often see them this far south, and not as strongly as that." He turns and calls out across the ship.

"Worry not. It is just a show of lights in the heavens. We have our wind at last, so jump to it and let us make for the foreign shore while the going is good!"

Lament turns to playfully mock Pieter but finds that everything has taken on a glowing halo. She looks back up at the sky, and for a moment before her vision returns to normal, she is sure that she can see the shadow form of mighty wings unfolding above her.

* * *

It is the evening of the second day, and the ships have made harbour. On the jetty, Lament and Pieter stretch their legs as the crews unload cargo, and cavalrymen lead their horses gratefully onto dry land. There is a more purposeful mood now, and an officer from Sir Humphrey's staff is ordering the troop, sending them up the dirt road to the camp on the edge of the town. He is a short, barrel-chested man with dark curling hair and an immense moustache that appears to be possessed by a life of its own.

"Captain Evyngar at your service, sir." Lament introduces them while Pieter does his best to avoid staring at the dancing moustache.

The officer looks up from the list he has been examining, and it is suddenly obvious why his facial hair moves unnervingly. At some point in his military career, he has taken a slashing cut from a sword across the lower part of his face, severing his lips and opening his cheek. Although the surgeon who saw to the wound had saved much of the flesh, he was incapable of helping with the damage to the facial nerves, which now twitch in perpetual motion.

"Greetings, Captain." There is a slight lisp from the damaged lips, and he nods at Lament in acknowledgement. His eyebrows raise as he looks up at the towering form of Seargent at Arms Hertgers, and then he turns his attention back to Lament.

"I am Lieutenant James of Sir Humphrey's general staff. I was told a week past to expect messengers from Her Majesty. Would I be correct in thinking that it is you?"

"Yes, Lieutenant. I carry a letter from the Queen for your commander." Lament raises an eyebrow at the news that they were expected. Dr Dee must have been rather confident of his plan to set the story in motion even before they had met.

"You can find a billet in camp for this evening. Sir Humphrey has been in conference with the Sea Beggars and is not expected back in the camp until morning. Or, if you would prefer to part with some coin, you may find lodging in the town. There is a tavern just beyond the gates that has become home to many of the officers. It is called De Zeven Sterren, so why not try there? The ale and wine are good, and the food is plentiful." A smile further twists the lieutenant's features and makes the moustache jerk alarmingly. Lament can't be sure that the tone is not in some way mocking.

"That sounds perfect, Lieutenant. Perhaps we will see you later, and if not, may God give you good ease." Lament and Pieter turn and head along the dock towards the town gate, and Lieutenant James stares after them for a short while before returning to his list.

* * *

Pieter has talked his way into the confidence of the tavern hostess, a short, plump woman with an eye for a large Dutch lad. She has begun to get tired of these skinny English gentlemen and their less than gentlemanly manners, so to be greeted in her own tongue by a roguish giant has put colour back in her cheeks and secured them a room.

In the taproom, they sit surrounded by gentlemen adventurers who drink and boast, but it is obvious that most have never seen battle. Lament weighs them with a practised eye and can tell that fencing lessons are the closest that the majority have got to the clash of steel. She sighs inwardly and wonders, *Was I ever like them?* and realises that she must have appeared that way when she first set out to find fame and adventure.

As a tomboy, she had much preferred fighting with the village boys, climbing anything big enough to present a challenge, and riding rather than the needlework her sisters practised diligently. She had pestered her father from an early age to be allowed to attend fencing lessons. As it transpired, her father had a close friend who had trained in the art of the rapier in Florance, and he consigned Lament to Master Antonio's none-to-gentle care, perhaps in the hope that it would break her of her unladylike ways. The lessons were hard and physically demanding, and Master Antonio did not care for anything less than perfection. Fortunately, Lament had what the Master described as a God-given gift for the blade, and she thrived, becoming strong, fast, and incredibly skilled. Master Antonio saw in Lament the adventurer and soldier, so he began to train her in the *spada da lato*, a heavier-bladed version of the rapier that could be used on the battlefield and not just in sporting contests and duels. After all, he was proud to say that there were more than a few swordswomen in the Italian states, so why ever not? Much to her father's dismay, Lament took to this new weapon with delight and worked until it was as agile as a rapier in her hand.

When the purges began to take place, it became unwise for a Florentine and a Catholic to remain in Her Majesty's violently Protestant realm, so Master Antonio went back to Italy. His parting gift to the sixteen-year-old Lament had been a beautiful, blackened steel wire hilt sword. The same sword she still wears at her hip.

A year later, Lament had killed her first man. A matter of honour, she had called it after the man had decried her as a roaring girl for her choice of male clothing and lack of interest in men, but she knows it was nothing more than to prove to herself that she could. After all, the accusations were not untrue. She had enjoyed tumbles with the stable boys but had much preferred the company of the servant girls. But the prying eyes of the Puritans had made her choices somewhat difficult, not least for her father and mother. And despite her father encouraging marriage prospects with various gentry, he had eventually retired, beaten by her obstinate refusal. Anyway, she had always been the apple of his eye, so against all sense, he found it difficult to remain angry with her.

So, shortly after the duel, she had, with her father's influence, gained a commission and joined a company heading for the Low Countries. She had not declared herself as a woman. Her small breasts had been easy to hide and had allowed them to think her a beardless youth. Her talent with a blade and reckless bravery had soon negated any problems with her gender, and all had accepted her. Those who made complaints soon learned that the young woman with the sword was not to be mocked or ignored. Lament had never looked back and had taken to the life as if she had been born to it. Perhaps that is the problem...

She now recognises herself in the posturing young men carousing around her. Untried, untested, many will break and run, and many will die. Most will have their fill of adventure within six months and take themselves back to English shores to boast of their victories and use them to help advance in courtly circles.

The rank and file, on the other hand... They will have been recruited from those who see fighting against the Spanish as their God-given duty or are too poor to reject the offer of regular coins and a full belly, even though the marketplaces of their hometowns are full of veterans of this endless war. Mangled and maimed, they sit at the base of the market crosses and beg for scraps and maybe a coin or two. No, those men can't leave when they have had enough excitement and slaughter. Those men are noticeably absent from the company around Lament.

Pieter has obtained for them trenchers of a thick pork pottage, and he is attacking his with gusto as he eyes the well-to-do young men who are drinking too much. He raises his bushy eyebrows at Lament as if to say, *here we go again!* Lament grins back, secretly hoping that none of them choose to start a fight that they will instantly regret.

As she scans the room, Lament finds her vision shifting, as if she is looking through a many-faceted gem that breaks up the image. She blinks hard, but the visual effect remains, and some of the men in the room begin to blur and take on a warped appearance, their faces becoming demonic.

She reflexively grabs the hilt of her dagger while the fingers of her other hand tighten on the edge of the tabletop. This is all she can think to do to keep herself grounded in what she takes to be reality. Looking over at Pieter, she sees nothing unusual about the big man, but when she turns to see who has just pushed their way through the outer door, she is greeted with a strange sight.

A tall, thin figure with a pallid face, almost corpse-like, strides into the tap room. He seems to be clad in countless strips of undulating grey that remind Lament of ribbons of dead flesh. Fastened to the grey strips are lead-coloured metallic objects in the shape of stars, moons, and thunderbolts. At the ends of the strips are jangling hooks and bells. As he moves, the whole ensemble seems to drift around him as if he is somehow underwater.

A pungent smell of ozone fills the air as if there has been a lightning strike, and Lament's fingers grip the wooden surface even harder.

"Hey, are you alright, my friend?" Pieter's massive hand claps Lament on the back, and the vision disappears as if it was part of a play at the Globe and a curtain has come down.

"Yes, yes. Sorry, big man." Lament pries her hand from the table and wipes it across a suddenly pale face, noticing for the first time the sweat on her brow.

"I am maybe a little tired still from the events of the past few days." She grins unconvincingly and raises her ale pot, and out of the corner of her eye, she notices that the tall figure is just a captain dressed in buff coloured doublet and hose slashed with scarlet and sporting a cloak of dark grey cloth shot through with a silver thread. His aquiline face is framed with chestnut brown ringlets, and a forked beard and moustache add to his debonaire appearance.

Lament smiles to herself. Dr Dee's ritual has taken more of a toll on her mind than she had thought. But then she catches a glimpse of the tall figure reflected in the decorative copper plates hanging on the wall, and for a moment, the death's head is there once again.

The room spins, and Lament fears she may fall from the bench. She is sweating profusely, and her hands are trembling a little. The ale sloshes over the edge of the pot, splashing the tabletop and dripping onto her breeks. She feels Pieter move closer to her and hears his deep, gruff voice whisper as best it can, "You had better not be coming down with the plague, Lam. You are sweating as if you have an ague. Do you not feel well?"

"I am sound in body, my friend, but I am beginning to fear for my sanity. I need some fresh air, and I need to tell you something that until now I thought was not important."

Pieter nods, a serious look on his scarred face. He downs his ale in one gulp and wipes the foam from his bristling beard. Then he pushes himself to his feet and smiles at his friend. "After you, Captain."

They are sitting on a breakwater, watching the sea reflect the lights from the harbour. Somehow, Pieter has managed to leave the tavern with a bottle of wine and a bottle of brandy. Lament suspects that he may have just scooped them up from a table or two as they were making their way to the door. It may have gone unnoticed, although it is more likely that the table's occupants chose discretion over valour, given the size of the light-fingered thief.

After taking a swig of brandy, Lament breaths deeply and then composes herself. She explains again something of the ritual Dee performed to the best of her memory. Then, after another drink, she continues.

"When I was recovering, Dr Dee explained what he called *truths* to me. I thought that, like much else he talked about, they were just fanciful imaginings of the moonstruck. But now I am not so sure." She stares out at the lights rippling on the dark water like old thoughts being carried away by the tide. "He told me that there are opposing forces in our universe. Not good and evil, more complex than that. These forces represent order and chaos, and they vie for supremacy through the agency of humanity. They encourage our wars, our religious intolerance, and our quests for power. They do this with a desire to manipulate those happenings, and because of the great releases of anger, hatred and pain, they can become manifest in our world and assume pre-eminence."

"Dee claims that they have a hand in all human conflict and would shape history as they play their war games, these things from another plane. But we only see them as mortal beings like us because to see them otherwise would drive us to madness. But I think I see them, Pieter." She passes the bottle to him, and he looks at her open-mouthed. "Dee said that the ritual he performed was needed to allow me to see what was hidden so that we can locate his damnable trinkets, but he also warned that it might mean that I see other things too... Pieter, I am beginning to see what should not be here amongst us, what I fear has leaked out of hell. This must be that which he called *witch-sight*. Either that or I am touched!"

Pieter fears no man or beast, but an atavistic chill crawls up his spine as he listens to Lament relate what she witnessed in the taproom.

"What has that bastard done to you? What has he plunged us into?" He takes a mighty swig from the brandy and then hands it back to Lament, an unusual look of pity softening his hard eyes. "What side does this Dee take then with his talk of Revelation and a new Eden? Are we aiding order or chaos by helping him?"

"That's a good question for which I have no answer other than to say that Dee believes the angels aid him and is, therefore, beyond the war between order and chaos. He believes that God sits apart from it all, above it all, and he would sit at God's right hand. I imagine that as part of his great dream of empire, he will crush all that does not conform to his ideals as the angels guide him." Lament swirls the brandy in the bottle. "At least we know that we can kill these creatures; we have been doing that without knowing for years, it would seem. Let us meet Sir Humphrey tomorrow and see where this campaign will take us. Until then, I think we should drink until God chooses to blot this from our thoughts."

# Chapter 7

Sir Humphrey has commandeered the town hall as his head-quarters while he waits in this town for his forces to assemble. The same gaggle of rich young men looking to make a name for themselves and prove their manliness are in attendance, most looking the worse for wear from last night's exploits.

Sir Humphrey himself stands on the far side of a large carved oak table that is strewn with maps and rolls of parchment; behind him, pinned to the wall, is a map of the Low Countries. He is of middling height with broad shoulders and a stocky phy-sique that betokens a man of action who has spent many hours in the saddle and many days on campaign. His auburn hair is combed straight back, and there is a little grey at the temples. Likewise, his close-cropped beard has a streak of grey running through it on the right-hand side. There is intelligence behind his hazel eyes, calculating intelligence that one would be wise not to insult.

"Lieutenant James, are all of the recruits accounted for?" The green eyes lock onto the face with the dancing moustache.

"Yes, Sir Humphrey. The five ships came in last evening, only half a day later than expected. Men and horses all accounted for, along with powder, shot, wheel lock pistols, and helmets to replace those lost by the pikemen when the barge capsized." The lieutenant makes to pass over his list, but Sir Humphrey waves it away.

"No, Lieutenant, I trust you to count correctly." Lieutenant James draws the list back and makes a slight bow of acknowledgement.

"Well, good sirs. As you are aware, I met with our friends, the Sea Beggars, yesterday. They stand ready with the support of half a dozen of Her Majesty's warships, and it is now time for us to fulfil our part of the bargain." He turns and stabs a wooden baton at a spot on the map to the north of their current position. "We march upon the port of Brielle. It will be our task to breach the landward defences and draw away the defenders as the Sea Beggars mount their assault from the sea. The Dons have a large contingent in place there, so the fighting will be stiff. But gentlemen, we will take Brielle, make no mistake!"

There is a rousing chorus of cheers. Even those with sore heads manage to find some enthusiasm.

"To work then, See Lieutenant James for supply quotas and Captain Bowcer for troop muster." Sir Humphrey indicates the tall figure in buff and scarlet with the silver shot, dark grey cloak who in turn nods his chestnut brown ringleted head in acknowledgement.

As the groups of officers break away to fulfil their tasks, Sir Humphrey shifts his gaze to the back of the room. There, by the large double doors, stand two figures he is not familiar with. His eye is drawn first to the most physically commanding of the two. A giant with a shaved head and a bristling red beard.

His shoulders look wide enough to block the double doors. But as impressive as he is, Sir Humphrey's gaze shifts to the second figure—tall, athletic looking, every inch the swordswoman. Shoulder-length dark hair pulled back into a loose ponytail and a thin diagonal scar cutting across an otherwise attractive face. Sir Humphrey takes note of their clothing as well. Not the extravagant spectacle for this pair but rather the practical, well-used, and well-padded leather doublets of veteran soldiers.

Lament stares at the man standing behind the map-strewn table at the far end of the hall. When they had first entered the room, Lament had experienced that peculiar and unnerving shift of perception once again. Clouds outside had moved away from the face of the sun, and a shaft of golden light had burst down from the large oval window in the far wall. The dust motes floating in the air had caught the sun's rays and sparkled like gold dust. As the rays illuminated Sir Humphrey, he seemed to grow in stature. But, to Lament, instead of becoming heroic, he became warped, as if his limbs were somehow constrained and in fighting against their bonds, they became twisted and malformed. He seemed to glow with a dazzling white light, and black eyes radiated a strange luminance from a face devoid of visible features.

Lament had squeezed her eyes tight shut and dug her nails into her palms. When she opened her eyes again, the scene had become one of almost normality. Many of the faces around her looked slightly blurred, as if their owners were shaking their heads rapidly from side to side. But in an instant, the clouds had once more obscured the sun and in the sudden gloom, everything had returned to how, in a sane world, it should be.

Now, the stocky form of Sir Humphrey has moved around to the front of the table and is beckoning for them to approach. Lament settles her breathing, and she and Pieter make their way through the officers vying for the attention of either Lieutenant James or Captain Bowcer.

"Good morning to you. I trust this day finds you in good health?" Sir Humphrey does not wait for a reply. Instead, he gestures towards a doorway off to his right. "Please accompany me to the mayor's office where we might talk in private."

He leads, and Lament and Pieter follow, the groups of officers parting before them like the Red Sea. The heavy door closes behind them, and they are suddenly in an oasis of calm after the urgent bustling and demands for attention in the main hall.

Sir Humphrey makes his way to an ornately carved desk and settles on the edge, a look of expectation on his ruddy face.

"Captain Evyngar and Sergeant at Arms Hertgers reporting Sir Humphrey. We carry a document from Her Majesty for your attention." Lament reaches inside the pouch hanging from her belt and produces the folded letter with the large, ornate seal that Dr Dee had given to her.

Sir Humphrey watches through intense hazel eyes as the letter is extracted and then handed over. He reaches out and takes the letter, but his eyes are still locked on the face of the captain. "I understand that you are in the service of Dr Dee. Is that correct?"

Once again, Lament is taken aback. How could this man know that when they have only been in Dee's employ for less than a week? There would have been no time for a message to have been sent ahead unless somehow this was all preordained...

Sir Humphrey sees the confusion that his words have caused. "Come now. The good doctor notified me of your arrival several weeks ago. It is common for agents of the Crown to join free companies engaged in the war against the Don." A knowing smile twists his lips in a non-too-friendly manner.

Pieter makes a growling sound, muttering something in Dutch, which Lament translates as a promise to do something with hot irons to Dr Dee's nether regions. She feels a growing sense of exasperation as she realises that she and Pieter have been holding losing hands before they even realised that they were playing a game.

"We have only just joined the service of Master Dee. Although he, on the other hand, apparently had us marked down for his employ before we had even met." Lament speaks through clenched teeth; there is a limit to her patience, and it is almost at breaking point.

Sir Humphrey laughs as he breaks the ornate seal on the letter. "The doctor does seem to have a knack for predicting the future. Perhaps he is not always accurate, but if you let fly enough arrows, a few are bound to find the mark." At last, his piercing gaze shifts from Lament to the letter he unfolds. He frowns as his eyes sweep across the neatly written lines of secretary hand that fills the paper. When he finishes, he folds the letter again and slips it into his doublet.

"You even warrant a mention by Her Majesty, it seems. You are to accompany us in the assault on Brielle, and then I am to make sure you have whatever aid you require to continue your *mission* deeper into Spanish-held territory."

Pieter glances at Lament. "Oh, happy days."

"Now, if you will excuse me, I have a battle that needs my attention. You may travel with the general staff if that suits you." There is a note of irritation in his voice, which is not lost on Lament.

"We require no special considerations, sir. We are more than experienced in the field of war."

Sir Humphrey fixes Lament with those light brown eyes once more. "Captain, I am well aware of your exploits. You and your comrade are not without a certain notoriety. But there does seem to be a generous element of mayhem that travels with you two, and I would rather it was overseen by myself until we part company." A tight-lipped smile settles upon his face. "I am sure that we can make good use of your *particular skills* when the attack begins. So no, there will be no special considerations."

* * *

"Is there truly an *element of mayhem* that accompanies us?" Lament wistfully asks the question as she adjusts the girth of her blue roan stallion.

"I would have said it was youthful high spirits," Pieter replies, barely concealing a smirk which quickly changes to a look of concern as the great beast, which he is astride, shifts unnervingly. He is not a natural horseman, having been very large even as a child, and therefore unable to find anyone willing to let him make their horse bow-legged. But they have managed to find him an old, dapple-grey Percheron that had once been a war horse but has spent the past few years pulling a plough.

"Ever the foot soldier, aye Pieter." Lament laughs as she swings effortlessly into the saddle. She shifts her weight, and the stallion moves off towards the advancing column of troops as Pieter tries to kick his horse into motion. Lament looks back over her shoulder and makes a clicking sound with her lips, and the great grey Percheron suddenly trots after her. Pieter clings on for grim death, scowling murderously at the amused faces around him.

Lament is finding that if she keeps focused, the strange visions of other beings do not become overwhelming. After a while, she can almost forget that they are always there, hovering just beyond her concentration. Mostly, the soldiers around them look like men, but sometimes, out of the corner of her eye, she will glimpse twisted demon visages or unearthly frozen faces like those of statues that are somehow alive. Although, if she turns to look, the faces are always what she would describe as *normal*.

The day drags on, and the column of soldiers does what columns of soldiers do, seemingly absorbing everything in its path.

Sir Humphrey's scouts are ranging far and wide now that they are in territory controlled by the Spanish, but there has yet to be contact with the enemy, and by nightfall, they expect to be in sight of the defensive ramparts of the port of Brielle.

"An attack tonight, do you think?" Pieter shifts his weight to ease his sore backside.

"Maybe. What would you do?" Lament wipes the mingled dust and sweat from her forehead. The weather is unseasonably warm.

"If the Sea Beggars are in position, then yes, I would mount an assault immediately. It would be a shame to give the Don a chance to put up a proper defence."

"Agreed. If the ships can give a good account of themselves, then I think the defenders will be forced to make a hard choice. From what I know of Sir Humphrey, he is not a man to hold back from an advantage."

"Good! I need to stretch my legs after being kidnapped into the cavalry. Some exercise will help to work out the stiffness in my poor arse." Pieter grins ruefully and once again adjusts his seat as his horse plods on along the raised roads that cut through the wetlands.

# Chapter 8

Brielle is shrouded in black smoke.

The Sea Beggars discovered, much to their amazement and delight, that the Spanish garrison had gone. That left a ragtag local militia to guard the port, and their less-than-spirited defence didn't go well. The Sea Beggars pounded the defences with their cannon until the militia were forced to withdraw behind the town walls. Then, six hundred men from the ships stacked barrels and carts against the gates into the town then set them ablaze. Before long, the main force was within the walls, and the sack of Brielle began.

Now Lament and Pieter, along with Sir Humphrey's company, guide their mounts through the smoking streets.

Drunken troops of the Watergeuzen stagger through the wreckage that they have created, on the lookout for more loot or further victims of their blood lust.

Dark tableaux are glimpsed as they pass alleyways. Women are thrown from one man to another to be raped and then butchered when their tormentors become bored or tired of the cries for mercy and move on in search of fresh sport. Children are used as targets for crossbow bolts or beaten to death against walls for the amusement of men who believe that because these people worship a different way, they are somehow less than human.

Ragged, broken figures hang from makeshift gibbets. Anything can be a gibbet if it is high enough for the victim's feet to be clear of the ground, and many of the towns folk of Brielle have met their ends hoisted from door frames and dangling from window ledges. The bodies bear the signs of mutilation. It is not enough to take a life, it seems; guts must be ripped out and breasts hacked off.

Lament looks on with cold resignation. After all, it's not as if she hasn't witnessed all this before. It's not as if she and Pieter have not taken part in the horror and desecration that comes when a town is taken by force and the troops are given free rein. But she had hoped that she had seen the last of it, and once again, she silently curses Dr Dee.

Some of Sir Humphrey's men are restless, bemoaning the fact that they have missed out on the killing and have lost their share of the spoils. They are mostly the young bucks who boasted of their coming exploits. Their blood is up, and they feel cheated while at the same time secretly grateful that they are not fighting hand-to-hand through the narrow streets. Still, that is the concern of their senior officers, and Lament looks over at Pieter, who shakes his head in mock despair and says, "There will be bloodshed tonight if the Watergeuzen boast too loudly of their victory."

Another town hall and another meeting of military men, but this time roistering and spilling wine and ale with careless disregard.

Captain Willem Bloys van Treslong of the Sea Beggars is entertaining the newly arrived English officers with the tale of how their ships sailed right into port with barely a shot fired against them. Indications are that the Spanish garrison had departed two days previously to deal with insurrection in Utrecht, leaving the town, for all intents and purposes, unguarded.

Lament gazes at Captain van Treslong from the corner of her eye. She has become aware that if she observes those around her in this way, she can see their *other selves*, if they have one, without becoming overwhelmed by the visions. Captain van Treslong seems to be enshrouded by a long, deep blue robe, the hood of which forms a cowl around an oddly angular, pointed face of translucent white. His eyes are inky black slits that slant inwards towards an almost non-existent nose above a pale-lipped gash of a mouth. Lament is reminded of nothing less than an eel...

Adjusting her eyes once again, the captain becomes no more ominous than a roguish buccaneer. Dark wavy hair brushed straight back. A full beard covers most of his lower face, the rest of which has been burnt brown by salt and sun. He is stocky and capable-looking, and there is a glint of mischief in his brown eyes.

Sir Humphrey is not pleased to be entertained by the captain. He would speak with the leader of the Sea Beggars, not a drunken officer. "Captain van Treslong! When can we expect Lord William to grace us with his presence? As amusing as your stories may be, I would converse with his Lordship so that I may assess what further part we may play in this, if any." He makes a sweeping gesture to indicate the totality of the town.

"Ah, Sir Humphrey." The captain gives an almost mocking

bow that causes some of his men to grin a little too openly. Lament watches Sir Humphrey visibly bristle.

"Lord William is currently with Captain de Graeff. The last pocket of resistance was at the Governor's mansion, and his lordship has gone to oversee the breaking of that." The captain's English is itself breaking under the assault of the wine he has been celebrating with.

Lament turns to Pieter and rolls her eyes. "Let's get out of here. I am in no mood to watch two cockerels square off against each other."

The giant sergeant turns, his bulk clearing a path for them as they head towards the doorway and the smoke and scream-filled darkness beyond it.

* * *

The night is lit by the burning hopes and dreams of the inhabitants of Brielle as Lament and Pieter lead their horses along the main street towards the marketplace, where they have been told the forces of Sir Humphrey will be billeted.

It's obvious that the English troops have been allowed to slip their leash, and now they are playing catch-up in the looting and destruction game that the Sea Beggars have begun. It is mostly the common foot soldiers, but they are being encouraged by the officers who seem to have decided that it is beneath them to take part. Yet they are happy to observe the brutal sport taking place around them.

As they traverse a crossroads, a hysterical shriek snaps Lament from the dark reverie into which she has sunk. She has spent the walk from the town hall trying hard to avoid seeing the twisted demonic forms which possess many of the figures capering through the night. What has become sickeningly apparent is that the great majority of these men are not possessed at all. They are just bad men. And that makes Lament wonder if there is any hope at all for God's favoured creations...

The shriek again. This time, it's more drawn out and with an awful note of despair as it fades away to begging, sobbing, the sounds of a victim trying desperately to bargain with a merciless predator.

Off to her right, Lament sees, in the sickly yellow flames issuing from a shop, a woman pleading against hope for the life of her husband and children. The man is lying on the dirty street, a group of soldiers around him. They are taking it in turns to stab him with their daggers. Not deep enough to kill immediately, but deep enough. The man twists and turns, trying to avoid the blades that pierce him. He makes no sound as if all his energy is now focused on nothing but enduring the torment, perhaps in the hope that it might stop.

A leering, drunken pikeman, his breeches around his ankles, drags the woman to one side. A child of around four clings to her skirts, but the pikeman grabs it by the scruff and tosses it howling into the burning shop. The mother's groan of despair is heard even above the laughter and the screams.

An older boy attempts to flee, but his legs are knocked from under him, and a fat, brutish man stamps him to death. The woman sobs, all fight gone from her, and the pikeman drags her up against a wall, his lust obvious.

Pieter looks across at Lament, whose face is a cold, hard

mask. He has seen this look before, and he knows only too well where it will take them. So, he draws his falchion, no need for the zweihander here, and follows Lament into the side street.

As Lament stalks towards the soldiers, she draws sword and dagger in a fluid motion across her body. By the time the drunken men notice her, she is a black silhouette against the inferno of the shop. A lanky youth, no more than seventeen, his face marked with scars from some pox, a stolen doublet clutched in his left hand and a bloody dagger in his right, turns to face the dark shape advancing towards him.

"Come to join in? This one's almost done, and you will have to wait your turn with his whore." He looks over his shoulder; the pikeman is grunting and thrusting into the sobbing woman, forcing her against the brickwork. As the lanky youth turns back, the leer on his face is replaced for an instant by a look of confusion and then terror as the dark shape comes into focus and a sword point flashes upwards, entering his open mouth and exiting through the back of his skull with its matted hair.

The others turn, suddenly sober, a pack of wild dogs facing a challenger to their prey. Looted goods are dropped as they fumble for swords or reach for the polearms they have lent against the wall. Their bleeding victim lies forgotten in the filth, but he is long past feeling and relief, his remaining eye glazing over in death.

They fan out, nervous, excited glances are cast, and then they attack in a rush. The first man forgets his lanky comrade, who has just collapsed to the ground. He catches his foot in the jumble of limbs and staggers forward, sword outstretched. The blade is parried away, and his momentum takes him straight onto the point of Lament's dagger. It slips in above his old breastplate, passing through the unkempt, greasy beard, and punctures his throat. Frantic fingers claw at the blade, shaving flesh from bone in their attempt to remove the steel and deny the inevitable. A gurgling moan escapes from blood-frothed lips, and then the blade is torn out in time to catch and deflect a badly thrust spontoon.

Lament moves diagonally to her right around the falling body. The weight of the spontoon carries it forward, and the inexperience of its wielder leaves his body wide open. A lunge sends the long blade of the sword into the man's groin, and with a howl of pain, he drops the weapon and crumples back towards the burning building. Lament leaps the two already dead and helps this third into the flames with a kick in the chest.

A thick-set fellow in a padded leather jerkin dashes forward. He has seen an opportunity to catch Lament in the flank. His short sword is held low, and he has managed to grab the buckler from his belt. Alongside him, another pack member roars incoherent threats and seeing the advantage follows the first, his polearm is held high, ready to thrust.

None of them has noticed the giant Dutchman who had slipped into the shadows on the other side of the road and now comes at them full tilt from the blackness.

Pieter's falchion, its wide blade catching the fire's glare, cuts down through the forearm of the polearm wielder and comes to a hard stop in the weapon's wooden shaft. He hits the man with an enormous shoulder armoured with a pauldron of engraved steel and sends him barrelling into the thickset fellow, who barely manages to keep his footing, his charge completely ruined. He throws his left arm up reflexively and manages to block the sword thrust that comes at him seemingly from nowhere. He knows it is luck, not skill, that saved him. But luck can be fickle, and he can't block the upward diagonal slash of Pieter's butcher's tool as it smashes up through his rib cage and ends in his armpit.

As Lament watches the man die, her witch-sight sees a twisting, smoke-like form of grey and blue writhe around the body. Ancient crimson eyes full of hate stare at her for a moment, and then the thing that had used him is gone.

Now, there are three.

The oldest of the gang steps forward. He is more experienced, and instead of drawing his sword, he produces a wheellock pistol, which is already primed. He is nervous but takes his time to uncover the pan with its embers and then sight down the barrel. It is only then that he realises he has two targets and only one shot. Does he shoot the huge bear of a man and risk just angering him further? Or does he aim for the slighter figure who seems to be able to dance through the carnage with consummate ease and risk missing her entirely? He is holding his breath as he tries to decide, and the lack of air in his lungs begins to make his hand shake.

"For God's sake! Just put a ball in one of the bastards!" The pikeman has finally been distracted from his rape, and as he fumbles with his breeches, he manages to thrust his dagger into the woman's now naked breast. Her eyes grow wide with resigned horror, and she slides down the wall without a sound.

The man with the pistol seems to come to a decision and swings the barrel up towards Pieter's snarling face. The dagger that suddenly sprouts from his chest is not within his expectations, and the pistol goes off high and wide. He looks down at the hilt and realises that the smaller of his two enemies must have thrown it. Blood dribbles down his greying beard, and then Pieter's falchion chops into his neck and drives him to his knees.

The pikeman has a look of contempt on his wide, flat face as he looks at the wreck of the man with the pistol. He reaches out to grab his pike and looks over to his last remaining companion. But that fellow has made a run for it. He watched as the others died, and then whatever courage he possessed fled the scene, and he swiftly followed.

"Fuck!" The pikeman turns, his weapon held across him in a guard position, and Lament notices a distortion of his face, that demonic malformation that seems to indicate possession.

It is over quickly. Pieter moves to the man's left, and as he swings the point of the axe-like head to cover the Dutchman, Lament steps in and feints at his chest. The pike swings back to counter the thrust in a vicious arc, but Lament has already stepped off her centreline, and she twists her body away and thrusts her sword through the cheek of the flat face and into the brain.

Pieter wipes his sword on the sleeve of the man who held the pistol and retrieves Lament's dagger. "We had best make ourselves scarce, Lam. That one who fled may yet come back with friends."

"Aye, let's get the horses and find this damned camp." As they turn away, Lament's eyes fall on the dead woman, and she sheaths her dagger, but it cannot draw a line under the waste of another innocent life.

* * *

Unseen, formless shadows drift across the town as it dies. Some seem to shudder in a sort of ecstasy at the slaughter and destruction; others just observe with a cold indifference. Even the shadows seem oblivious to the presence of each other as if they exist in separate realms that only cross in this sad, mortal world.

# Chapter 9

Morning has found Lament sitting on a crate outside the storehouse where she and Pieter spent last night. She is cleaning her sword and tending to the edge, keeping it keen with a whetstone. Pieter tips a bucket of water over his head and shakes the drops away noisily.

They had managed to buy a bottle of brandy from a group of Dutch sailors, and along with sausage and bread from Sir Humphrey's quartermaster, they had settled down and let those who still had designs on finding some adventure wander the streets of the town.

"So, the visions are becoming less then?" Pieter squeezes water out of his great bush of a beard as he asks the question. It was a conversation begun last night, but Lament had been in a dark mood and had preferred drink over the conversation.

"I think so. Either that, or I am just becoming used to the witch-sight. Whichever is the case, they are becoming easier to cope with. Dee's sorcery has found a home in my skin."

"But nothing that might be one of Dee's baubles?" Pieter is hopeful of a quick conclusion to this adventure.

"Sadly, no, my friend." Lament laughs at the big man's

disappointment. "Just these spirit creatures that possess men. I don't believe we have enough luck to chance upon one of the good doctor's objects here."

Pieter shakes his head with disappointment and then shudders despite himself. "Makes my skin crawl what you have described. To think they are all around us..." He glances out into the awakening camp as if he might see some vision of hell's own creatures.

"It would seem they have always been there. But at least we know that we can send them back whence they came."

"Aye, as you have said. At least that is some comfort." He looks across the makeshift camp that is the market square and sees the figure on horseback heading towards them. "Looks like we have company."

Captain Bowcer sits astride his palfrey and eyes Lament and Pieter with what might be considered hostility masquerading as disdain. He does not think it fit for an officer of his station to be dispatched as an errand boy to fetch these two soldiers of fortune. They look less the worse for wear than most of the camp, but he views them as no better than the common soldiers. Still, he has been commanded by Sir Humphrey to fetch them, and so he must.

"Captain. You and the sergeant are required to attend Sir Humphrey at the Governor's Mansion." He is curt, and Lament does not look up from sharpening her blade, which makes him even more belligerent.

"Did you hear me, Captain?" He nudges the palfrey forward. It senses its rider's mood and twists nervously.

At last, Lament looks at Captain Bowcer. Blue-grey eyes

stare up at the man wrestling his horse around to face her. For a few brief moments, there is once again the impression of a thin, pallid face and the floating grey ribbons with their metallic decorations, but that passes almost before it has fully formed.

"I bid you goodmorrow, Captain. You seem somewhat vexed."

Bowcer's face flushes, and he agitatedly slaps his horse, annoyed that he appears to be not in control. "I am engaged in the business of dealing with the troops, Captain, and I do not take kindly to being used as a messenger when I have more pressing matters to attend to!"

"Well, you had better be on your way then, Captain Bowcer. We would not wish to detain you further." As she speaks, Lament extends her sword out to arm's length and, closing one eye, sights along its keen edge. Bowcer is only too aware that the tip of the sword is pointed directly at him. His face colours still darker, and as his horse turns yet again, he looks over his shoulder.

"It would be wise for you to make your way to the Governor's Mansion with all due haste. I will bid you good day, and maybe our paths will cross at some more convenient time, and we can find out if you are as good a swordswoman as your reputation would have us believe." He kicks his horse away and forces bleary-eyed pikemen to dodge back into the tents from which they have just emerged.

Lament raises her sword and mockingly salutes the captain's rapidly disappearing back.

"Have we lost another friend? That does seem to be our curse. How bitterly disappointing." Pieter grins and spits into the straw that is scattered on the storehouse floor. He makes a mental note to watch Lament's back when that particular streak of piss is nearby. Yet another name on a long list.

The Governor's Mansion is not as grand as it once was, although it has been spared much of the carnage meted out to the rest of the town. That is due to the good graces of William van der Marck, Lord of Lumey, leader of the Watergeuzen.

Lord William has just finished speaking with Sir Humphrey as Lament and Pieter arrive. William van der Marck is a rangy fellow with a full beard and a somewhat piratical air about him. He reminds Lament of an older Walter Raleigh. She had briefly met Raleigh during a campaign several years before. She instantly had marked him as a rogue, a likeable rogue, but a rogue nonetheless, and one who had tried on several, mostly unsuccessful occasions, to bed her. Lord William leaves the same impression. He bids Sir Humphrey a good day and heads out towards the docks to get a report from Captain van Treslong. He nods at Lament and Pieter as he passes and is gone out into the daylight.

Sir Humphrey turns his attention to the new arrivals, and a shadow briefly crosses his face. "Good day to you, Captain Evyngar, Sergeant Hertgers. I trust you slept well?" The question seems loaded, and Lament senses what is to come.

"We did, sir. Is something troubling you?"

"Captain de Graeff's pickets came across one of our men in a state of panic and blathering incoherently last night. He claimed that a sword-wielding she devil and a giant had materialised out of the darkness and murdered his comrades as they celebrated victory. He seemed to think that they could have been Spanish assassins left behind to wreak havoc amongst us. I think he and his friends may have had too much drink and found themselves in a quarrel with the wrong persons, and he only just escaped with his life. What think *you*, Captain?" Sir Humphrey raises a quizzical eyebrow as he watches the mask that is Lament's face. Lament allows that mask to crack slightly into a thin smile.

"Ah, these things happen when men celebrate with drink and slaughter. They could have got themselves into an argument with another gang over sharing the spoils. Tempers can become frayed rather thin where loot is concerned, especially as we arrived rather late to the party. And drink can play havoc with a man's memory..." Lament cocks her head to one side, aware that the witch-sight is causing Sir Humphrey's face to blur alarmingly, and she fights it back under control. "But why ask me this, sir? Surely this is a matter for your officers to handle?"

Sir Humphrey sighs; he looks weary. Having marched his men to battle only to find that they were too late, the anticlimax is making him, or perhaps *that* which possesses him, irritable.

"Come, Captain! When a witness describes a giant and a woman wielding a black-hilted sword, it is wise to look to those fitting the description. I know not what happened and care even less, but rumour will spread amongst the men, and I will not have unrest in the ranks." He places his fists on his hips and addresses the whitewashed ceiling in an attempt to control his temper. "I have agreed to give you aid in your mission, but I can't, in all good faith, have you travel with us further. Therefore, you will ride with Captain de Graeff and a company of Dutch dragoons to the city of Mechelen. There is an agent of the Privy Council there who can arrange further assistance for you."

Lament nods her head once in acceptance of Sir Humphrey's

decision. There is no point contesting it. She does not want to be there any more than Sir Humphrey desires her company.

"Captain de Graeff leaves at noon. Be sure you are in his company when he departs." Sir Humphrey turns away, and it is nothing less than a contemptuous gesture of dismissal.

Lament says nothing; she just stalks from the room. Pieter stands for a moment, looking at the back of Sir Humphrey. He opens his mouth to say something about discourtesy but then closes it and makes a mocking bow noticed only by several of Sir Humphrey's aids and strides after his captain.

"Is this a good thing? Did the doctor not put us in this company for a reason?" They are strapping their few belongings, plus some extra items they have acquired, to the saddles of their horses. Pieter is not his usual happy-go-lucky self. He is not at all sure that this new course of action will not bring about some failure to comply with Dr Dee's contract and, therefore, result in all the threats that their failure would entail manifesting.

"Come now, Sergeant," Lament grins over at him, "it is unlike you to worry about trivialities!"

Pieter grunts and continues to strap his great zweihander sword to the saddle.

"There is nothing that the good doctor seeks here. I get no sense of anything other than the occasional glimpse of these entities, and besides, he said that we would find the first object in Naarden, which is not high on Sir Humphrey's plan of action at this moment. So, I believe that it would not serve our cause to tarry here amongst these would-be heroes and addle pates. Let us away to Mechelen and see what this intelligencer of the Privy Council has to offer."

Something more akin to his normal smile settles on Pieter's wide face, splitting his bushy beard. "Aye, you are right. No good reason to remain in a town with these arses. Let us go and find a city filled with even bigger ones!"

* * *

A fine drizzle descends as they leave a smouldering Brielle to the tender mercies of its conquerors and set off into the Low Countries.

Captain de Graeff is an amiable professional soldier, and his men are well-disciplined, seasoned troops. Lament finds herself liking de Graeff despite her usual indifference. The slim, athletic-looking Dutchman with straw blonde hair and a pointed beard to match has a ready smile. His cornflower blue eyes seem constantly to be attempting to contain some jest or other, and, unlike many of the other officers that Lament has observed, he doesn't seem to be harbouring an unearthly parasite.

Pieter is happily conversing in Dutch with the other men. Lament's Dutch is not quite fluent, but she can follow along and catches mention of Pieter's great size, a common topic of conversation, and questions about where he hails from. There is much laughter, and Lament relaxes a little as she no longer feels the threat of imminent violence. Not that it concerns her much. She has lived with the risk of sudden death, hers or another's, for so long that it is like a well-worn cloak that she always seems to wear. Comfortable and familiar, but a weight nonetheless that feels good to take off when she can.

"You wore out your welcome with great rapidity, Captain

Evyngar, no?" Captain de Graeff gives her a mischievous smile, settling his wide-brimmed hat more securely on his head. "Something to do with an encounter with members of Sir Humphrey's soldiery, was it not? However, who is to say what might have occurred during the plundering last night? My men and I spent much of it patrolling the countryside around the town, and there was no need for them to be involved in the murder of their own people, be they Catholics or not." A look of distaste passes over his angular, handsome features.

"I believe that my sergeant and I fitted the description of two *ghosts* who may have taken exception to the level of depravity on display and meted out some form of their own justice. And, as you say, Captain de Graeff, who is to determine what might have happened... But tell me, sir, why do we go to Mechelen?"

De Graeff smiles again and nods, acknowledging Lament's desire not to discuss the reason that they have been banished from Sir Humphrey's retinue. "Cities that were staunchly Catholic are beginning to make noises that they would welcome the forces of William of Orange. We are to join with those forces, and if the intelligence is correct, we may walk through the gates of Mechelen as allies. That, of course, is the plan. We will have to see what the reality brings to us."

# Chapter 10

A week has passed as the troop made their way past flooded dykes, often leading the horses on foot or travelling on commandeered flat-bottom barges. The bargees have mostly been friendly, but as they approached the Brabant, there was a definite change in mood.

They have ridden past columns of refugees fleeing from cities that have suddenly changed allegiance from Catholic to Calvinist. Those fleeing are not prepared to take the chance that the new forces entering their cities and towns will not take the opportunity to engage in rape and looting despite assurances.

Heading southeast, they have entered a landscape of open fields and waterways that have allowed them to skirt some of the more settled areas which may hold Spanish garrisons.

* * *

Scouts have reported a large body of pikemen and cavalry travelling along the main highway that runs along the far side of the dense woods in which they are camped.

It is Captain de Graeff's habit to send out scouts in all

directions when they have made camp. This helps to avoid any unpleasant surprises, and in this case, the riders who were tasked with heading east have returned rapidly with news of the much larger force. They assure de Graeff that they were not spotted, and when pressed, they respond with indignation at the slighting of their skills. De Graeff laughs at their bluster; he knows the abilities of his men only too well.

"Shall we take a look at this war party, Captain?" He already knows the answer as Lament and Pieter are up and saddling their mounts almost before the question is fully asked.

They follow the scouts back into the densest part of the woods and take a course heading northeast to get a look at the head of the column and the officers leading it. The sun is sinking as they leave their horses with one of the scouts and make their way through deep blue shadows to the margin of the trees.

"I would wager that they are heading for Antwerp. They could make camp outside the city before nightfall." De Graeff eyes the officers at the front and frowns. "Do you know those men, Captain?"

"Indeed, I do." Both Lament and Pieter nod in confirmation. "That is Sir William Stanley. A renegade gone over to the Spanish with his English and Irish troops. There is rumour that he pays men to go into England to act as assassins against the Queen."

"They appear to have little success then!" De Graeff grins at his humour, and then he narrows his eyes in the failing light. "And who is that just to their rear?" He points at a group of riders who, even from this distance, look to be of a different stock.

Lament follows his gaze, and as she does, she feels her

perception begin to shift, something that has mercifully been absent since they left Brielle.

The setting sun appears to illuminate them as if they were in a heat haze, the figures growing larger and mutating. Unlike the entities that possess the likes of Sir Humphrey and his officers, these are gaudily dressed and appear wreathed in fire. They are no less disturbing to gaze upon, but whereas the others seemed imbued with a cold stillness, these seem to writhe as if in constant motion. And there, in their midst, is a figure astride a large grey stallion with eyes that glow like hot coals. He looks like nothing less than a jester. Like the ones that are common amongst the street entertainers, in the theatre, and at court. But London has never seen a jester such as this one, dressed in multicoloured clothes and wearing a curved sword in the style of the Turks as he sits astride his horse and laughs with the other strange, shifting things around him. His skull is long and narrow, and it looks as if he is wearing a mask, although the shape and design of that mask seem to continually mutate into different forms. Long dark hair flows out from beneath the wide brim of his hat, fluttering in the otherworldly breeze that seems to accompany these creatures.

The whole column suddenly, to Lament's witch-sight, takes on the semblance of a hellish carnival parade. Demonic beings cavorting in procession across a land turned to boiling purple and blue clouds.

"Captain! Are you well?" Pieter's huge hand grips Lament's shoulder, and he gives his friend a quick, violent shake. This is no place for anyone to be without their wits, and Lament is staring in slack-jawed amazement.

De Graeff looks on with concern as Lament shakes her head and blinks repeatedly as if to expel the remnants of a nightmare from which she is just awakening. She reaches up and pats Pieter's hand.

"I am good, my friend. I was dazzled by the reflection of the last of the sun's rays for a moment and could not see straight." Looking now, she can see once again the line of English and Irish troops and their officers in the vanguard. The odd group behind Sir William Stanley, his captains and lieutenants come momentarily into sharper focus. They are dressed in the Spanish style, and they have a disdain about them that is evident even from this distance. All except the one on the grey stallion. He seems aloof even from the others. His black hair and narrow beard frame a pale face that still has something of the everchanging mask about it, and he runs a gloved hand through his hair before replacing the wide-brimmed, dark purple hat with its cockade of peacock feathers upon his head. And for a moment, Lament could swear that the pale face turns towards them, and a knowing smile crosses it before turning away once more.

One of de Graeff's scouts signals that there are outriders from Sir Williams's column making a sweep of the area, and so they disappear back amongst the trees and silently make their way back to camp.

* * *

Captain de Graeff sits on a fallen tree. The morning mist rises from the damp ground and softens the forms of his men as they go about the business of preparing themselves for another day's ride. He can see the horses tethered just off the edge of their camp, and they wicker greetings to their riders as they are tacked up.

But his attention is taken up by the strange Englishwoman travelling with them. He and Captain Evyngar have become, if not friends, then at least good allies during their journey. He trusts the woman, probably more than he trusts most. There is an unwavering certainty about her but also some sense of doom that seems to weigh heavy, and there are those marks on her skin. Lament rarely reveals more than her bare forearms. But now and then, when she washes, she pulls up the sleeves of her shirt, and the strange geometric patterns on her skin show up like faded ink just below the surface. The first time he noticed them, de Graeff could not help but express his amazement. Lament, on the contrary, seemed self-conscious of them and quickly covered them. The explanation that they were markings she had gained while trading with the Moors years before seemed a little false, although de Graeff had decided that a woman's business was her own and had left it at that.

Lament and her constant companion, the giant Sergeant Hertgers, are fine company and more than useful in a fight. So, de Graeff is willing to ignore the odder elements, such as Lament's strange, almost fugue states like the one she appeared to enter as they watched Sir William Stanley's column of troops pass by into the night.

De Graeff stretches; he would still take the seemingly doom-laden English swordswoman and the colossal sergeant over any of the men that Sir Humphrey had brought to them in their fight against the Spanish. They were either nobles seeking a name or vagabonds and curs who had been dragged from the gutters of England and promised coin and a regular meal if they killed Catholics. He is tired of seeing his country scorched for the sake of ideology. *This war*, he thinks, *will make paupers of us all.*

* * *

Today, there is a sense of anticipation in the air. They are two days short of Mechelen, and there is a company of Spanish troops blocking their path. They have been positioned to intercept any Calvinist force sent to garrison Mechelen now rumour has it they will throw open the gates and embrace the protestant forces of Orange.

De Graeff's men are readying for the fight. Nervous excitement and bravado run through the men like a shiver on a winter's night. These are good, solid soldiers, but every man has a cognisance of his mortality before battle. It is only in the frenzy of combat that they become, at least in their thoughts, immortal. Until they are not... And the men they will face are Tercios, the shock troops of the Spanish. Although, and this brings some heart to Captain de Graeff's men, they are far short of battalion strength. Questioning the local population has given them a possible answer – it would seem that the main part of the battalion has marched to Antwerp, the same destination as Sir William Stanley's men. But both Lament and Pieter have faced the Tercios before, and they know that only a fool would underestimate even a diminished force.

"At least they are cavalry, thank the Lord. Facing their

pikemen would have been an unwelcome task." Pieter eyes the edge of his great two-handed sword as he makes his observation.

"You will not be using that butcher's knife from horseback, my friend. Or have you seen the musketeers lining up on yonder ridge?" Lament nods to the east, and the low bank formed by a dyke. There, a row of men in steel helmets are setting up their firearms on musket rests.

"Aye, Captain. I thought I might take a few of the men and skirt around the edge of the field before you lot make your charge. If we can dissuade those bastards from pouring shot onto you, it might just make your task a little easier. Besides, riding one of those beasts is one thing, fighting from the back of one is quite another! I prefer to have my feet planted on solid ground when I am killing. And you know that I haven't given Utricia here any exercise in a while." He pats the flat of the long blade affectionately and grins that broad grin that splits his red beard in two.

Lament laughs as much at the fact that the big Dutchman has named his sword after his mother, something that, even after all these years, causes Lament amusement. But, as Pieter likes to remind Lament, "You have never met my moeder. If you had, you would understand."

Pieter has gone with a dozen men. They have disappeared into the tall reeds that skirt the edge of the road where the Spaniards have laid their line. The Tercios await, drawn up in formation at the crossroads, their horses impatiently pawing at the ground. On the bank of the dyke off to the left, the musketeers are now in place. There has been no attempt at concealment. The Spanish know that de Graeff's force must advance towards them or turn tail and retreat, and so they must face whatever lies in store for them, even if it is a deadly barrage of shot.

Water swirls around their ankles as they push silently through the sedge and reeds. It is muddy but not enough to slow their progress.

Pieter holds up a big hand, signalling a halt, and he crouches low and peers through the screen of grasses at the backs of the men above them. They are ranged out along the dyke's flat crest, musket stands pushed into the surface and big, unwieldy wheellocks pointing down onto the road along which de Graeff's dragoons will charge. There are thirty of them, and Pieter can hear their jests as they prepare to inflict carnage on the slowly advancing horsemen.

Checking along the line of his fellow Dutchmen, Pieter can see that they all have two wheellock pistols, each primed and ready to fire. He smiles a tight-lipped smile of grim satisfaction and draws his pistols or dags as his English friend calls them. They will even the numbers before closing in.

The horses walk forward towards the Spanish. It is almost leisurely. There seems to be no haste for the slaughter to begin. The Spanish horses match their pace, but Lament knows that they are only waiting for the guns on the ridge to open up and inflict their damage before they charge.

There is a moment of eerie silence and then a crackling sound like heaps of dry branches being broken. The soldiers on the ridge begin to fall, and as they do, Captain de Graeff raises his sword and signals the charge.

Sergeant at Arms Pieter Hertgers was known as *Red Pieter* by his fellow Landsknechts. Because of his red hair but also because of the battle rage that engulfs him, turning the laughing, womanising giant into an engine of death. Right now, he can feel *Red Pieter* crawling up through the darkness inside him, and he welcomes him like an old friend. Just for a moment, he wonders if he carries a demon such as the ones Lament can see on other men. But the moment passes swiftly, and after discharging his pistols, he takes the hilt of Utricia in both massive hands and roars his battle cry as he storms up the bank.

The Spanish line is in chaos. They can't turn their guns on the attackers at their rear, so they must drop them and draw swords or grab polearms. Some manage to get shots off at the advancing line of de Graeff's cavalry, and a few heavy lead balls rip into men and horses, but most go wide.

At first, they are stunned as to how their comrades are falling around them, but these are seasoned professional troops with an officer who knows the business of war. Still, nearly half their number fall dead or wounded to the pistols of those who now charge at them from the reeds below.

Pieter cleaves his way amongst the enemy. His sword is sharp, but its mere weight alone is enough to knock men off their feet and break bones. Its reach is terrifying. The men with him know to give a wide birth to the great length of steel that is hacking off limbs and caving in torsos with sickening ease.

Not that the others are not equally engaged as they spread out amongst the rapidly recovering musketeers. It quickly becomes a desperate hand-to-hand melee as men wrestle each other down to the ground, and a few locked together roll back down into the reeds, where the grizzly work of killing continues.

As Pieter kicks a snarling Spaniard off the bank, he glances down onto the road below. There, the two forces of cavalry have met with the thunder of hooves and a clash of steel. But a shout from one of his men snaps his attention back to the job at hand, and he curses as he realises that the Tercios had suspected an attempt to take the bank. As he watches, there is a force of two dozen pikemen rushing from the hidden end of the ridge where it intersects the road.

"Look to your work! We have company!" He roars the warning to his men and runs towards the newcomers, his sword sweeping low as he goes, cutting through legs and felling startled Spanish who had thought the enemy an easy encounter.

A horse rears in front of her, falling backwards as its rider takes a lead ball in his chest and drags the animal with him in his death throes. Lament deftly shifts her weight, and her horse responds by moving aside and past the flailing limbs. They have not had to endure the withering blast that could have come from the muskets, but the few shots that do rain down on them still do terrible damage. Lament bends low over the horse's neck and extends arm and sword. The blade skewers the first rider she meets, and she allows the blade to flex as she withdraws it and passes the man, now dead in his saddle. She parries a blow from her left and then slashes across to her right, feeling the edge of the blade bite deep.

She kicks her mount on between two brightly plumed Spanish, slashing left and right as she goes. Then suddenly, she is through the enemy line, and she turns the blue roan back towards the brawl she has just broken through.

"Not now! For Jesus' sake, not now!" She cries out in alarm as the witch-sight takes her without warning.

The mass of fighting men has become a scene from hell. They appear to be fighting on a boiling, shifting terrain of dark liquid colours and evilly glowing clouds of mist. Men are no longer men but have the faces and forms of beasts that shift and warp in fantastic, unearthly delight at the dreadful work they undertake. The Tercios all seem to embody some extravagant, mythical form. Bright swirling colours emanate from them while flames dance around their bodies. By contrast, de Graeff's men have a sickly silver-grey appearance like disembodied spirits, ghosts raised from some unknown ancient marsh where they drag down the unwary. Their garments float around them as if they are underwater, and while the Spanish give off constantly changing luminous clouds, the Dutchmen leech a pale vapour that seems as cold as winter. Even their beasts have taken on new and terrible forms. Scaled, spiked, terrifying chimaeras that thrash around them or rotting skeletal forms burning with malevolent green fire.

Lament has reined in her mount, and, for a moment, she stares with an open mouth. Then, she narrows her gaze and urges her horse on again. Demons or not, there is bloody work to do. Work she knows only too well.

Pieter's wild charge causes the advance of the pikemen to falter. They are too closely packed as yet to use their numbers and weapon reach to their advantage. They were not anticipating a berserk giant with a huge sword to suddenly be in their ranks. Their captain bellows at them to form a line, but several slip and fall onto the roadway below in a tangle of polearms and limbs. But they are seasoned troops, and they are already beginning to form up and brace against this unexpected enemy. Big as he is, they know that they can use their extra reach to end him once they can bring their weapons to bear.

From behind him, Pieter hears a roar of muskets, and some of the pikemen in front of him go down. He glances over his shoulder to see several of his men drop the muskets they had taken from the Spanish in their first charge. They close in behind him, forming a wedge on top of the dyke.

"Well, sergeant, what is your pleasure? The rest of the lads are dealing with the musketeers, so do we attack?" The young, lantern-jawed Dutchman wipes blood from his brow and smiles at Pieter, pale eyes shining with a crazed intensity.

"Aye, boys! Before they can get line abreast. Let us drive these Papist fuckers back over the edge!" He surges forward, but this time at the tip of a bristling wedge that splits the Spanish in two before they can become a deadly wall of pikes.

Men of both sides go down around him, and his booted feet slip in the blood and viscera that is coating the grass and quickly turning the earth beneath to copper-stinking mud. But the press of bodies is too tight to let him fall, and so he pushes on, hauling one Spaniard off his feet and using him as a shield as he drops his useless zweihander and draws his falchion. He pushes the squirming pikeman before him, letting him take the thrusts of the weapons of his men. When the legs give way, and he becomes a dead weight, Pieter kicks him forward, leaping after with the broad blade of the falchion, chopping into anyone unfortunate enough to be in his way. He knows that this is a desperate action and that if the Dutch soldiers to his rear give way, then they will be surrounded and cut down. He grins a savage, wild grin and gives himself to the will of God, mayhap an Old Testament God.

Slashing right and left, Lament clears a path back into the heart of the fight. Snarling, deformed faces glare at her from under outrageous, exaggerated helmets and broad-brimmed hats. Plumes of fire crown them, and embroidered designs or gilded engravings writhe across them like a nest of adders.

The tip of her sword finds an inhuman face, and the owner of that face screeches as he throws up his hands before slumping dead from the back of his beast. Two riders close on her, and she lets them come. The first, with a vulpine look to his features, sweeps in with a heavy longsword looking to unseat Lament. He swings the blade in an upward arc as he urges his mount across Lament's path. The second, a strange, flabby look to his purple face with octopus-like tentacles sprouting out around his head in a bizarre mane, rushes in headlong, an axe held high.

Lament steps on her left stirrup. Her horse responds perfectly, side-stepping across the approach of the first, whose blade sweeps up and wide. The savagery of the slash, coupled with the weight of the sword, causes him to overextend and twist in the saddle. As he does so, the mount of the second attacker crashes into him, and Lament takes the opportunity to empty the barrel of the pistol she has drawn into the first man's armpit. Such a small orb of lead, but when it contacts flesh, it appears to obtain an obscene magnitude that belies its seeming insignificance. The vulpine features twist in an agony of hatred and lost opportunity as the ball snaps ribs and mangles nerves before coming to a halt deep in a collapsing lung.

The impact of the horses colliding throws the mortally wounded man clear, but the second grimly keeps his seat and goads his frothing beast out of the tangle and back towards

Lament. Lament kicks hard, and as they draw level, she flings the pistol from her left hand into the tentacled face and uses the distraction to cut beneath the raised axe and open the flabby purple throat.

She finds herself clear again and realises with shock that most of the Spaniards are either down or attempting to ride away. An unguarded back presents itself, and she cuts the undulating man thing down. She learned a long time ago that the only *fair* thing in battle is being alive at the end of it. Honour and chivalry are both things that poets and playwrights can celebrate, but when you stand knee-deep in gore, they are far from your thoughts – and the dead care nothing for them.

The visions of hellish creatures begin to fade as the fight peters out, and Lament spots a group of her Dutch companions in arms dismounted and gathered around a fallen form.

A sigh escapes her. Perhaps a release of the tension of violence. Or maybe an expression of sorrow. Even she is not sure.

There, on the trampled earth, surrounded by his men, lies the broken body of Captain de Graeff. A savage cut has severed his thigh just above the knee, and there is a neat hole in his breastplate above his heart. Astonishingly, he still clings to life, eyes searching those around him as if seeking some miracle, some reprieve. Lament dismounts and kneels beside him, taking his hand in hers. The captain's eyes focus for a moment on Lament's.

"Did you *see*? Did you see what they are, what they became?" A spasm of coughing takes him, and his eyes search the heavens. Lament looks at the man she would happily have called friend and wonders, *did he see what I saw?*

"What did you see, Lennaert? What was it they became?" But Captain Lennaert Jansz de Graeff does not answer.

Pieter and his six remaining men descend from the crest of the bank. With them is a prisoner, the captain of the musketeers. He is limping and, in general, looks a little worse for wear, although he has the good fortune to still be breathing.

The young Dutchman with the lantern-jaw forces the Spaniard to his knees, and he is no longer smiling as he looks at his captain dead on the dusty road.

"Ah, tis a shame. May the Lord grant him mercy; he was a decent man." Pieter claps Lament on the shoulder as she stands up, almost sending her back to her knees with the weight of the gesture.

"Indeed, it is a shame." Lament stares at de Graeff for a moment, and then, with a shrug that only Pieter notices, she turns to her giant sergeant. "Well, big man, you did marvels up there and made quite a mess by the looks of it!" Lament forces a smile at her friend, who is covered in blood and gore. Utricia rests across one shoulder, already wiped clean on the cloak of some fallen Tercio. He looks more like a mythical creature summoned from a pagan vision of hell than a man.

"It was good to get some exercise after all of the sitting on that fat beast." True to form, he makes light of what was a near-run thing. It could have all ended very differently up on the dyke. Lament raises an eyebrow and smiles a more genuine smile. It is hard not to get caught up in the great Dutch bear's bravado.

"And who do we have here?" She nods over at the kneeling Spanish captain.

"Oh, this is the officer in charge of the bastards up on yonder bank. Thought he would surprise us with a flanking manoeuvre, but he didn't consider the difficulty of pointing all those pikes in the right direction while trying to climb a slope."

"And being attacked by a *monster*!" the Spanish captain adds with a surly grunt.

Lament moves to stand in front of their captive while de Graeff's men are dealing with his body and the rest of their dead and wounded. Lament is now the only senior officer in the troop, and she automatically assumes command.

"So, sir, I understand from some of the locals that you were part of a larger force. Why, pray tell, where you left behind?"

The Spaniard sits back on his heels. He is of medium build and once may have been athletic. But he is in his late thirties and has begun to let himself get too fond of wine and sweet-meats. He had thought this his last campaign, returning home with gold and prestige. Now, his shoulders slump, and his long moustaches seem a foolish embellishment for a defeated man.

"There was unrest among the men. We have not had pay for a long time. When the battalion was ordered to march to Antwerp, there was dissent, and it was decided to leave a small force here to intercept any who would head to Mechelen, made up mostly of those who were vocal in their demands for pay. I was one of the officers left with them to make sure that they did not just desert and pillage the local villages. Although it would seem that the other officers have made their escape." A look of distaste crosses his face, and he stares down into his lap. "What will become of me senior?"

"Well, I think that very much depends upon what other information you care to share with us…"

Lament stares after the departing figure of Captain Iago Hernandez. The good captain has been very forthcoming with information, at least the little that he is privy to. He has given more detail about the troop build-up around Antwerp and his belief that it will presage a response to the invitation of some of the cities to the Calvinist troops of Orange. He has also given a good account of the arrival of several Archdukes and Dutchesses who have been given command of some of the forces of Phillip of Spain. They seemingly have a free hand in dealing with those considered by Rome to be heretics, while the Duke of Alba and his son wage a more concerted war effort further north.

Hernandez is a man who is sick of being let down by his command and is now just grateful for his life. He disappears into the twilight along the road south.

As she looks away, she doesn't notice the young lantern-jawed Dutchman follow Hernandez into the dark. After a short while, he returns, quietly cleaning his dagger, a haunted look in his pale eyes. He saw no reason why one of the hated Spanish should walk free after the death of de Graeff, his Captain. But maybe, if he lives, he will regret that impulse one day...

"Well, Captain Evyngar, you have a company of men to command again." Pieter pushes the ostrich-plumed barret further back on his close-cropped head. A mirthless grin plays on his heavy lips. He knows that this is the last thing Lament wants, yet somehow, they are going to have to work with the hand that fate is dealing them.

"Yes, sergeant. You had best get those men who can ride into the saddle, and let's find somewhere with a surgeon who can look to the wounds of those who need care. Then, my friend, after food, drink, and perhaps sleep, we should finish the journey Captain de Graeff started and get us to Mechelen." Lament feels none of the bravado she seeks to impart. The visions seem to take a toll on her that she is only now beginning to recognise. After each event, she has started to become more detached, to feel less solid, as if she is slowly becoming a ghost. A weariness is gradually overtaking her that, if she stops to think on it, may well have been coming before she ever laid eyes on Dr Dee.

# Chapter 11

Lament has discharged her duty. Captain de Graeff's company of dragoons is now billeted inside the walls of Mechelen. Though they would have happily kept Captain Evyngar as their commanding officer, Lament has other tasks to fulfil.

Mechelen itself, like many of the cities in the Low Countries, has opened its gates to the troops of William of Orange. He, in turn, has left a garrison under the command of Bernard van Merode while he continues his advance towards Mons. Unfortunately, the portly van Merode is of the opinion that Lament and Pieter are now at his disposal. And so, while evading the attentions of van Merode, they have managed to make contact with the agent of Dr Dee, one Master William Sterrell.

Sitting on the one good chair in the third-story lodgings of the intelligencer, Lament rocks the chair onto its back legs and leans against the wall, her sword lying across her thighs. Pieter sits on the storage chest by the bay window and looks out across the city through the open shutters. A buxom young woman hanging washing over a line strung between the houses has caught his eye, and he grunts appreciatively. Lament smiles at her large friend's ability to be oblivious when something takes his fancy.

William Sterrell is a tall, thin, fair-haired young man. He sports a wispy beard and has watery, pale blue eyes that look, judging by the pink rims, to be permanently irritated. He brings a wooden tray from the back of the room and places it onto another chest, which serves as his table. The tray bears a jug of wine and three mismatched drinking vessels made of pale green glass. As he fills the glasses with the deep red wine, he glances calculatingly at this swordswoman perched on his good chair. He has been instructed by Dr Dee, via coded letters, that he is to provide guidance and assistance where possible to these soldiers of fortune. He has also received a purse of coin to help facilitate this. Although his previous requests for funds had gone unheeded, therefore he feels a little less obliged to be free and easy with the monies he has been given.

Lament has already given Master Sterrell a document containing the information she managed to ascertain from the Tercio captain and a description of the troop column of Sir William Stanley that was heading for Antwerp. The neatly written document lies on the chest alongside the tray, and Sterrell's eyes pass over it again as he finishes pouring and hands the glasses to his guests.

"You say there were Spanish officers in the vanguard of Stanley's force?"

Lament takes the proffered glass and nods, taking a sip before answering. "Yes, I would estimate that there were a dozen or so. Hard to tell as the light was failing, and there was one in particular who had an odd look about him. Sort of like a street entertainer, a fool, a..."

"*Jester?*" Sterrell finishes the sentence for her, and Lament nods, eyes narrowing suspiciously.

"Indeed, sir. How did you know that?"

"There have been reports coming in from other agents of a new senior officer in the Spanish ranks. The story is that he came from the Americas with the fleet guarding the treasure ships. There is talk that no one knew who he was, that he just walked out of the jungle carrying the head of one of the local native princes. They were not even sure he was Spanish, although he spoke Spanish fluently. And, as far as his appearance goes, they call him *El Arlequín...*"

"The Harlequin." Lament knows enough Spanish to understand that nickname and to see the truth in it.

"Yes, quite. Seems he is a ruthless bastard. He has been making something of a reputation for himself fighting the Turks, and now it would appear that he has come to join the fight for the soul of the Low Countries."

Master Sterrell quaffs his wine, eyeing the bulk of Pieter as he does so. The glass of wine is lost in the huge Dutchman's great paw as he sits, seemingly unaware of the conversation, and blocks out most of the light from the window. He has caught the eye of the buxom lass, and he is happily making faces at her as she giggles and flushes pink.

"And what news have you for us from the good doctor?" Sterrell can't help but notice the edge in Lament's voice as she mentions Dr Dee.

"I received letters regarding your good selves not three days past. They came with a courier who will pass back this way in a week and take my reports and your gathered intelligence back to London with him."

"How did that scrawny crow know we would be here?" Pieter doesn't glance away from his quarry beyond the window, but it is obvious that he has been paying close attention.

Sterrell laughs nervously as if he is suddenly afraid that Dr Dee might somehow be able to hear the Dutchman's insulting tone. "Dr Dee would appear to know a good many things, sergeant. He casts horoscopes for Her Majesty, and it is said he can observe things at a distance through his sorcery. He has an uncanny knack for knowing when I have useful information for him almost as soon as I know it myself. His couriers always seem to arrive at the timeliest intervals."

"And these letters?" Lament knows enough about Dee's abilities to not be surprised.

"Yes, well, I deciphered them and then destroyed them as instructed after memorising the content. The doctor would have you make your way to Naarden. He has information that one of the things he seeks is most definitely in that city. He does not enter into further detail, and I suspect that you have some knowledge already regarding what that might mean." Lament nods but doesn't offer any explanation, and so Sterrell continues.

"I fear you may have more difficulty leaving the city of Mechelen than you did entering it. Van Merode is keen to garner and keep all the fighting men he can. He knows, as do any with an ear to the ground, that the Dons will not take the opening of the gates to Calvinists lightly. All the cities who chose to change allegiance will be marked for reprisal, and I suspect that will be sooner rather than later." Sterrell drinks and wipes a dribble of wine from his thin beard before going on.

"The gathering of Papist troops at Antwerp is a sure sign that the tide will turn again. The Duke of Alba and his son Fadrique Álvarez de Toledo will not hesitate to make examples of all those who have slighted them. It will soon be wise for me to leave here, but as I said, you may find it less easy to depart. Van Merode is intent on making a stand. Orange has left him with instructions to hold this city, and by God, he intends to do so! And, of course, that means keeping all his troops. There is a general order that no fighting man may leave the city without written permission, and that is never given." Sterrell's watery eyes regard Lament carefully. Here is a woman who will not take kindly to being constrained, and he senses an undercurrent of potential violence in these two servants of Dr Dee that he would not willingly arouse.

Lament glances at the bulk of the sergeant, who is still flirting, if now a little more half-heartedly. "I think we need to be planning our exit from this fair city, Master Hertgers. That is if you can tear yourself away from the local wildlife."

Pieter snorts, and his huge shoulders rise and fall as he laughs. "We could kick our way out and be gone before they know what has hit them. The gate guards looked less than interested in their work." He glances over at Lament, who knows from experience that he is only half joking.

Sterrell shakes his head, fair hair falling over red-rimmed eyes. "Van Merode has a squad of men, mostly well-paid mercenaries, who he sends after those who seek to break his general order. I am sure you would give a good account of yourselves, my friends, but I fear that there may be too many of them even for you!"

* * *

Two days have passed, and Lament has done her best to keep them out of sight of van Merode and his officer staff. Truth be told, it hasn't been difficult. Mechelen is a large city, and if they do not attempt to leave, they can wander at will.

They have observed the mercenaries that William Sterrell gave them warning of. Mostly German and Danish, from what they have seen. Large, quarrelsome brutes who walk the streets as if they own them. Lament and Pieter have steered clear of them so far as it would be far too easy to get into a fight with these thugs.

Pieter has kept himself occupied, humping the lass from the building opposite Sterrell's garret. Lament is content that the big sergeant is out of troubles way for the moment, at least until the wench's husband gets back from the markets of Leuven to the south. He has been gone now for eighteen days, and she expects him home within the next ten, so it would be wise for them to be on their way to Naarden before then.

The tavern in which they are currently drinking is a large and rowdy place. The ale and wine are good, as is the food. It is frequented by both Catholics and Protestants, and they seem to get along without animosity. Sterrell has told them that there has never been much dislike for either persuasion within the city walls. The reason that the gates were thrown open to the forces of Orange was more about expediency than religious conversion.

The aldermen of the city saw the writing on the wall, as it were, and rather than be besieged by the advancing Calvinists, they chose to be seen as graciously welcoming them in like long-lost brothers. However, this has not prevented an exodus of a good number of Catholics. There are some, even in a relatively free-thinking city such as this, who would use any difference to settle scores or gain an advantage at the expense of others.

Lament slumps back on the bench in the corner they have taken to occupying. Her long legs stretched, hat on the table beside her. It gives them a clear view of the entrance and the passageway to the yard at the rear. A young woman idles next to her, her arm linked through Lament's and her ample bosoms pressed against the lounging swordswoman as she leans forward to engage in a heated conversation with the girl sitting on Pieter's lap opposite them. They are arguing about the merits of the latest fashions that have found their way to the city from Florance. Lament has long ago given up listening and stares through the small, dirty window into the square beyond. An ornate fountain splashes at its centre, and a group of youths show off for the girls who are sitting on the fountain's low stone wall.

Pieter kicks Lament's foot and nods over to the doorway where the long, lean form of Master Sterrell is just easing his way past a pair of intoxicated merchants who are busy slapping each other on the back and praising each other loudly. They bump into Sterrell, almost knocking him over a table, and after a mocking apology, continue with their celebration of successful business dealings. Sterrell looks at them with daggers for eyes but says nothing as he heads towards the corner.

"Ladies, could you entertain yourselves for a while? We have matters to discuss, and I fear they may bore you somewhat." Pieter gives the girls a coin each to assuage the pouting and a gentle slap on the rear as his girl slides off his lap. Lament's girl leans in and kisses her on the cheek.

"Be seeing you later, Captain", and she winks archly at her before the two of them head off giggling, past Sterrell and the boisterous merchants.

"Master Sterrell, good day to you, sir. And to what do we owe the pleasure of your company?" Lament eases herself upright on the bench, massaging the life back into her numb leg muscles as she does so.

Sterrell swings himself down onto the bench beside her, and Pieter empties the dregs from one of their companions' cups into the rushes on the floor and refills it with ale from the jug on the table.

"I have information of grave import." Sterrell leans in over the table in a confidential manner, nodding his thanks to the big man opposite as he accepts the cup. He glances around to ensure he is not overheard and then leans in still further and, in a low voice, begins. "An agent in Antwerp has sent word that the troops gathering there are preparing to move. He has intelligence that the Duke of Alba has ordered all Catholic forces in the north of Brabant to muster. The signs all point to one purpose." He pauses to take a drink and add to the drama. "He is coming here to take back this city for Phillip of Spain and the Pope. To pay back the insult that is perceived to have been offered and exact revenge." He downs the rest of the cup and reaches for the jug.

"How long?" Lament has a sudden ill feeling about their situation.

"The courier with the message arrived this morning. So, given that they will be mustering a large force and awaiting the arrival of, the intelligence claims, the son of Alba, Fadrique Álvarez de Toledo, to lead them, I believe that we have less than two weeks before the Dons are hammering at these city gates!" He takes another drink. "But there is more. I have also heard that Bernard van Merode is getting cold feet despite his orders from Orange. He is now to be faced with an overwhelming force, the reality of which is causing him to make plans to leave the city with his men."

"Is this not good news, though? Surely it means we will be able to leave unaccosted?" Pieter looks at Lament for confirmation, but before she can comment, Sterrell shakes his head and answers.

"Alas, no, at least not just yet. Van Merode would keep Calvinist troops in the city for as long as possible to prevent the good folk of Mechelen from getting suspicious and panic setting in with the possible result that they turn on van Merode's men before they can exit. I think, my friends, that you will have to remain here for another week before van Merode makes his move to leave. I will be gone within two days at most. There is work for me to do in Lille, it would seem, and if truth be told, I am none too keen on being anywhere near when the Spanish attack!"

* * *

Six days after the departure of Sterrell, van Merode has made his escape, and his forces have left the city. Thus has begun an exodus of Protestants who can see exactly how the wind is blowing. That wind, like an omen of things to come, carries the smell of smoke with it as Lament and Pieter ride away from Mechelen across a long stone bridge. They skirt around the mass of those who are now becoming refugees in their own land and head east towards Flanders and, hence, north to Naarden.

A message arrived with a courier just after sunrise this morning. William Sterrell, as good as his word, had promised to give them warning of when the Spanish forces might arrive, and it seems that they have moved with greater enthusiasm than anticipated and are now no more than twenty miles to the north.

Van Merode's troops have fled south, and all that is left to protect Mechelen are four companies of foot soldiers and two hundred cavalry, the real garrison of the city. But both Lament and Pieter know that they will be swept away by the army and ordinance of Fadrique Álvarez de Toledo, and mercy is not something that will be in plentiful supply.

Yesterday, Pieter went to pay a final visit to Sophia, the young woman whom he had seduced from Sterrell's garret window. He warned her of the Spanish approach, but now her husband has returned. He, like many other Catholics in the city, is not perturbed by their imminent arrival. So, like a dutiful wife, she will wait with her cuckolded husband, even against Pieter's dire warnings. As they ride away, there is a sadness about the red-bearded giant that is most unusual. He is a realist and knows what is most likely to happen and that yesterday was the last time he would see the pretty young lass. But unaccountably, he can't square that away, and an unpleasant feeling lies heavy over him.

As they reach the far end of the bridge, a sound makes them turn in the saddle and look back. A collective groan of despair escapes the line of grim-faced people. In the distance to the north, columns of smoke are rising into the cold grey air. Black smoke mingles with the low cloud to take on the appearance of a shroud. All know that farms and homes are burning. All know that the Spanish are here.

# Chapter 12

For three days, the Spanish outriders have stalked them. The forest is seemingly endless and ancient and was meant to be their escape route. The Spanish have other ideas.

They appear to Lament when she catches sight of them through the dense undergrowth, as demonic half men half dogs. They seem to give off a dark vapour, like the clouds in an approaching storm, and she can hear them baying like the hounds of hell.

Yesterday, they were almost flanked as they were driven into a deep defile amongst the trees. But before they could be trapped, they charged their tired mounts through the startled Tercios, leaving three men dead and two more brutally wounded. Now Lament and Pieter lead their horses on foot up a steep slope strewn with huge moss-covered rocks. Tangled roots from the elm trees that tower above them make the climb difficult for the mounts, so they pick their way slowly and carefully upwards.

A crossbow bolt skitters across a boulder, kicking up clumps of moss as it disappears into the undergrowth. They have been spotted once again. Shouts in Spanish ring out, and Lament hears a call for pistols. It will not be good if they are caught out in this place with no decent cover. The rocks will only provide a limited reprieve, and they both know that to be pinned down here will end in a drawn-out coup de grâce delivered eventually by the more numerous riders following them.

A shallow gully running across the face of the slope provides welcome relief. For the moment, they can move more quickly, the horses finding safer footing and greater purchase on the firmer ground. The angle of the gully leads them further upwards, and a huge slab of sandstone juts from the side of the slope, acting as a natural defence against Spanish projectiles. But they can already see the gulley's end, and beyond it is a long clearing to the tree line at the summit. A clearing that will leave them completely exposed.

"What reckon you, Captain?" Pieter gazes up at the open space before them and then back the way they have come. The shouts of their pursuers are getting louder, and it is clear that men are working their way across the lower slope to come at them from two sides.

"I like not our odds, my friend. I fear we will need to make a stand. We can't charge the horses on this ground, so outrunning the bastards is no longer an option." Lament ducks as a lead ball ricochets off rocks above them, spraying shards of stone. Then, she notices the fallen tree lying partially across the sandstone outcrop. She glances at her companion and then back at the tree, and then a smile crosses her lips. "Big man, do you think you could dislodge that fallen tree?"

Pieter eyes up the task and shrugs. "I would guess so. To what end?"

"It would make a pretty mess of our friend's plans to come

across the slope below us if that tree trunk were to go crashing down amongst them..." Lament raises her eyebrows and smiles again. It has now become a challenge.

The big Dutchman hands the reins of his horse to Lament and strides purposefully over to the tree. As Lament ties both their horses to a knotty root sticking out from the side of the gully, Pieter puts his large hands against the trunk and gives it an exploratory push. There is some movement, and he quickly surveys as much of it as he can without poking his head up above the outcrop.

Lament takes a pistol in each hand, having thrust two more into her belt and moves back down the gulley to catch the Spaniards coming after them along that path. She looks back at Pieter, who has turned his back to the tree and, squatting down, has wedged his broad shoulders under it. The red-bearded face looks back at her.

"Try not to get shot, Captain." He grins.

"And you try not to burst anything." Lament grins back.

"Aye, I will try not to shit myself!"

"God give you strength, big man. Or at least may the devil lend you some of his." Then she turns away to face whatever might come up the gulley from below.

Pieter squares his shoulders and gradually straightens his thighs. There is resistance, but then the trunk begins to shift and slide back over the fulcrum of the sandstone. He clenches his teeth and pushes his hands against his massive legs. The tree is moving, but something is preventing it from going past the tipping point.

He lowers himself back into a squat, and the tree settles

again. He will need to take a look at what is stopping the trunk from falling, but that means leaving cover. He shakes his head grimly and begins to scramble up the outcrop.

A helmeted head pokes out from behind a moss-covered boulder and then disappears in a pink mist as Lament empties the first of her pistols at point-blank range into it. The body falls backwards, and the helmet clatters down amongst the stones, empty now of the ruined head.

Another appears and just as quickly falls away, a black hole suddenly in his throat. The others become cautious, and Lament swaps the pistols over, knowing that the next Spaniards will not make such easy targets.

A crossbow bolt thuds into the bank beside her, and she whirls and fires, but the bowman is already back behind cover. She exchanges the discarded pistol for her sword and moves further down the gulley. Now, they rush her.

Pistols fire as she dodges from one side of the gulley to the other. The shots are close, but not close enough, and she fires her last primed pistol and draws her dagger. Blades in both hands now, she rushes them before they can bring more shot to bear on her.

They are tough, these Spaniards who appear to her with the faces of dogs. But whether she would have chosen to be in this situation or not, this is what Lament Evyngar was born to do, and at this moment, she would have it no other way.

She catches a sword thrust with her dagger, turning the blade as she slips sideways. Her riposte takes the man through the thigh, and she is past him, leaving him clutching the wound. She dodges back out of range of a heavier blade and quickly steps back in, intercepting the backhand slash, and drives the dagger beneath the sword arm. There is resistance. It feels as if there may be mail hidden beneath the leather jerkin. Lament drives forward, bending her arm to use her body's weight to force the blade home. Mail links give way, and the Spaniard lets out a gurgling groan as the dagger enters his lung.

There is a chopping sound from further up the gulley behind her. Lament uses the embedded dagger to turn the man, putting him in the way of his fellow attackers, and risks a glance. Pieter is up on the outcrop, his falchion rising and falling against something on the far side that Lament can't see.

The heavy falchion blade hacks into the branch, the one branch that is preventing the fallen tree from rolling down the slope.

Pieter is aware of the Spaniards on the slope beneath him. They have become highly animated at seeing their quarry so exposed. Shouts ring out, and there is coarse laughter as they sense an end to their long hunt. But the Dutchman continues to cut at the branch with grim determination even when what feels like a red-hot iron pushes through the pauldron and the flesh of his shoulder.

With a growl that masks the pain, he gives one more mighty chop, and the branch separates from the trunk. He slides rapidly back over into the gulley, and thrusting the falchion into the soft earth where he can easily reach it, he once again turns and puts his shoulders beneath the edge of the tree. The pain in his left shoulder is intense, but he grits his teeth and begins to straighten his thickly muscled legs.

For a moment, the tree trunk remains intransigent, balancing on the sandstone, and Pieter has the horrible feeling that the branch he has cut is not the only culprit. He allows the trunk to settle back down slightly as he draws a great breath. Then, with a roaring battle cry, he surges upwards for all he is worth, and with a creaking of timber, the tree trunk upends over the rock and begins a devastating journey downwards.

The Tercios, who have been carefully making their way across and up the slope, freeze in horror. They had primed their pistols and cocked their crossbows for the reappearance of the hulking figure who had inexplicably left cover to stand on the outcrop and chop frenziedly at a fallen tree. But now it is plain why he would put himself in harm's way because, above them, the tree trunk is descending and bringing stones and scree with it. As one, they come back to life and, in their panic, crash into one another, slowing down any escape.

It seems the entire slope is moving down onto them, and there are screams as the first of them are caught and crushed by dead timber and moss-dressed rock. Two of them leap aside as the main part of the trunk rushes by, only to be swatted by the trailing roots as the tree catches on a broad boulder and spins wildly. Limbs break, and torsos are mashed to a pulp.

Those few left mostly undamaged, look up from the wreckage to see a giant figure once more astride the outcrop. This time, he rains down rocks and branches onto the prone figures. Lumps of stone large enough to crack bones thud down amongst them, and suddenly, there is no more movement from the men who would have crept up the slope.

Lament kicks a man in the face as he tries to regain his footing on the slippery scree. She feels the jaw break, and the

Spaniard cartwheels over. A well-aimed thrust causes her to twist violently to allow the blade to pass between arm and torso, slicing her arming doublet but not flesh. Then she clamps his arm hard against her side, trapping the blade, and she moves in close to prevent a cut on the withdraw. A dark, bearded face glares at her. There is still a look of the hound about the features, although she can see the human crawling beneath it. She punches the face hard with the quillons on the hand guard of her sword, leaving a bloody mess before cutting down and stepping back to open the Spaniard's neck with the razor edge of the blade.

And it is over. The remaining Tercios flee as fast as the terrain will allow, curses flying back at Lament. She wipes sweat away from her forehead on the sleeve of her doublet and, for the first time in days, realises just how filthy her clothes have become. A noise causes her to turn, sword at the ready. It is Pieter leaning on the hilt of his falchion, which he has just thrust through the chest of one of Lament's previous victims who had not quite given up his life. The man gurgles and gasps, bloody froth running from between his writhing lips before he goes suddenly still.

Lament's grin dies upon her lips to be replaced with a frown of concern. Her bear-like companion is unusually pale, and there is blood darkening his massive left shoulder. Lament quickly wipes and then sheaths her blades and moves forward to give aid.

"A lucky shot, Captain. I fear I have been stung. But no worries, I did for those on the slope. The tree trunk proved to be a fine cudgel!" Pieter half smiles and half grimaces. He tries to raise his left arm, but it barely moves from his side as the damage becomes obvious after the heat of battle has faded.

"Well done, Sergeant. I did not request that you get shot though, that I fear was a little careless." Lament moves in quickly to support her friend as he sits down heavily. She unbuckles the straps of the pauldron and then uses her dagger to cut away part of the stitching of Pieter's gambeson and surveys the wound. There is a hole clean through the outer muscle of the big Dutchman's shoulder. It is a blessing that the lead ball is not still in there, but its path has dragged in fabric and fragments of metal and opened a large wound upon exiting below the lower edge of the pauldron's rear. At least it has missed the bone.

Lament leads the horses back to where Pieter sits, still leaning on his sword. From her saddle bag, she takes a relatively clean linen shirt and rips it into strips. A bottle of brandy appears, and she tips it over the wound before handing it to the cursing Pieter, who quickly downs the rest. Then, Lament packs the wound with cloth and binds more around it. She stands back and surveys her work. She has done the best she can, and hopefully, it will stop the bleeding, but they are in dire need of a surgeon.

Supporting Pieter's weight as best she can, she helps him to get into the saddle and leads his horse along with her own up the gulley and into the clearing. They are still deep in this ancient forest, and Lament looks at her friend and knows that this will be a close-run thing.

"Don't look so grim, Lam. It was a fine fight. I just need some rest, a comely wench, decent food and drink, and I will be fixed up just fine." But it is clear that even Pieter does not fully believe his own bravado.

# Chapter 13

Tied to his saddle, Pieter rocks with the motion of the Percheron as it plods its tired path through the trees. Lament rides alongside, keeping them both steady. She blinks bleary eyes, wishing that the endless forest would indeed end and that there would be food, sleep, and some help for her ailing friend.

Unable to clean the wound or close it sufficiently, there is foulness setting in and a fever that drenches the Dutchman in sweat and delirium. Lament can do nothing to aid him except keep them moving forward.

The sun begins to sink on the second evening since the fight on the slope. Lament guides them through a thicket and then a stand of birch trees that point at the reddening sky like silver spears as if the earth would impale the void above it in some jealous rage.

As the trees thin, Lament smells the smoke. Wood smoke curls through the air like a long-forgotten memory. It brings Lament out of her reverie with a shock. Fading light does nothing to aid her blurred vision, but *is that fire light?*

She almost cries out in joy and perhaps desperation in case this is just a phantom conjured by her desire. She kicks her tired horse forward, pulling Pieter's horse along after them. There, in a small clearing at the edge of the birch, is a hut. The glow of firelight spills out from around the sides of an animal hide curtain that hangs across the doorway. Smoke curls from the smoke hole in a roof covered with turf. To one side is a smaller structure, perhaps a wood store, that leans against the hut and is surrounded by a low wattle fence over which several goats eye them with suspicion.

A howl, not too distant now, sounds from the forest behind them. The wolves have been following for the last day, and they seem to sense the desperate state that the two are in. Shadowy shapes emerge from the thicket, and a fog of breath rises from the snarling muzzles. Unnervingly yellow eyes shine in the sun's last red rays. Lament reaches for a pistol and her sword, but the wolves stop in their tracks. They pace along the edge of the thicket but don't pass into the birch trees.

Lament becomes aware that there are other hulking shapes amongst the trees, and as she looks around, she can see that they encircle the clearing. At first, her tired eyes do not register what they are, and so she stares hard at the closest shape in the dying light. They are standing stones. An ancient ring of stones surrounds the clearing, and as she turns back to face the wolves, she sees that they are already slinking away, snapping at each other in their frustration, those lower in the pack whimpering as they avoid the ire of their leaders.

A superstitious chill runs down her spine, but here is shelter and fire, and so with pistol still in hand, she draws the horses closer to the hut.

She is only a few yards short of the hut when, with a groan,

Pieter slips from the saddle. The makeshift bonds with which Lament had tied him finally give way, and with a heavy thud, the big man hits the moss-covered ground. One foot is still in the stirrup, but fortunately, his horse is too tired to do anything but stand and look at its now prone rider.

Lament swings herself from her saddle with far less than her usual athleticism and moves her tired, aching limbs as quickly as she can to aid her friend. As she pulls the boot free of the stirrup and lowers the leg to the ground, she hears movement from the doorway of the hut, and a red firelight spills out into the gloom.

The woman is standing there in the doorway, a dark silhouette holding the hide curtain to one side. Lament blinks and half raises a hand to one of her pistols but changes her mind and goes back to tending her ailing comrade. She kneels by Pieter's head and checks that he is still breathing. Yes, the Lord has not taken him just yet.

She is only dimly aware that the woman is squatting beside her. She looks Pieter over, moving the dirty dressing on his shoulder and wrinkling her nose with distaste at the smell that emanates from it. Wild hair and shadow obscure much of her face, although Lament is sure at that moment that her eyes glow with an unnatural light. She says something to her in a language that could be Flemish, and Lament shrugs and indicates that she doesn't understand.

"My apologies, I don't know what you are saying." She manages in Dutch.

"Help me get him inside. I need to tend to this wound, or your friend will die." She responds in Dutch, and Lament nods and stands wearily. Together, they drag Pieter's massive body towards the entrance.

"He is a big one, is he not?" She smiles at Lament as they manhandle the unconscious Pieter, and that smile takes Lament by surprise. The light from the fire illuminates a young, attractive face beneath a tangle of dark hair. She is not what courtiers would describe as beautiful, but there is a sensuality to her features that renders Lament speechless. She nods stupidly and carries on hauling.

Inside the dwelling, it is more spacious than it would at first appear. There are doorways leading off to other areas with heavy, surprisingly expensive-looking drapes that can be pulled across to close them off. The wooden frame that supports the roof is dense with bunches of dried plant material and other objects that Lament can't identify. In the centre of the room is a fire pit which glows welcomingly, and over it stands an iron tripod from which hangs a cooking pot.

Lament takes all of this in as she helps drag Pieter across to the bed of fresh straw that the woman heaps up on the hard-packed earth floor. Then she sits down with a bump, her head swimming. It has been days since they have been able to rest, and her concern over the Dutchman has driven her on long after Pieter had passed into uncaring delirium.

The woman is squatting next to Pieter and cutting away the remains of the gambeson and the shirt beneath it. She shows surprising strength as she levers Pieter's massive bulk to one side and cleans the exit wound at the back of his shoulder with a wad of cloth. As she rinses the now gory fabric in a basin of fresh water, she glances over at Lament and smiles gently at her. "Rest.

I will tend to his wound, and then I will make some food. But you should rest. You are safe here."

And with the fire's warmth lulling her, she pulls himself back against one of the upright beams that support the roof frame and, almost against her will, closes her eyes.

* * *

Beatris pushes the dark tresses from her face, quickly plaiting them down one side of her head with practised fingers. She has thoroughly cleaned the wound in the shoulder of the big warrior, picking out shavings of metal and threads of fabric and leather. It is now packed with a mixture of herbs and honey, and beneath the clean bandage, she has applied two dozen maggots to eat away the foul flesh. It will still take all the giant's obvious strength, but she has dribbled other herbs between his thick lips to help break the fever and aid in his healing. Another day, and he would have been beyond even her help.

Next, she adds water and root vegetables to the cooking pot, lowering it down closer to the fire, and while that begins to heat, she removes the saddles from the horses and rubs them down with straw, talking to them quietly and leading them to an area of good grass next to the goat pen. She carries the saddle packs into the hut and places them by the door. Her dark eyebrows arch as she peeks inside the long, oiled leather bag and sees the mighty zweihander nestling there.

Now, she looks down at the sleeping form of the other woman. She has slid down the beam where she had positioned herself and is lying on the floor. Carefully, she removes her weapons and her boots, placing them on top of a chest in one of the side rooms. As she loosens Lament's doublet, she sits back on her heels in sudden shock. A fine, greyish tracery pattern is visible on the skin of her upper chest. With cautious fingers, she pulls aside her shirt to reveal more of the markings that have been a constant companion since Dr Dee performed his ritual.

Her eyes grow dark, and she raises them to the herb-covered roof. Words come from her lips. Words that Lament would not understand even if she were awake to hear them. Words that were old even before the drowning of Atlantis.

A shimmering begins in the air around her. A dark luminescence that moves with an almost sentient life, like some strange sea creature from the ocean depths that has found its way to the shallows. The shimmer touches Lament, and the marks upon her glow for an instant and then fade back to their dull form.

Beatris begins to hum a song she vaguely remembers from her childhood, and the shimmer in the air fades away. This woman and her wounded companion did not chance upon her by accident. There is something this one has to offer, something that can be traded. For good or ill, she is here now, and the wheel of fate has turned once again.

Lament wearily opens her eyes and blinks. A woman stands over her, a dark shape against the fire's glow. She begins to struggle upright, but her limbs feel like leaden weights, and a strange soporific wave sweeps over her, causing her body to refuse the urge to awaken. She vaguely recognises the woman, and her tired mind tells her that she helped them and that all is well.

There is a deep, rich scent in the air. It reminds her of the incense burnt at Mass but mixed with another, unidentifiable aroma, which is somehow darker, more intoxicating than the re-membered smoke drifting from the priest's censer. It seeps into her, and all urge to fight fades away. Her eyes begin to close once more, and as they do, the shape of the woman seems to flicker in the air like a candle flame caught by a sudden breeze. A smile touches her lips. *How odd*, she thinks. Then she is asleep once more, and the woman covers her with her cloak fetched from the saddle bags and gently lifts her head to place a straw-filled pad beneath it.

A vaguely remembered song drifts through the hut, mingling with the smoke of burning herbs and incense, and Beatris goes out into the moonlight that has pierced through a break in the ragged clouds and listens to the call of the wolves far away in the forest.

* * *

Lament's dreams are filled with phantoms. Her sleep has not been easy since they left England; there is a darkness there that is worse even than the re-lived horror of the battlefield. Now, she stands at the foot of a tree the likes of which she has never seen. Its branches reach out and up towards the stars in the firmament, and they are baren of leaves. But something dangles from the branches in dense clusters, swaying gently, although there is no wind.

It is dark at the base of the impossibly huge tree, and she must shift her position to gain some meagre light from the river of stars that runs across the inky black of the void above. And there they are. Hanging from the branches are the broken bodies of men, women, and children. Some are naked, others wear out-landish dress that she does not recognise, and all have the same look upon their grey, rotting faces, a look of desperate horror.

She backs away from the tree, although she knows that she will need to retreat a considerable distance to be clear of the branches and their fruit. As she does, the sky ripples, and the same purples and greens that she saw in the sky as they crossed the Narrow Sea bleed across the darkness. There is a coldness that cuts through to the marrow of her bones, and colossal wings, or perhaps an idea of them, flap up and along the path of the stars.

She tears her eyes away for fear that she may look upon the face of the eternal, and none can do that and remain in their right mind. But she also fears that there is no god out there that she could ever worship. That there is something out there beyond her knowing that loathes the squirming humanity that struggles for life. Something that plays an eternal game of chance with the lives of men. Shadows that are cast by nothing laugh at the endless race towards death.

She runs unthinkingly from the shadow of the tree, and there before her, another shape appears from the rising mist. A head-less cross, such as those on the high moors of England. It leans to one side as if the earth beneath it can't sustain its weight, and perched upon its apex is a large black crow that watches her through eyes that show no pity. The bird cocks its head to one side, and in that motion, Lament knows that it is Dr John Dee who is looking for her from another land. Seeking to judge her and find her wanting.

# Chapter 14

There is a blueish mist rising from the damp earth this morning. A weak sun tries its best to penetrate the clouds of vapour and manages to thrust ghostly fingers of light between the spears of birch. But despite this, there is little in the way of illumination.

Lament sits on the threshold of the hut, her cloak gathered around her and shudders involuntarily at the mist. It reminds her too much of the headless cross and the night-black crow. She would very much like a good bottle of sack to help wash away that dream.

She had woken to the grey light of dawn filtering into the hut and had lain for a while in a drowsy confusion as her thoughts had gradually fused to form a narrative that made sense of her surroundings. Across the room, she could make out the bulk of Pieter, and she had made her way over to him, stretching out stiff muscles as she went. The great bear of a man was lying in deep sleep. Beads of sweat stood out on his face and neck. He is still in a fever, although less than a day ago when he had begun to shout out in his delirium. Lament pulled back the edge of one of the blankets covering the massive frame and looked at the expertly dressed wound. She nodded, satisfied that her friend had been cared for, and covered him again with the blanket.

A need to relieve herself became suddenly pressing, and she headed out through the hide covering and into the weak dawn light and the mist. Then, back to the hut, helping herself to a wooden bowl and a ladle of vegetable potage simmering over the fire. Now, as she sits in the doorway and enjoys the sensation of the potage filling her belly and wishes for a bottle of sack, her thoughts turn to the woman. She has not seen hair nor hide of her this morning, although, to be fair, her looking has not yet been extensive.

A movement. A darker shadow amongst the trees, detaching itself and coming towards the clearing. The mist makes it look like it is changing shape, and the hairs on her neck stand straight. Getting to her feet, she reaches for her dagger and, for the first time, realises that she is without weapons. Shaking her head, she berates herself for her lack of awareness, but that is quickly forgotten as the shadow emerging from the mist takes on female form. And it is only when the form stoops to retrieve clothing from the top of a flat rock that she realises this other woman is naked. She continues to advance while she pulls a shift over her head and then wraps a shawl around her shoulders. There is no sign of embarrassment or coyness.

"Good morning, my Lady." She makes a small curtsey.

"I am no lady, but may God give you a good day, madam." She bows to her, noticing the look of partially concealed suspicion that quickly crosses the woman's features.

"All of those carrying swords are *Lords or Ladies* to a wise woman until she can get the measure of them. Better a little flattery than a beating or worse – my *Lady...*" There is humour on her full lips, but her amber eyes do not smile, not yet.

Lament bows again to show that she understands and moves aside to allow her to enter the hut. She brushes past her, and there is a smell about her that fills Lament's senses and leaves her feeling like a speechless fool for a few moments.

"Thank you for giving aid to my friend. I was greatly feared for him." She nods in the direction of the sleeping giant.

"He is not free of the shade gate yet, my Lady. But he is a strong one, and me thinks he has a lust for life that will carry him back to the land of light." She stares hard at the unconscious form as if she can see more there than just a wounded soldier.

"He would not have lasted another day if we had not hap-pened upon you. And please, stop calling me *my Lady*. I am Captain Lament Evyngar, and I am at your service."

"We shall see..." At last, the eyes are smiling. "And you may call me Beatris."

Pieter sleeps on. Dead to the world as Beatris changes the dressing, cleans the wound of the leaking puss and swaps the engorged magots for fresh ones. She drips more of the herbal draught into his mouth, and he seems to go even deeper into the fever-fueled slumber. There is more than a touch of the poppy in this tincture.

Lament brings wood for the fire and stacks it on top of what is already there. She has checked the horses, tending to their hooves and searching for any sign of lameness. So far, they have been lucky, but there could be unseen damage waiting to make itself known.

She sits on a three-legged stool and watches, fascinated, as the dark-haired woman tends to the snoring giant. There is a vivid memory of her nakedness approaching through the morning mist.

"How is it that you survive out here on your own?" she asks the question more to break her own enraptured staring than to gain an answer. But she would like to hear that answer.

"Can a woman not survive on her own merits as you do? Just because I don't carry a sword doesn't mean that I am helpless. And *out here* is not without its benefits." She glances over her shoulder at Lament, and her dark hair obscures much of her face.

Lament holds up her hands in apology as she turns to face her, but she sees that Beatris is not offended by her question; rather, she pokes fun at her. "In truth, madam, I meant more that it is a wonder that you live so well in this wild place."

"Well, Lament, I have been here for many years, and I am visited often by folk who seek me out for my skills." Beatris sits on a carved wooden chest opposite her and stares deeply into her blue eyes with amber ones that appear to contain flecks of gold. Lament finds herself captivated and not a little unnerved. Captain Evyngar is hardly a blushing virgin, and she has stared violent death in the eye more times than she cares to remember, but this young woman sees right through to the core of her. And something more...

Beatris leans in and takes her hands as she tries to compose her thoughts. "You did not come to me by chance. The fates have brought us together. To what end, I yet do not know, but I believe that we need to make a trade." For a moment, there is a look of pity, of sadness in the gold-flecked eyes, and then it is gone, leaving Lament to wonder if she imagined it.

"What trade do you speak of? We have nothing of value that we can give you unless you desire a city stormed or a man killed. These are things that we are well versed in. May God have mercy upon us." She squeezes her hands gently. There is a little desperation that she may somehow disappoint her.

"Just you, Lament. That is all that needs to be traded." Once again, that look, and Lament goes to pull her hands away, but Beatris holds on tightly. Before Lament can speak, she continues. "I have a knowledge of things that few possess. Folk come to me to hear what their future may be or to gain insight into things that are hidden. Oh, I heal the sick as well, but most are more interested in knowing how they will fare in love and war than having boils seen to!" She releases one hand, and with her long fingers, she moves aside the neck of Lament's shirt. "Whoever put those marks upon you has cursed you more than you can know." She glances at the revealed skin, and Lament gasps and snatches her hands back to cover them up once more.

"I saw them last night as you slept. It was then that I knew you were more than just soldiers of fortune. Those marks single you out as one who can walk between the worlds, although it becomes obvious that you are unaware of this."

"I see... *things*." Lament whispers the words. "There are things abroad in this world that have no place outside of Hell, and I can see their true forms as they ride mortal men for their perverted pleasure."

Beatris looks at her with gentle amusement. "I would be more surprised if you didn't see things! You spoke in your sleep last night. There was mention of someone called *El Arlequín*. You have seen this creature?" Lament nods, and she continues. "There are omens and signs regarding one in jester's garb." Her eyes take on a remoteness as if she is observing something through a great distance of space or time, or perhaps both. "He has forgotten who he is. He plays the fool and spreads discord while he dances a jig of destruction. It suits the others on both sides to let him, to allow him to play the cards as he chooses, rather than have him remember. *They* have also forgotten who he truly is. He could end them all that one... He always was a naughty boy..." The faraway look softens into a sad, affectionate smile.

"What do you know of all this?" Lament is in a state of bewilderment, but Beatris shakes her head to clear it and will not be drawn further.

"That is not for me to tell, even if I knew what answers to give that you would understand. But I can help you in other ways. It seems to me that you have been tethered in this half-state, for what purpose I do not care or wish to know. I would, though, offer you freedom. A freedom granted to few mortals. The freedom to move beyond the clutches of death itself. To break the contract made by our ancestors that in exchange for knowledge, we should live finite lives." Beatris snaps her fingers to emphasise this breaking.

"To move beyond death's clutches... How?" Lament would humour this entrancing woman, feeling that perhaps this is merely a metaphor. But something in those amber eyes is deadly serious, and she realises, perhaps too late, that for Beatris, this is no allegory meant for seekers of spiritual peace.

"There are those who can walk between worlds. Those who are not bound by the conventions of time and space. They can step beyond this tragic Earth as easily as you step through a doorway into another room. And they do not just enter other spheres. No, they can pass through the boundaries of time itself, existing wherever they would." Those eyes with their sheen of gold stare with rapt intensity at something that Lament can't see, can't even imagine.

"I can give you that potential, my Captain. To step beyond the threshold of the *moment*, to be encompassed by the possibility of *eternity*!"

Lament stares, uncomprehending, as the seconds seem to hang expectantly in the air between them. "And how does this work?" Is, at last, all she can think to ask.

Beatris smiles with some sympathy for the captain's bewilderment. "At first, it may occur during some moment of crises, which may seem quite trivial. But as you experience more episodes, you will learn to gain control of when and how they occur, and you will be able to remember them. In the beginning, they will just seem to be waking dreams."

"But *how* does this work?" Lament asks again, desperate to understand.

"Ah, Lament. That I cannot fully explain. I think that there are no words for it, at least not in any language I know. But what I can tell you is that because of the designs you now wear upon your skin, you exist in all points in space and time at once. And if you accept my bargain, you will be able to move to any of those locations at will. You will never be the victim of mortal constraints again. You will be God-like! Isn't that what all men want?"

"I am no man!" Lament sits back, and she suddenly feels a

weight upon her. Perhaps it is the weight of a destiny that she is not yet aware of...

"No, no, you are not. You are more than the sum of man and woman. I can see that you are not possessed of the ruthless ambition and greed that most display given the opportunity. But, Lament, whether you chose it or not, you are now marked until your dying day with something powerful. Why not control that power rather than be the pawn of others?" Beatris, eyes burning bright, leans in towards Lament and strokes her cheek.

Mind whirling, Lament sighs. What harm will it do to play along with this folly? The woman caressing her face is saving the life of her friend, and if that were not enough, she feels a deep desire for her.

Her mind made up, she frowns. This is some form of heresy, of that she is sure, but then her ties to whatever god is in fashion were loosened long ago. She fears that she has already committed enough heresy to damn her to the everlasting purgatory that surely is waiting. "You said a trade. You would offer me this *freedom* but in exchange for what pray tell?"

"Lie with me and give me a child. That will be our trade. And in exchange, I will make you invisible to death, a walker between the worlds." Beatris smiles a smile which Lament can't read.

"You jest! If you had not noticed, I, like you, am a woman and not equipped to give you what you require in trade." Lament thinks that there must be some riddle to this that she does not understand.

But Beatris shakes her head. "You truly have no idea of what you have become, do you? You have been moulded by forces beyond your ken and then thrown like dice to see how you fall.

*But you do not have to be at the mercy of some cosmic game of chance!* Captain, you have within you the potential to be either sex or none. You hold within you the essence of the hermaphrodite angels. You are all possibility!" Standing, she takes a bottle from the chest upon which she has been sitting. "Will you trust me, Captain, as you trust me with the life of your comrade?"

Lament watches her, mouth opening and closing in unformed words, and she nods without knowing why. Beatris pours brandy into a glazed beaker and hands it to her. She takes a deep drink, feeling the burning liquid heat up her throat and chest.

"I would have no wish to live forever, even should such a bargain as you suggest be possible. I am no divine being! I have regrets about having lived just one life, and the things I have seen and done should one day either be erased or judged by whatever awaits when we die." She finishes the brandy, and Beatris offers more, which she gladly accepts.

"There may be much beyond your control and understanding. But perhaps you would not be displeased by the thought of lying with me? After all, am I not pleasing to the eye?" She smiles at her, hands on hips, and the smell of her fills Lament's senses once again. Her head is spinning. There is a strange bitter aftertaste to the brandy, and Beatris takes the beaker from her before she can drop it, and at that moment, she knows she is lost.

* * *

Lament lies on her back on a bed covered in wolf pelts. She is naked, and although she can move, she has no desire to. Unbidden, her thoughts go back to the chamber of Dr Dee and the ritual that was performed upon her. She was naked then, and something about this is similar, although this is far more enjoyable.

Beatris sits astride her. Wild hair sweeps across Lament's face and breasts, and Beatris tosses it backwards over her pale shoulders before leaning forward and kissing Lament again. Fingernails dig into the muscles of Lament's shoulders, and Beatris moves her body against her. There is an urgency in the movement, and Lament responds to it, holding her hips and aiding the movement. Beatris arches her back, and her breasts gleam with sweat. A chanting has begun, and for a moment, Lament does not know where the alien sound is coming from. Once again, ancient words spill from Beatris' lips, and Lament feels as if her skin is burning. She looks down at her body, and the patterns that mark her skin are alight like intricate rivers of molten metal, quicksilver that flows like water. She cries out, and Beatris looks down upon her from somewhere in the black void beyond the Earth, and her eyes are the colour of obsidian. They swallow Lament whole.

* * *

She wakes on a bed with furs partially covering her. Beatris lies beside her, limbs draped across her, breathing deeply. Something in the back of Lament's mind tells her that, somehow, she has become part of a larger, more complicated tale yet again. But her memory of last night, even though not complete, sweeps away any doubts. Perhaps because it is not whole, it makes it easier to ignore the uncanny parts that, after all, must have been a dream.

The trade that Beatris spoke of can surely be nothing but superstition. If she wants a child and has chosen Lament for the *father*, then why not? She is a pleasure to look upon, and it is not as if this playacting can be anything other than that.

She rubs her head. There is a dull ache behind her eyes as if she had drunk too much last evening, but she only remembers having two beakers of brandy... It begins to dawn upon her that the brandy might have been drugged, something that seems to be becoming commonplace in her more *unusual* encounters, and as she thinks that she might search the hut, there is movement beside her.

Beatris lies on her side. Her eyes are half open, and she regards her with cat-like intensity. She strokes the patterns on Lament's breasts and smiles at her slightly bewildered expression. "My Captain. I told you that there would be a bargain struck between us. Your seed for something that I have the power to grant." She puts a finger to Lament's lips as she opens her mouth to once more state the obvious. "I know that you do not want my part of the trade or even believe that it is possible, but that is precisely why you are the one human who may have it." She levers herself up onto an elbow and gazes deeply into her eyes.

"Forces greater than the ambitions of men have already been released on the day that you were given those marks. But they are not chains that bind you to a blind fate, not if you will it otherwise." She moves across Lament, the weight of her body pressing warm against her. Lament's mouth is dry, and she can't speak as she once again watches those eyes grow dark. "Will you accept the bargain, Captain?"

Beatris' lips are barely inches away from Lament's, and despite herself, she finally manages to whisper, "Yes, I accept."

"Then we must fully consummate our agreement, for I fear it will be now or never."

Lament grabs her and rolls on top. She stares into the suddenly liquid darkness where the amber eyes once were, and in some way, there is still a hint of gold, a star field of shimmering motes. Then she is inside Beatris, and she feels the strange throb of maleness that is suddenly present, alarming but in a way not unexpected, and the strange designs that crisscross her flesh come to life once more in a burning net that snares her body. But there is the feeling that the net is stretching, tearing, being pulled apart as they move together on top of the furs.

She sees in Beatris' eyes the beginning and end of all things. The birth of all creation and the stagnation and death of it all at a place where time ends. Then, there is nothing but darkness, and the world falls away.

# Chapter 15

The familiar voice of an old friend, a comrade, drags at the edges of consciousness until the curtains part, and like one of Master Shakespeare's plays, Lament finds herself once more on the stage of waking.

Lament stretches and pushes the furs off herself and looks around. She is alone in the room, a room which looks faded and barely used. She shakes her head and swings her legs off the bed. Her breeches are on the floor, along with her shirt. Pulling them on, she stops as she hears the voice again. She had thought it a dream, but now it has some urgency to it.

"Forsooth, I could murder a jug of good ale! And is there no meat? Lam, are you awake, my friend?"

Lament grins and throws aside the curtain that separates the rooms. It tears, and she snatches away her hand in alarm at the fabric, which suddenly seems ancient. Stepping into the main area of the hut, she is confused by the dusty, drabness of everything. The bunches of herbs hanging from the roof beams are dried and dull with age. The fire pit smoulders with embers, and there is the smell of pottage from the cooking pot, but the hut has a ramshackle air to it that she can't accept as being real.

Pieter is sitting on the far side of the fire, wooden bowl gripped in his massive fist and greedily ladling pottage into his mouth. He waves the hand holding the spoon at Lament in greeting, splashing food around him. There is no dressing on his shoulder, and the wound there has closed over, leaving a purple circle about the size of a shilling.

Lament stares at her large friend in bemusement. "Well, met Sergeant! I knew you had the constitution of a bear, but I did not think to see you up so quickly or healed so well." Pieter grunts something through his food, waving the spoon again. Lament continues. "Where is Madam Beatris? I must congratulate her on the efficacy of her healing."

Pieter wipes his mouth and beard on the back of his thick forearm and looks questioningly at Lament. "Who do you ask for, Lam?"

"Why the young woman who has been our host and ministered to your wound. The owner of this abode."

The Dutchman reaches out to scoop more food into his bowl, the same quizzical look on his face. "I know of no *young woman*, Lam. There has only been an old crone who has given me herbs and cleaned this damnable wound. I was incapable of much movement on account of the infection and the fever. She told me you had come down with the sweats due to dragging me through the forest for days and had taken to bed."

Lament laughs and shakes her head. "No, my friend. We arrived here two nights past, and Beatris has been tending to you. I have certainly had no sweats!"

Pieter puts down the bowl, the food forgotten, and looks at his friend with concern. "Are you sure you are yet well, Captain?

We have been here for nearly two weeks. The crone checked my wound first thing and then put the pot on the fire before going out to fetch water. She said that your fever had broken and that you, too, would be up and about this morning." The look of distress on Lament's face takes Pieter by surprise. They have been through many things together, but this is the first time that he has seen the captain at a loss.

Lament rushes to the doorway of the hut and steps out into the cool morning air. The horses are happily eating grass with no care. But the area next to the hut no longer has a serviceable fence, and there is no sign of the goats. The vegetable plot and herb garden are there, although both have seen better days, and the thicket that marks the edge of the forest proper seems closer, even obscuring some of the standing stones.

Turning back towards the hut, Lament is stunned to see how rundown it appears. She stumbles back through the entrance, pushing the old stiff hide that hangs there to one side. "The old woman – how long has she been gone?"

Pieter looks up at the dry-looking herbs hanging in the roof beams as if they will supply the answer before replying. "Maybe an hour? No, thinking about it, perhaps more like two. Captain, what vexes you so?"

"What does the old woman look like? There is a wild urgency to Lament's questioning that finally causes Pieter to realise that there is something very much amiss.

"She is just a crone, ancient by the looks of her. The Lord knows how long she has lived out here on her own. The only remarkable thing about her is her eyes. They seem to have gold in them depending upon the light." The big Dutchman watches as his friend grows pale, the colour fleeing from her usually sun-browned face. Then Lament almost runs back into the room in which she had awakened and returns equally rapidly with their weapons. She places Pieter's swords on the ground next to him and proceeds to buckle on her sword belt.

"Something is very wrong here. I fear there may be witch-craft, and I would confront her when she returns." Pieter is used to trusting Lament, whose instincts have saved them on many an occasion. So, he does not question her but dresses as quickly as his wound will allow in clothes from his saddle bags. Then he goes to sit back by the fire, Utricia resting across his knees.

They wait until gone noon, but the woman, any woman, does not return. Lament remembers that Beatris had told her that folk would visit her for her *skills*, and that must mean that there is some town nearby, or at the very least a village. So, she saddles the horses and collects their possessions along with an earthen-ware jar holding a paste that Beatris has been using to salve Pieter's shoulder. Then they ride from the clearing and back into the forest, but this time, there is a worn path for them to follow that leads them further west.

As they ride away, a woman watches them go from the shadow of a standing stone. She hugs herself and hums a half-forgotten song. A smile plays upon her lips at the new life already growing inside her while sadness clouds her amber eyes for the fate of one of those she watches disappear amongst the birch trees. She brushes dark tresses from her face and turns towards the clear-ing and the bleating goats that require milking in their pen next to the hut in the clearing.

* * *

It is dusk when they spy the lights of the town in the distance. The forest is behind them, and they have come upon a well-made road.

Pieter has attempted to question Lament about her unease, but on each occasion, Lament has avoided answering. She is conflicted. Beatris saved the life of her friend, and she can't say that she did not enjoy their congress, even if it was *odd* to feel so male, but perhaps there is more truth to this *trade* than she would have liked to believe. Now, they ride on in silence, although Lament knows there will be more questions when they get to the town. Then maybe she will feel like answering them...

* * *

The tavern is inviting. The war has yet to touch these people's lives, and they welcome travellers with coin to spend.

Pieter slides his bulk into a high-backed wooden chair and waves at the serving girl, a big grin splitting his red beard. As he orders wine and food and flirts with the girl, Lament sits herself in the chair to Pieter's right. They have a good view of the taproom and the entrance – some habits never die.

She scans the customers as they sup their ale and wine. They are obviously well acquainted, and amongst the friendly banter and more serious conversations, there are glances cast towards these two strangers. Curious glances rather than suspicious or aggressive, but then these two do not look like they would be an easy target for any with ill intentions.

The girl brings a jug of wine and two glasses, smiling at the still-grinning giant. He watches her swish away between the tables to fetch their food and gives a long sigh before pouring Lament and himself a drink.

A well-dressed fellow, the grey at his temples and in his spade-cut beard marking him out to be in his middle years, approaches their table. He makes a small bow and smiles openly at them both. "Good evening, friends. May the Virgin bless you." A Papist, but they have been used to playing the game when the need arises, and Lament's Catholic heritage serves her well on these occasions.

"May the Lord bless you too, sir. Would you care to join us? We would seek information as to our location and have news of what has been occurring in the world." Lament gestures for him to sit. Her Dutch is not perfect, but after years of being in Pieter's company, it is passable.

"I thank you, good mistress. But how is it you do not know where you are?" He holds out his glass as Pieter proffers the wine jug.

"Ah, it's a sorry tale. We ventured into the forest and got ourselves impossibly lost, wandering for days until we came upon a hut and a woman who gave us shelter and pointed us in the right direction." Lament notes their new companions raised eyebrows at the mention of the woman.

"You say you saw this woman, and she gave you aid?" He leans in, keen interest on his face.

"Yes, do you know of her? There were pagan standing stones around her dwelling, and she professed some skill as a healer."

Maybe it is best to dissemble rather than give away too much of the true story.

The man crosses himself and shakes his head. "She was well known in these parts, but we thought her long dead. None has seen her this past fifteen years or more, and she was old then. Folk would seek her out for her remedies, and there were tales of other *things*. It was said that she could tell the hour of a man's death but that she could change that hour if the right bargain be struck. Witch many called her, but when sickness came knocking, they still went to her. I remember my mother seeking her out when my father became unwell. I was only a child myself, but I recall how my mother returned with herbs, and after a few days, my father recovered." He looks wistfully at the smoke-darkened ceiling. "Local legend would have you believe that she has been there since the time of the Romans, came with them as a slave from the east and escaped to live wild in the forest." He laughs as if it is a fine jest.

Lament stares at him dry-mouthed, her surroundings forgotten.

"Aye, her name was Beatris, I seem to recall..." He continues speaking, but Lament hears nothing. Her world contracts to darkness as her mind tries to make sense of what this man tells them.

Pieter eyes his friend. The expression on her features suggests that she is lost somewhere in thought, and it may take a moment for her to navigate back to the place in which they sit. Pieter promises himself that he will ask Lam what precisely did happen at the hut of the old woman and not accept obfuscation. But now, as their newfound companion begins to look with concern at Lament's vacant expression, he changes the subject. "Prey tell friend, what news of the war?" Pieter refills the man's glass; his deep, rumbling voice captures the man's attention.

"Ah, savagery, sir. There has been the sacking of a city across in Brabant. The Spanish Fury, they call it." The fellow gulps his wine, warming to the subject.

"What city would that be?" Pieter fears that he already knows the answer.

"That would be Mechelen. The fools opened their gates to the Calvinist heretics, and the Duke of Alba took the city back, or rather his son did. And despite the cities Catholics welcoming the Spaniards, the troops were unleashed upon the city." He takes another swig. That strange look that folk get when they relate the misfortunes of others shines in his eyes. "Three days, sir, three whole days they were left to their own devices. Slaughter, rapine, and pillage. Much of this against the good Catholics." He crosses himself. "Ah, it's a bad business, but they have themselves to blame. No good can come from having truck with Protestants!"

"Aye, that would seem to be the case." Pieter swallows his anger along with more wine, and at that moment, the serving girl returns with plates of fowl and hunks of dark bread.

"I will leave you to your repast and wish you God's ease, and I hope you have no further cause to get lost in the forest." He bows, laughing at his jest, and makes his way back into the middle of the tavern.

Lament picks moodily at the food, but her thoughts still distance her.

"Did you hear what our friend had to relate about Mechelen?

I fear that they have no love for those who do not bend the knee to the Pope in these parts. It would be wise if we made ourselves scarce come the morning." Pieter knows that practicalities will bring Lament out of her reverie.

"Aye, let us not tarry here any longer than we need. We will avail ourselves of a room tonight and then be gone at first light. Let's find out from the tavern keep which road will lead us to Naarden, and let us fulfil this damnable quest that Dee has set for us."

# Chapter 16

A bushy red eyebrow arches. "Tell me again, Captain. You lay with the old crone... more than once!" Pieter would be laughing if it were not for his friend's dark mood and the uncanny sense that they have both been in the presence of the supernatural.

"Again, yes. When I lay with her, she was not an old crone but a young woman, if indeed it was the same woman. Perhaps it could have been her granddaughter? I do not know, but a trade was offered, and I am not sure who got the best part of it, for I am not sure if I received anything. But at least you are mended, big man, and we do not seem to be any the worse for our encounter." Lament can see Pieter from the corner of her eye, and her massive comrade nods as if in agreement. She knows that there may come a time when they are in their cups, that the Sergeant will bring up the subject again, but for the moment, he seems satisfied. In truth, Lament has related the whole story except the offer Beatris made to aid her in cheating death and the fact that Lament herself seemed at some point to possess a phantom cock. That is too mad to even contemplate being real, despite what last evening's tavern companion hinted at.

"It seems we must head north then." Pieter chooses to change the conversation. He would rather think about the task at hand than dwell upon the weird.

"It would seem so. The tavern keep was adamant that we should head north and try to hire the services of a boatman to take us through Zeeland and, hence, into Holland. He believed us to be in the service of the Spanish, perhaps couriers, and I did nothing to dissuade him of that notion."

"So, we travel in ever-decreasing circles. Pity we did not get word from Dee before we wasted time going in the wrong direction!" Pieter shakes his head at their nonsensical wanderings. He stretches out his left arm and rotates the shoulder. It is healing remarkably fast, but there is still an ache in it, possibly brought on by the Autumn chill that has begun to creep into the air.

* * *

An obliging boatman, obliging due to the coins handed over to him, has navigated them through the series of canals and waterways in his flat-bottomed boat. Ghostly islands of reeds inhabited by squawking waterfowl have loomed from the mist that has never fully cleared, and for days, it has seemed they travelled through some world between heaven and earth, a purgatory for those who have lost their faith.

They have overnighted in the houses of the boatman's seemingly endless extended family, all of course at an extra cost. But Lament must agree that it has saved them a much longer and more perilous journey over land. At the very least, they have avoided the parties of Spanish outriders who are rumoured to be scouring the countryside to the east, and every day, Pieter's shoulder gets stronger.

Now they are back upon dry land, south of Utrecht, and once more in friendly territory, or so it would seem.

The countryside teems with refugees fleeing from the on-going chaos in Brabant, and they have tales of a strange Spanish commander with jester-like looks who brings an unearthly fog and darkness with him when he is present. Mechelen was not the only city to fall foul of Alba's wrath. The blood stain that spreads across the map of the Low Countries shows no sign of drying up. The columns of infantry and cavalry that clog up the roads would only seem to indicate that more is afoot.

Lament urges them further north, and they agree that it would be unwise to become entangled with any of the companies that they ride past. On occasion, when they are questioned by someone wanting to know their business, Lament shows them the seal on the letter given to her by Dr Dee. That, and the implication that they are on urgent official business, does the trick and allows them to pass without further hindrance.

* * *

Against her better judgment, Lament agrees that they should make a stop in Utrecht to refresh their supplies and try to gain any gossip that can be had regarding Naarden.

They ride through an arched entrance and into the stable yard of a large inn. Dismounting, Lament hands her reins over to the yard boy as Pieter instructs him to feed and water the mounts and to be very careful not to allow any of the contents of the saddlebags to mysteriously disappear. He grins at the boy and tosses him a coin before following Lament towards the door to the taproom.

A figure clad all in grey watches them from the side of the taproom counter. He smiles with malicious glee as Pieter recognises him and swears loudly.

"It is a fine pleasure to see you as well, my giant friend." Garrat Blexham makes a mocking bow to the Dutchman, and then he turns towards Lament. "Good Captain Evyngar, it is glad I am to find you still alive!" There seems to be an implication that he is less pleased by the continued good health of Pieter.

"You had my master worried for a while, disappearing from his sight as you did. He sent me hence to intercept you at this place which his astrology suggested you would reach - if you were still breathing."

Pieter positions himself alongside Garrat and, before he can object, places a heavy arm around his shoulders like old friends well met. "Ah, worm. I should pluck your head from your shoulders and search inside to see if you have any sense. Why are you here to vex us further?" Pieter gives a none-too-gentle squeeze, and Garrat groans, panic flashing across his eyes as he looks imploringly at the silent captain.

"Shall we avail ourselves of a nice quiet booth, and you can regale us with your story." Lament nods towards the dark wood partitioned booths at the back of the taproom, and Pieter guides the sweating Garrat in that direction. "Well then, Master Garrat, what is it that has caused you to scurry hence at the black crow's bidding? And prey tell what you infer by *disappearing from his sight?*" Lament leans in uncomfortably close while Pieter maintains his overly friendly hug.

The innkeeper makes his way over, a wary eye on the three of them. He is not too sure what is afoot, but he has seen enough trouble in his establishment to know that there could be more very soon. The scrawny grey-clad youth is not a serious threat; he is an ex-soldier, and he can still handle himself, but he knows killers when he sees them, and the other two have all the hallmarks of those who trade in death. He says a silent prayer; he is very much hoping to grow old and spend time with his grandchildren. "My friends, good day to you. Can I fetch you drink? We have a fine Rhenish that I think discerning gentlefolk such as yourselves would enjoy. And there are boar sausages, fresh made. Could I tempt you?"

Pieter smacks his chops noisily. "Yes, friend. Two bottles of the Rhenish and three servings of the sausage if it please you."

So, it looks as if trouble may be averted. The innkeeper heads back to the counter to fetch drink and shouts to his wife in the kitchen to plate up some of the boar.

The wine and food are delivered to their booth, and Lament and Pieter seem more relaxed, although Garrat still looks as if he may bolt at any moment.

"You were saying Master Garrat?" Lament slices off a large chunk of the dark boar meat sausage and takes a bite, her eyes fixed on Garrat.

"Dr Dee told me that you had passed beyond his sight; that is the ability of him to see you in his shew stone. He had been privy to your exploits up until then, and you suddenly up and vanished *poof!*" Garrat makes a mime of opening his hands as if what they held has suddenly disappeared. "And then you re-appeared to him, and his reading of the stars had you in its story once again. That is why he sent me here to meet you. His readings told that you would indeed be here on this day, and here you are!" Garrat looks as surprised as they do.

"But why did he send you? It can't be just to enquire after our health?" Lament watches Garrat fidget uncomfortably as he must now come to the bones of the task Dee has set him.

"I am to remind you that you have a job to do, a job that has consequences should you fail to complete it. The doctor was none too happy with his inability to see you and would know why you are not yet in Naarden." He quickly takes a drink, perhaps seeking to hide behind his cup as Pieter scowls at him like some angry demon from the fiery pits of hell.

"Oh, we know well the mission we are set upon and the price of failure. Our disappearance from Dee's sight was not of our choice. You may tell the doctor that maybe he is not the only one who has occult knowledge and that it would seem that sometimes it can be impossible to avoid straying into the orbit of such a person." Lament waves her eating knife to emphasise her words. "But tell me, Master Garrat. How do you come to be here if he knew not where we were? You must have begun your journey hither whilst we were still invisible to this *shew stone.*" Lament sits back against the carved dark wood of the booth. She is heartily sick of the machinations of those who practice sorcery, but she has a strong suspicion that she is a long way from being free of them.

"Oh, Master Dee raged when you were lost from sight, but he looked to the stars and drew the charts. He saw that if you were still drawing breath, you would likely as not be here on this day. So, he dispatched me hence. Another man might have thought it a fool's errand, but where the doctor sends me, I go and do not question it."

"And so, you came all this way to chide us for our lack of progress on the off chance that we would be here?" Pieter releases Garrat from his grip and holds him at arm's length, the better to see him.

"Not entirely, sergeant. For you see, the doctor has further intelligence on the artefact in Naarden that he desires. It is a map etched on a disk of bronze. Do not ask me its import or even what it doth show; he has told me that is none of my concern. But he is in grievous need of it and has had word that it has been moved from its previous location and now resides in the centre of Naarden under lock and key."

"Why does he not use his magics to locate this map? He has us dance a jig around the Low Countries while all this time he could just tell us where to look!" Lament feels her frustration boiling over, and she knows that it would only take a misjudged word on Garrat's part for him to be the recipient of that frustration.

"No, good Captain. That is the rub! The doctor can see a great many things of the past, present, and future, but he can't see these things that he so badly desires. These are objects of strange and ancient power, and they defy his best attempts at location by occult means. This is why he sent you because only *you* can find them when you are close. This is what he bid me tell you as he knew you would question his methods."

"Tell me then, what exactly is this *shew stone* that you and the doctor seem to put much faith in?" Lament has heard this object mentioned enough to pique her interest.

"Ah, I have only seen it twice and know nothing of its workings, but it would seem to be a wondrous thing! It is a mirror made of black stone that was brought back by the Spaniard Cortés from the New World. Dr Dee says that the very act of removing it from its natural home and carrying it across the ocean caused a twisting of the fabric of the world. It sounds like the talk of madmen and philosophers to me, but I know he prizes it highly, and through it, he can observe distant actions. He may be watching us even now." Garrat looks around as if expecting to see eyes floating in the very air. Pieter grunts and makes an obscene gesture, hoping that it will be suitably witnessed.

Much as Lament has no reason to like or trust the grey-attired servant of Dr Dee, she believes that the man is telling the truth. She looks across at Pieter, who is busily shoving another sausage into his mouth and sighs. "We had best to Naarden then and at least get Dee one of his baubles." Pieter nods in agreement, and they both look back at Garrat.

"Tell the devious old crow that we will obtain his map for him. In fact, by the time you reach him, we will most likely have it in our possession."

"Ah, I think you misunderstand Captain. I am here to accompany you to Naarden, and when you have secured the map, only then will I return to the doctor taking it with me." Garrat draws back in his seat, not sure which one will hit him first. But Pieter just rolls his eyes and swears under his breath, and Lament stabs the last sausage on the plate in a way that suggests she sees it as the orchestrator of all her ills.

# Chapter 17

Naarden is in something of a turmoil. Following the sacking of Mechelen and then Zutphen, the city elders are resigned to the fact that they are not prepared for an effective defence. They are in negotiations with the Spanish in an attempt to avert the same *Fury* that has descended upon the other cities, leaving them smoking charnel houses. They are offering to give supplies to the Spanish in the belief that this will be enough to stay their bloody hand.

Lament and Pieter are under no such illusions, and now the search for Dee's map has gained a new sense of urgency.

The motley bands of musketeers, pikemen, and irregulars who make up the city's garrison all have an air of defeat about them. There are few of the demonic entities inhabiting these soldiers and driving them on. The forces of chaos and order seem to prefer to be on a side that is likely to win. It appears to be a very human trait to side with the underdog. Lament smiles at her philosophical musings as she watches yet another group of local recruits drilling in the square, even though the city has already been offered up on a platter. She decides that it can only be an attempt to keep up morale.

They have taken up lodgings overlooking the square, and now they must discover the location of the map. Lament questioned Garrat as to its probable location, but his response was consistent – Dr Dee does not know, but Lament's witch-sight should enable her to locate it. How? Once again, Garrat doesn't know, but he has been assured by his master that Lament will know when she is close.

So, they must walk the city until some higher compass points them in the right direction. Lament hasn't a clue what form this divine inspiration will take, but she does keep bringing them back to Marktstraat and the Great Church. However, it is an easy landmark.

"Is there nothing Captain? Not a tingle in your gut? Not a host of spirits pointing the way with golden trumpets?" Garrat slumps down onto the low wall surrounding the churchyard and rubs at a sore calf muscle. They have been walking on the cobbled streets all day long, and his humour is wearing as thin as the soles of his boots.

"Do you not think I would have made some sign addle pate? I like this no better than you." Lament takes the leather strip from her shoulder-length hair and combs her fingers through it before retying it. She stops. "We have not yet been into this church, am I not correct?"

"You are right, Captain. We have yet to set foot in that den of Papistry." Pieter takes a few swings with his left arm. The wound is healing nicely, and the stiffness has almost gone.

"Judas! I think we may have been walking in circles for a very good reason. We need to search inside; I think our prize may be contained within." As she gazes at the church, the air around it seems to ripple like the heat coming off the ground on a hot summer's day, even though it is currently drizzling.

They slip over the low wall and pick their way through the gravestones. The door stands open, and inside, there is the strong smell of incense. It is cool, lit by candles and the weak rays of the late afternoon sun as it filters through the stained-glass windows. Pools of coloured light stain the tiles of the floor, and they walk the length of the church between the wooden pews.

At the altar with its tall gold crucifix from which Christ looks upon them with tormented, judgmental eyes, they stop and look back down the nave. It would appear to the naked eye that it is just a house of God if a Catholic one. But Lament is beginning to see something else. It is as if she can see the bones of the church, the things that lie below the surface. A blue glow seems to emanate from the floor in the centre of the church. No, not from the floor, but somehow beneath it. She walks back to the place it is brightest and points. "Something is there, something beneath us."

"There must be a crypt." Garrat searches the tiles for evidence of a trapdoor, running his thin fingers around the edges of the tiles.

Pieter glances at Lament and heads off to the only other visible door off one of the transepts. As he opens it, there is a startled cry of indignation. "How dare you enter the house of God bearing weapons! And you have the look of a Calvinist about you! We have an accord that all are safe to worship as they will in this city, but we do not trespass into one another's holy places." A short, plump priest clad in a purple cassock bustles out of his inner sanctuary, waving hands at the amused red-bearded giant before him.

Pieter scoops him up and places him to one side as he ducks through the doorway, and the priest's face turns a darker shade of puce, and he focuses his ire on Lament. "Brigands! I will have you all hung for this. I will summon the Watch!"

"Father, calm yourself." Lament eyes the purple cassock and thinks that they may have more here than they bargained for. She holds up a hand to appease the angry priest. But the loud noises emanating from the vestry do nothing to aid in his return to a state of peacefulness.

"There is no way below in there; just alter wine and fine vestments. All the trappings of Papistry." Pieter stands in the doorway with his meaty fists planted on his hips.

"I am not a simple *father*; I am Bishop van der Croon, and you will address me as such. And what do you mean by *no way below*? What exactly are you looking for? I want you out of God's house right now. I will fetch the Watch, mark my words." Bishop van der Croon builds himself up for yet another tirade, but Lament clamps her hand across his mouth and pushes him down onto a pew.

"Apologies, your eminence, but there are chambers beneath this church, perhaps a crypt. I would gain access to them. Allow this, and we will leave you to your conversations with the Lord." As she mentions the spaces under the church, the bishop's eyes widen, and his indignation is replaced with terror. Lament removes her hand, and it is obvious that the rapid breathing has nothing to do with having had his mouth covered. "What ails you, Bishop? You have a look about you as if I had asked you to show us the very gates of Hell. We mean you no harm, but there is something hidden beneath that we will not leave without."

"There *are* vaults beneath the church. But there are other things in those depths. A villain came not two months gone. He brought with him cart loads of crates and a letter from the Holy Roman Emperor, Rudolph II himself, requesting that the villain be allowed to store the boxes where he saw fit and aid be given to the man who would follow. Thus, the crates have become resident in the vaults." The Bishop takes a deep breath, and there is perspiration on his top lip. Lament looks at the man inside the robes for the first time and sees a weak character, body become corpulent, with the face of an ageing cherub who maybe has less than holy vices. This is a man who enjoys his God-given authority over others, but he is also a man who is deeply afraid of something. "Count Godard van Ijzendoom is the man's name. He arrived in the dead of night and has spent much of his time since in the vaults with his boxes. I fear he is doing the Devil's work even if it is with the blessing of his holiness." He dabs at the sweat on his forehead with the sleeve of his cassock.

"What is it that you fear so much about this van Ijzendoom?" Pieter sits his bulk down in the row of pews behind the Bishop, who leans back and part turns his head as he answers.

"I believe him to be a necromancer and dealer in magic. He barely shows himself in daylight and only then with his two heathen henchmen, and there are sounds that emanate from the vaults at night that are enough to drive a man mad! I would be rid of him if I could..." There is a pleading look in the small eyes, a desire to make a deal even if it means going against a higher authority.

"So, Father. How do we descend into these vaults?" Pieter senses rightly that this man will not stand in their way if they can remove his *concerns*.

"I am a Bishop." It is said very quietly, almost as an afterthought.

"My apologies, Bishop. You are not in your finery and Popish trappings. And where are your minions? Surely you do not look after this grand church all on your own... But more importantly – where is the entrance to the vaults?" Pieter observes a flash of wounded pride.

"My *minions,* as you call them, do not tarry as the sun begins to set. And it sets early at this time of year. I was only still here because I was collecting something to take to a meeting of the city elders on the morrow." He sees that these men are running out of patience and gathers himself together. "The entrance you seek is in the churchyard. You may not have passed it unless you came into the grounds from the east. There is a low stone building with an iron-bound door. That is the entrance to the crypt and the vaults." He decides to take a chance on these heretics. Maybe they can remove the necromancer, or mayhap they will die trying, either way... "I know not what you want from the vaults, and I must say that I do not care. But you would be performing a service for God, however you choose to worship Him, by sending van Ijzendoom to the hell that so surely awaits him."

"So, we are *doing God's service* now, are we? No longer *brigands* when you want something from us!" Pieter looms over the Bishop from the pew behind.

"I may have judged you hastily." The sweating cleric edges forward as he feels the giant's breath on the back of his neck.

Pieter laughs and slaps him on the shoulder. "No offence taken, *Bishop,* 'twas a reasonable mistake."

"Enough talk; let us get what we have come for and be away from here. If your necromancer is below and he seeks to stop us, then he may well find himself roasting in hell fires before his allotted time. Now, show us to this entrance." Lament signals the Bishop to his feet. There is an obvious reluctance as he realises that he must accompany them at least part of the way, although this is tempered by curiosity and avarice as to what might be concealed within the crates. Perhaps if these soldiers kill van Ijzendoom, then there may be rich pickings to be had. And he can always set the Watch on them when they have played their part. So, he gestures them onward towards the doorway.

Out in the churchyard, the light is fading, and the Bishop takes a lantern from inside the doorway.

"Good Captain, what is happening? Why have we left the church in the company of this servant of the antichrist?" Garrat does not speak Dutch and has, therefore, no knowledge of what has just passed between Lament and the Bishop. His genuine dislike of all things Catholic is not feigned. He has never been anything other than Protestant and has grown up indoctrinated by the hatred that has spread throughout England.

"This, Master Garrat, is Bishop van der Croon, and he is about to show us a way into the vaults. So be not too harsh with him, for we may soon have Dr Dee's map." Lament follows the Bishop along a gravel path that skirts the periphery of the church, and Garrat follows close behind, a sudden look of excitement upon his pale face.

They reach the low stone structure that holds the way down

to the vaults, but the door is locked, and the Bishop shrugs helplessly. "He has taken all of the keys."

Pieter pushes against the door, but it has been made to resist force, and his shoulder is still not healed enough to risk charging it. "We could shoot the lock, although I fear that might attract unwanted attention." He draws his falchion to attempt to pry the door open, but Garrat places a hand upon his arm.

"Allow me. I was not always in the employ of the doctor." Reaching into the pouch at his belt, he produces a leather roll, which he places on the ground and opens. The roll contains lock picks, the tools of the trade for a house diver. As the others look on, Garrat examines the lock and then selects skeleton keys and picks from the roll and inserts them into the lock. There is much intense concentration accompanied by whispered exhortations and profanity. Then, there is a loud click, and with a look of triumph, Garrat pushes the door open.

It is only Lament's unnaturally fast reflexes that save Garrat from the quarrel that fires from somewhere within. Lament pulls him out of line with the door as she hears the snap of the crossbow releasing, and the missile travels a hair's breadth past his skinny frame. Unfortunately, the Bishop is not so lucky. Standing square on to the doorway, eager to see what is inside, he takes the quarrel full in the chest, and he dies with a surprised look on his ageing cherub's face.

"So, we can assume there are traps then." Lament's irony causes Pieter to smile as Garrat pats himself all over, not quite believing that he has not been hit. He stoops and collects his tools as Pieter takes the lantern from the ground by the body, and they peer cautiously inside.

There are stone steps leading down into what would appear to be a dimly lit chamber. The rest of the stone structure is littered with barrels and baskets that look as if they once held food stuff or other supplies. But Lament's interest lies on the back wall directly opposite the door where a metal bracket holds a large crossbow and a thin cord stretches from its release mechanism through a counterweight and to a ring set on the back of the door.

"This could only have been set from inside, so methinks that this van Ijzendoom is at home. Therefore, we proceed with caution." Lament runs her fingers along the cord and must give some credit for the skill of the trap. She turns as she hears a grunt and sees Pieter dragging the Bishop through the door by one ankle, the cassock riding up to reveal a fat arse, and then propping him in the corner behind some barrels.

The Dutchman looks up and grins. "Well, we don't want any-one stumbling over the little fat bastard, do we? I would say our necromancer might be enough trouble without a visit from the Watch."

They descend the steps slowly, aware that there could be more lethal devices lying in wait. The lantern casts a peculiar, sickly glow on the stones of the stairwell, and then they are in a broad corridor that runs away from them. There is light. Candles set in iron sconces illuminate the corridor as it transitions from the entrance and becomes something else – the vaults.

Pieter and Garrat gasp in superstitious awe at the images painted on the wooden panels that clad the sides of the vault walls. Biblical images from the Old Testament fill the right-hand wall in a profusion of colour and detail. On the left-hand wall, scenes of hell and damnation scream out at them in lurid detail. As good Protestants, Pieter and Garrat see terrible heresy, but Lament grew up Catholic, and although she has never seen images quite like these, she is not offended by them. She recalls hearing of a Dutch painter called Bosh, whose visions of what awaits the damned have been vilified by those of all religious persuasion for the hysteria they have caused. Perhaps these are similar? Lament's attention is caught by a depiction of the Garden of Eden to her right. Is it a trick of the flickering light, or is the serpent really moving amongst the branches of the tree?

"Jesu, preserve us!" Garrat backs away from the images of the inferno on the opposite wall. The mix of lantern and candlelight makes it seem as if the fires of Hell are truly ablaze and the souls of the damned are writhing in torment. Perhaps it is just the cleverness of the artist, but it makes the blood run cold.

Another passage crosses this one at right angles, and as they approach it, there is the sound of a voice droning what Lament thinks, from recent experience, can only be an incantation. She holds up her left hand in warning as she quietly draws her sword. The ceiling of the vault seems no longer to be a painted depiction of the heavens but to be filled with billowing clouds. As Lament cautiously peeks around the corner in the left wall, there is a drawn-out groan that seems to come from the walls themselves.

The new passage is a vision of lunacy. The walls are entirely covered with images of devils and demonic forms, punishing the sinners who have now to pay the eternal price for their transgressions against God. In the centre of the passage is a figure clad in garments of a deep maroon slashed with gold panels. A hood covers his head, and a cloak falls back across his shoulders as he stands with his arms raised. The droning voice comes from that dark cowl, and as the companions round the corner, it rises to a crescendo of inhuman sound.

The arms sweep down and are thrust forward as if he is throwing something towards them, and suddenly, the images on the walls of the vault are no longer on the wooden panels.

The groaning has turned to howls and shrieks and a tittering that threatens to make lunatics of them. Then suddenly, they are in the midst of it, and surrounded by demons, they fight.

Pieter's falchion hacks out in a vicious arc, chopping into scaled, reptilian things that hop and skitter on two legs. The blade cuts deep and spills a luminous fluid of a bilious yellow colour, but there seems to be little lasting effect because the things keep coming.

Lament fends off a flapping horned thing that looks as if it has been freshly dipped in crimson paint as she attempts to aim a pistol at the necromancer. There is no shot to be had. The demons swarm around him like some protective shield as they work their way towards those they have been summoned to destroy.

"Ideas would be welcome, Captain!" Pieter thrusts a cowering Garrat behind him as he frantically slashes at the creatures that approach. A tentacled horror explodes out of nowhere, vile purple suckers' mouth at the air as if already tasting human flesh and souls. The big Dutchman backs away, cleaving through the nearest fleshy appendage, which whips back into the bubbling slime-green and black body and then begins to grow anew.

Lament risks a glance over her shoulder. The other arm of

the passage behind them contains the crates that the Bishop mentioned. They could provide a temporary barrier, or perhaps they should attempt a fighting withdrawal to the stairs. But the grotesque shadows moving on the floor in that direction would seem to indicate that the images on the walls there have also come to life.

"Make haste to the crates behind us. Mayhap there is another way out!" Lament fires the pistol into the grinning jaws of a hairy, ape-like thing that staggers backwards with a sizeable part of its head missing. The large wooden boxes provide cover for the moment, making it less easy for the creatures to get to them. It can only be a temporary reprieve.

Lament looks on in horror as the far end of the corridor beyond the necromancer begins to fill with a ghastly light, and in that light, figures take form, and it is a form she wishes she did not recognise. They are too vast to fit into the confines of the vault, but somehow, they are there. Terrifyingly beautiful, the fallen angels begin to materialise, and Lament feels the markings upon her skin burn.

With a grunt, Pieter pushes a large crate from the stack onto the demons who are trying to swarm over it. There are crunching sounds, and the things writhe, trapped beneath it for a moment, and then the crate bursts open, spilling out its contents. A crystal orb, similar to one Lament has seen in Dr Dee's chambers, rolls from the wreckage. To Lament's witch-sight, it glows with orange flame.

"Throw that thing at that bastard!" Lament points at the orb, not really knowing what else to do. Fortunately, Pieter does not need further prompting to violent action, and he scoops up the orb in a massive fist and hurls it with all his might along the corridor. They watch in amazement as the demons avoid the orb's flight, and then, with a resounding thud, it strikes the hooded head of the necromancer, spinning him around and knocking him from his feet.

Time seems to slow. The demons halt their headlong charge, and many of them turn to look at the fallen human who has summoned them while others mill around suddenly aimless. There is a flickering in the light behind where he stood like distant summer lightning, and the archdukes of hell begin to fade, anger written on their perfect faces.

The necromancer struggles to his knees, one hand pressed to his face, blood running freely from a smashed mouth, and before he can try to speak again, Lament draws her other pistol and fires. The ball hits him in the throat, and he falls once again. Then, like a pack of savage dogs turning upon a fallen leader, the demons descend upon him. They tear at him and hoist him up, and en mass, they carry him away with them, back into the walls.

There is silence, broken only by the crystal orb that rolls from where it fell back into the centre of the passageway and comes to a stop in an indentation in the stone flag floor.

Lament realises that she is holding her breath. They are all holding their breath, and as she exhales, she begins to laugh, the tension leaving her in a rush. Pieter joins in, shaking his red bristling head. The laughter is only just on the correct side of sane, and it could easily become hysterical.

Garrat crouches by a large open crate, and he is trembling uncontrollably. Now that he is breathing again, he is making small sobbing noises. He wipes his face on his sleeve, not wishing the others to see the tears on his cheeks.

On the far wall is a depiction of the fallen angels wreathed in the smoke and flames of the pit. And there, where the demons had retreated, taking their human victim with them, there is a scene of torment and suffering. Beastly diabolic forms tear apart and roast a struggling figure dressed in maroon and gold.

A shiver runs through Lament, and she starts as Pieter comes up behind her, silent despite his size.

"What say you we get gone from this place, Captain? I will fight any mortal, man, or beast, but there are things here that should not be in our world. Let us get this cursed map and leave this tomb." Pieter chooses not to stare at the paintings; they pull at his mind in a way that he would prefer to forget as quickly as possible.

Lament finds it difficult not to stare. She gradually backs away from the wall and turns towards her friend. "Aye, big man. Let us get what we came here for and escape into clean air." She gazes around the passageways with their boxes, barrels, and crates. Now, she is not fighting for her life, and she can once again see the strange phosphorescent blue glow that marks her goal.

Taking her dagger, she pries the lid from a large crate that sits next to an image on the wall of Golgotha and the crucifixion. A sad-eyed Christ looks towards heaven from the cross, a crown of thorns circling his dark, bloodstained forehead, and in the background, in silhouette, Judas hangs from a tree, thirteen pieces of silver scattered on the ground beneath him.

She pushes the lid to one side, and Pieter manhandles it out of the way. The crate is filled with all manner of things, most wrapped in cloth or straw to protect them. Lament knows what she is looking for and doesn't waste time examining the strange books and intricately wrought instruments that she removes. Then, under a large tome that is held closed with a brass lock and seems to be bound, *Lament shudders*, in human skin, she finds a disk wrapped in dark green silk. It is about the size of a buckler, and compared with many of the other items in the chest, it appears unimposing. But as she unwraps the silk, she reveals a map, a map unlike any she has ever seen before. There, on this metal disk, is etched an image of the world but showing continents that she can't name and in detail that she can scarcely comprehend.

"Master Garrat, is this it? Is this what Dee so desires?" She looks at Garrat with some sympathy. It is plain that he has pissed himself and has been unmanned by the experience. It is not unusual for a first battle to have that effect, and given their adversaries, maybe a little slack is in order.

"Yes, yes, that is it." Despite all that has just occurred, Garrat can't take his eyes from the disk with its chart. He knows it means that he can return to London, something he dearly desires, and it also means that his master will be very pleased. And there were rewards promised...

"What is so important about a map?" Pieter stares over Lament's shoulder and, for the life of him, can't understand why it should be of value. Unless, of course, it is a map to treasure.

"Dr Dee called it the *Map of the Ancient Sea Kings*. He values it greatly; I have heard him make mention of it when talking about the colonies in the New World and something called the

*Northwest Passage.*" Garrat clearly does not care much for the details as long as it is his ticket home. Lament wraps it back in its silk and hands it to Garrat, who hugs it to his chest.

"Do you want to take any of these other goods? They look like they may fetch a pretty price." Pieter holds up a gilded mechanical instrument that has a series of orbs on concentric rings about a larger central one.

"Take what you will, my friend, but I want nothing from the hoard of this van Ijzendoom and his sorcery." And she turns away, ushering Garrat towards the entrance. Pieter shrugs, tosses the instrument back into the chest and follows them.

In the crystal orb that sits on the flagstone floor, a smoky shape takes form, and for a moment, it would seem that bright eyes study them before they are gone back up the steps and into the night.

# Chapter 18

Garrat has gone. He joined a group of English merchants who had made a collective decision to flee Naarden before the Spanish could make their presence felt. So, this morning, he bade them farewell and sailed away with the merchants and their heavily laden barges heading towards Amsterdam.

Inside a leather pouch is securely ensconced Dr Dee's precious map. His intent once he reaches Amsterdam is to find passage on a trader bound for England, and hopefully, by then, the ill effects of last night's carousing will have dissipated, at least from war drums beating in his skull to a dull ache. His attempts to blot out the memories of the events in the vaults by downing copious amounts of wine and brandy were only a partial success, despite the assistance of Lament and Pieter. His sleep, once he finally collapsed, was still haunted by the visions of hell that had somehow come to life and attacked them. Even though he had managed to avoid seeing the final act in the necromancer's demise, the sounds that had filled that loathsome crypt had been enough to drive him to the very edge of reason. Waking tangled in twisted bed linen and drenched in sweat, he had cringed at every shadow and curled, whimpering in his rank fear until the dawn drove the visions from his mind, at least for the moment.

It was with little regret that he put Naarden behind him. Glad would he be to be back in London where he only must avoid the cutpurses, plague, and perhaps a dose of French pox.

Lament and Pieter have other problems. The Bishop was not alone in the church. The rector had just finished sweeping the flagstone path running around the church's perimeter and was replacing the broom in a store cupboard when he had seen them leave the church and make their way around the building. His curiosity had been piqued, although because the Bishop was escorting the group and seemed to be conversing amiably with them, he had not been concerned. After all, the strange fellow who was using the vaults often had visitors, although they usually came bearing objects concealed in boxes. He had learned to avoid the entrance to the vaults; the strange, muffled sounds that emanated from there caused him great unease.

It was not until the morning when he began his rounds of the church grounds, that he noticed that the door to the vaults was ajar and, after tentative exploration, discovered the body of the Bishop propped inside. He immediately sounded the alarm and summoned the Watch, and before long armed men were searching the vaults while the captain of the Watch sent out orders for his men to be on the lookout for a swordswoman in black, a thin man dressed all in grey, and a red-headed giant.

As they make their way back to their lodgings with the intent to gather up their belongings and put some leagues between themselves and Naarden, they find their way blocked by a group of soldiers. Soldiers who are pointing muskets and crossbows directly at them.

The captain of the Watch strides out from behind his men. He is a man in his late thirties with a bristling moustache and curling hair that is brushed back and held in place by a wide-brimmed hat that sports a red feather. He wears a steel cuirass and a short skirt of steel plates that protect his upper legs. He has the look of an angry lobster as he taps his baton against his thigh. "Sirrahs! Hold fast! You are to accompany us to answer questions in connection with the murder of the Bishop and the ransacking of the vaults of the Great Church."

Lament raises her hands in resignation. There are too many weapons pointed in their direction for foolish heroics. She glances over at the big sergeant just to make sure that he has not decided on a different course of action. But Pieter has followed suit and raised his massive palms in supplication. Lament nods and gives a faint smile. Her vision suddenly turns to deep swirling greens and purples and then piercingly bright metallic hues that seem to have turned everything into a mosaic which rushes inwards like a whirlpool. She is pulled towards that whirlpool over its spinning lip and into darkness. The last thing she hears is the uproar of men shouting and the startled exclamation of a familiar voice.

* * *

*I open my eyes, stomach still in my throat from the drop into spinning darkness. It is still dark, but it is the dark of night rather than the void, and it is not complete blackness. The lurid light of flames illuminates a scene totally alien to me, yet somehow familiar.*

*Tall buildings surround me as I climb over the rubble that has fallen in great heaps into the streets. I realise that I am not alone; dark shapes move around me with a sense of purpose. At first, I think demons once more beset me, but something clicks into place in my mind, and I know who these men are and why they look so strange. I know that the large round disks that sit on either side of a corrugated tube that descends to a metal container and the black hood which holds all this tightly over their heads is called a gas mask. And even as I fathom this out, I find myself pulling one of these masks over my head, gaging slightly at the stink of what I know is rubber.*

*There are enormous lights, searchlights? That project beams of light up into the night sky. As I stare upwards between towering buildings, I see a shape appear from the blackness to be illuminated by the searching finger of light. A silver-grey thing like a whale in the sky, too massive to be floating in the air, manoeuvres itself above the buildings. My mind does yet another convoluted flip, and I know that grey thing is an airship, and suddenly, everything rushes in and clicks into place.*

Cannons boom from the aerial gun platforms and incendiary shells rain down upon the city of London. Other shells follow, and I pull my mask tight as they explode around us, and clouds of gas begin to fill the spaces that were once busy streets. Like a fog, *a real pea souper*, it rolls in and across us.

There is a cry of alarm and panic from my left, and I watch helplessly as one of the new recruits, I can't even remember his name, struggles too late to get his mask over his head. The chlorine gas caresses him, doing its work. In the confines of the street, and with no wind to thin it out, we might as well be on the ocean bed. The youth, and he is only just of fighting age, drowns in the air, waving his arms in frantic circles, all hope of putting on the mask gone. As bloody froth begins to spill from his distended lips, I look away. I know that death in another form is coming.

Long ropes are falling from the gondola suspended beneath the Zeppelin, and dark figures begin to slide down the ropes.

We duck under cover as machine gun fire from the turrets on the gondola rakes through the toxic fog. I draw my.455 Webley and take aim at one of the descending shapes. The combination of impaired vision because of the gas mask, the swirling gas, and the sudden sideways drift of the Zeppelin causes my shot to go wide. Bullets rattle across the half-downed wall in front, causing me to duck, and as I come back up, I steady the heavy weapon on the top of the brickwork. This time, I do not miss. A dark figure convulses on his rope and falls into the clouds of gas.

The other members of my unit are already firing with rifles and small arms as they pop up between bursts of machine gun fire. More of the figures drop from the sky like puppets with their strings cut.

I hear another noise. More Zeppelin engines, and I turn to see Corporal Barrat looking up and along a side street. "Fuck!" His muffled exclamation is very apt. Fuck indeed. Three more of the grey cigar shapes have appeared from the darkness, and they are already discharging their *Selbstmordkommando*.

It is not unusual for them to come in pairs, these giant, floating bastards, but four at once... This is going to get messy.

"Warren, get over here!" Private Warren uses the shattered

masonry and the tumbled remains of a broken staircase as cover and quickly makes his way over to me.

"Yes, Captain?"

"Get back to battalion command and tell them that we need at least one more unit. Try not to get shot." He can't see my grin behind the mask, but we all know each other well enough by now, and I think he gets it.

"Yes, Sir. Would the Captain like me to bring back a cuppa?" Yes, he gets it. He vaults a fallen beam and disappears into the gas.

The Hun send their men, crazed on amphetamines, strength-enhancing drugs, and painkillers, with no hope of return. Many of them have been surgically altered by the sorcerer scientists of the Second Reich, tubes and wires disappearing into their suppurating flesh, gas masks stapled permanently to their faces. Seemingly already more dead than alive, their job is to cause as much damage and destruction as possible. Our job is to stop them.

We are specialists, trained in close-quarter combat and gymnastics, and yes, fuelled by our own heady mix of stimulants. We can run across the city's burning skyline and play these invaders at their own game. We have little choice. Since the expeditionary force was driven back out of France and the French forces were overrun, we fight this war on our own soil. Every attack could be the herald of an invasion, so every attack must be repulsed with maximum prejudice.

The newly arrived Zeppelins rain down machinegun fire and more gas shells. One of the searchlights is hit and goes dark in a fountain of shattered glass and screaming men. We continue to aim at the descending figures, like spiders coming down on threads from their floating web. But we know that we will have to wait for them to land before we can engage them fully. Because at that point, the machineguns on the Zeppelins' will go quiet so as not to hit their own men.

Corporal Barrat nudges me, and I follow the direction of his nod and see through the gas that Blue Unit have taken up position across a small garden area at the entrance to the tube station. I wrack my brain. Russell Square, that's the name of the station.

The first Hun has made it to the ground, and the floating guns have begun to go silent. I unsheathe my sabre, transferring the Webley to my left hand for the moment. I watch as the lads produce the array of weapons which they have come to rely on when it comes to the business of face-to-face killing. Foot-long blades with spiked knuckle duster hilts, clubs and hammers customised to resemble medieval maces. Broadswords and axes commandeered from museums and private collections. And, of course, the fixed bayonet.

Like a motley army raised from the depths of Hell, we ready ourselves, and I give the nod to Sergeant Coles. He points the flare gun up into the sky and fires. The streets are bathed in a red glow, turned a nauseous purple by the toxic mist, and the black shapes are coming, loping like mutated apes. Flat glass eyes, spiked steel helmets, weapons at the ready.

I stand and fire. The time for hiding behind cover is done. My shot hits the German in the chest and knocks him backwards off his feet. The second shot blows the lower part of an arm off a second approaching figure. The Webley is a fearsome pistol.

Shots are returned. At first, I think that they have carried down a machine gun, but I see that several of them hold automatic pistols. I have heard of these; they are Austrian and can fire eight hundred rounds per minute, although they fortunately only have a sixteen-round magazine. But that is more than enough. Two of my men go down, and then there is a barrage of fire from the direction of the tube station, which cuts the leading Germans almost in half. Blue Unit do love their shotguns.

We charge. Leaping over rubble, zig-zagging the potholes in the road, we close the distance. The Webley is back in its holster, and in its place, I have my trusty short axe to complement my sabre.

The collision is sudden and bloody. To my left, I see the sergeant thrust a long metal spike, which he has welded to a brass cup that fits over his fist, through the eyeglass of a gas mask. The point exits the back of the head, and the man drops twitching. I twist to one side and parry a bayonet thrust with the axe. As the man comes level with me, I cleave him open with my sabre, letting him pass and fall to the ground behind me to be stomped on by another of my men.

In the hellish glow of a second flare, I can see a bulky figure in the centre of the street. This one has a blackened steel full-face helmet from which protrudes tubes for a concealed gas mask. A steel breastplate covers his torso and protects his groin and upper legs. Painted across the armour are the words *Tod vom Himmel,* which my rough German translates as *Death from the Skies.* He is a big bastard. He needs to be to wear that armour and carry the gun he levels at us.

"Machine gun!" I shout a warning as the bullets start to fly.

One man drops, shot through the hip, while the rest of us scatter to whatever cover we can find.

The Hun we are already engaged with follow us. Their comrade with the machine gun doesn't seem too fussy about dealing out friendly fire to his own side. I can see men rolling together in the debris, locked in a grim embrace. Masks are ripped from faces, and panicked men, burning from the chlorine, flail desperately at their foes.

One of my boys, a stocky East Ender, sits astride a German and slams a large chunk of concrete containing metal reinforcing rods up and down onto his face. Very quickly, there is only a rubber bag of mush in a helmet. He glances over at me, and I see a crazed look in his eyes, exultant but horrified by what he has done. A burst of machinegun fire ends him.

I crawl forward, and the armoured Hun advances towards us. I intend to close the range and use the Webley to shoot off one of his lower legs, but as I manoeuvre around a fallen beam, another attacker rises from the body of his victim and throws himself on me. He has a spiked club that crashes down towards my head. This would be my last moment if not for the wooden beam. The club catches it, and two of the wicked spikes dig in, bringing it to a halt an inch from my helmet. I kick out, frantic to get some space and manage through blind luck to catch him in the knee. Balance gone, he drops onto his wrecked leg and the tip of my sabre. It goes into his thigh about six inches, and by the sudden spurt of blood, I know it has cut his femoral artery. He takes another swing at me, a dead man trying to take me with him. I block with the axe, and a stream of guttural curses emanates from him. Using the inner curve of the axe blade, I drag the club downwards and outwards. As the momentum causes him to fall towards me, I punch the axe head forward into the side of his neck, crushing his windpipe.

There is a loud burst of firing from the tube station. They are concentrating fire on the armoured machine gunner. But though he staggers under the volume of fire, he does not fall. In fact, he turns his attention to Blue Unit, and I hear screams as he rakes them with murderous intensity.

Pushing my assailant's body away from me, I look for an opening to attack. But there it is, a horizontal fountain of flame that engulfs the steel-clad Hun, causing him to pirouette, burning, as through the drifting clouds come our reinforcements led by a flamethrower unit.

An explosion somewhere behind me, and I am flung to the ground. I roll onto my back, checking that my mask is intact and that I have all my limbs. Lying here, I look up at the silver-grey shapes of the Zeppelins and see smaller shapes flying amongst them. The Sopwith Camels are airborne at last, darting around the giant shapes like angry hornets.

Fire. The night sky is suddenly ablaze as the gas bags of a Zepplin are ignited. It is a beautiful and terrible sight as it crumples and sags, the flames running astonishingly quickly along its length. It veers away across the rooftops, looking for a place to die. Perhaps we will be lucky, and it won't come down on top of us...

* * *

A voice calling her name as if from a forgotten dream.

"Jesus, be praised! Lam! Lament, are you well?" Pieter's big hands check the prone figure for signs of injury and then haul her to her feet. The Dutchman holds his friend upright at arm's length as he stares into the blank face. "Captain, we need to be gone from here." He shakes Lament in his urgency, causing her head to wobble like a dancing marionette.

Lament's eyes begin to focus despite the shaking, and she is aware of the flames and smoke around her. There is a moment of panic as she clutches at her face and finds no mask, and her eyes dart reflexively upwards, searching for something in the sky above. "Where are the Zeppelins?" The confusion in Lament's voice is tinged with yet more panic as she twists desperately to look around her.

"What? Are you moonstruck Captain? We must be away from here. The Spanish are within the walls, and they are in a killing mood. They have marched the towns folk into the Guild Hall and fired it." Pieter still holds Lament by the shoulders, but he no longer shakes her. "If it had not been for van Ijzendoom, I would not have found you. But we must go now, for I fear the odds are too great even for us!" Pieter gives Lament his biggest grin even though his eyes show his concern.

At van Ijzendoom's name, Lament's head snaps up, and her eyes become clear as the world, this world, rushes in, and the *other* world is relegated to dream-like phantoms. "The necromancer is dead! We witnessed him perish. What madness is this?"

"Ah, Captain. I have much to tell but now is not opportune. I will relate all once we are beyond the clutches of de Toledo's butchers." Pieter gestures for them to move, and Lament nods. The screams and the stink of burning are now all too real, and she follows the red-haired sergeant as he heads towards a lightly guarded breach in the city wall.

Pieter stops briefly to collect their saddle bags and his zweihander from the ditch in which they are hidden, and then, blades drawn, they advance upon the unwary Spaniards.

# Chapter 19

They have ridden the stolen mounts hard and put ten leagues between themselves and Naarden before stopping to rest the horses. The road to Amsterdam, like many of the roads they have travelled, is congested with groups of refugees who had the good sense to flee the doomed city before the arrival of the Spanish.

"What in the name of all the hells happened to you, Lam?" Pieter lets his horse join Lament's at the water trough. It is not as large as the old Percheron he was riding, and because of the pace they have set, it has struggled under the Dutchman's weight.

"I do not know my friend. One moment, I was standing with you, awaiting arrest by the City Watch. The next, I was in some strange London fighting against soldiers who came from the sky!" As she relates all she can remember, Pieter stares on in superstitious awe.

"Was I struck on the head? Were they just dreams of my befuddled mind?" Lament shakes her head, not believing her own experience even though it felt totally real to her.

"You were not touched by anyone. One moment, you were there, and then you were gone as if the earth had just swallowed you up. I thought that the Watch captain would fall into a swoon. They searched everywhere while I stood surrounded by pikes." He cups his hand and splashes water over his face, rubbing it across the red stubble on his massive head. "That was three days past."

"Three days! But I could have been in that other place for no more than a few hours if I was there at all. You say I vanished without a trace?" Lament feels the ground reel and leans against her horse to steady herself as Pieter nods in confirmation that it has indeed been three days since they were halted by the Watch. "And what of van Ijzendoom? He is dead, is he not? Tell me what happened after I... I *disappeared*."

Pieter takes a swig from an earthenware jug of ale that they purchased from a fleeing merchant who seemed pleased to make a sale even under his current circumstances. He hands it to Lament and takes a deep breath before beginning. "When it became obvious even to those addle pates that you were not hiding under a cobblestone, they marched me off to the gaol. There, they questioned me about the Bishop, the vaults, and about your vanishing trick. I denied having been to the church, but it would seem the rector was on the grounds and gave a fulsome description of us, and it was he who discovered the unlucky Bishop in the entrance to the vaults. And as for yourself, well, what could I say?" He shrugs. "The Watch was dispatched again to widen the search for you, and I was left sitting in a cell awaiting the magistrate. But the next day, I was visited by none other than van Ijzendoom himself. I did not believe it was him at first, but it seems that it was one of his acolytes left to catalogue the artefacts who took it upon himself to summon the demons, and it was that inept fool who was dragged off to Hell." Pieter shudders at the thought.

"The necromancer has friends in high places, as we know from the things the Bishop let slip. He was given free rein to visit with me as he saw fit, and I imagined that he would be most vexed by our adventure in the vaults and the theft of part of his patron's collection. But no. He was much more interested in your vanishing, and he questioned me on that at length. Of course, I could tell him nothing, so he began to ask me to confirm other things that he had become aware of." The Dutchman scratches at his hedge of a beard.

"Such as?" Lament's interest is peaked further.

"Such as how you came to be in the service of Dr John Dee. How you can see otherworldly entities that possess certain folk. He also asked regarding our meeting a witch in the forest."

"How is he aware of these things? It's not as if I have distributed a pamphlet advertising our exploits!" The jug halts midway to her lips, and Lament shakes her head in consternation.

"Ah, I did put that matter to him. He was most forthcoming with an explanation, albeit a cryptic one. He stated that *Dr Dee is not the only one in possession of a scrying stone*. 'Twould seem that this van Ijzendoom can divine the goings on of a subject using his magic in the same manner that the black crow Dee can. As I said, he was most interested in you and your disappearance. He returned later that day, saying that he had performed *some sort of working* that had shown him when and where you would reappear but could not say where you had gone. He also vouched safe the knowledge of the impending Spanish attack and massacre, then he escorted me from the gaol and bid me

God's speed, encouraging me to find you and flee the city with all haste."

"Why would he give you aid in such a manner? Was there no talk of recompense? I find it hard to believe that he would act as our benefactor from the goodness of his heart." Stoppering the jug, Lament slips it back into a saddle bag.

"Aye, that is the truth. I have the feeling that we have not seen the last of van Ijzendoom and that he has some designs upon you."

They walk the horses, allowing them to pick at the long grass that borders the road. There will be a need to stop for the night if only to give their mounts some rest. They know that they are safe from the Spanish forces, so a farmer willing to let them sleep in his barn would be a satisfactory result – if they can find one.

"This *other place* you say you went, what do you make of it?" Pieter looks down at his feet as he asks the question rather than look at Lament.

"I know not. It is already fading like a dream. What seemed to be so real, and the things of which I had knowledge, now are difficult to grasp. When I put my thoughts to them, they slip away like eels in dark water. I fancy that this vanishing is more of Dr Dee's doing. Something linked to his ritual that he neglected to mention. As for that vision of lunacy, it may perhaps be the stress placed upon the human soul by such occult and dark practices. Phantoms of a mind stretched too far."

Pieter nods, satisfied that the answer lies with the man who set them on this infernal quest. Yet another thing for him to be called to account for when the time comes. But he does not see the look in Lament's eyes. For Lament remembers more than she would admit, and in her thoughts echoes the words of Beatris, *I will make you invisible to death, a walker between the worlds,* and she grows cold despite herself knowing that this at least is not the fault of Dee.

* * *

The guards at the gate are more cautious than usual. Armed men are to be questioned now as word reaches Haarlem of the sacking of Naarden.

"Ho, friends. From whence do you come?" The large gate sergeant looks them over with a practised eye. He is a big man and is not used to being dwarfed, so he puffs out his chest, making the quilted gambeson swell and somehow look even more grubby than it is.

"Good sergeant, we have recently fled the Spanish Fury visited upon Naarden, and we seek refuge in a city that still values freedom and is loyal to the Prince of Orange." Lament does her best to show some deference to the man. The last thing that they need is to ruffle the feathers of a minor authority figure who could deny them entry to the city and a decent inn. Pieter does *his* best to look less menacing, a fixed grin plastered across his broad face.

"You have come from Naarden? We have had reports from other travellers, but you are soldiers. I would value your assessment." It is obvious that he seeks gossip that he can trade for ale or wine when his watch is over.

"The Dons have done what is their want and let loose their dogs on the good citizens of that unfortunate city. The burghers of the city tried to buy their safety with supplies, but the Spanish entered en mass. They drove the populace into the Guild Hall and set it alight. Thousands burned. As far as we know, they are still raping, murdering, and pillaging." Pieter shakes his head as he relates the events.

"Could nothing be done? Could the garrison not hold them at bay?" There is a slight undertone of accusation in the gate sergeant's voice. Perhaps these two *soldiers* could have done more if they had not fled.

"If only good sir. It was the might of the Spanish force, and they were allowed to just walk into the city. Much of the garrison had already abandoned Naarden to its fate, and the militia were blown away like straw in a gale. We were lucky to escape, but we did leave several Spaniards who will never see another dawn." Lament drops her hand to the hilt of her sword in emphasis, her voice hardening. She will take no accusations of cowardice from a man who spends his days bullying travelling merchants.

"I am sure you are right, friend." He holds up a hand in a half-hearted gesture of conciliation. "Pass through, and if it is a good tavern you seek, then head for the docks and look for the Ships Rest. Tell them Sergeant van Ginkel sent you." He watches them as they ride past and along the crowded cobble street before his attention is dragged back to the next travellers seeking admittance at *his* gate.

"So, will we try to find this *Ships Rest*?" Pieter smiles broadly and rolls his eyes.

"I rather think not." Lament laughs. Sergeant van Ginkel will have to forgo his commission for recommending customers on this occasion. Plus, whatever further fleecing is done to weary, naive travellers. Besides, this is not their first time in Haarlem, and they guide their horses through the crowds towards the main square.

* * *

The days have passed pleasantly enough. They have diced, drunk and whored in the company of many soldiers from many countries who have come to the Netherlands to fight against the Spanish and what they see as the heretical doctrine of the Pope and maybe to return home wealthy. It has done them good to rest from the search for Dee's mystical toys and has allowed Lament a chance to learn to control the witch-sight visions of the other-worldly entities that possess so many of these men of war.

As she has become more accustomed to the sight of these beings, they have become more of an irritation than the shocking revelation that they originally were. She has found himself drinking and laughing with several *things* that bear more of a resemblance to animated blueish corpses than to the men she knows them to be. The mere fact that she can ignore these creatures and go on as if all is perfectly *normal* makes her wonder whether she has lost something of her humanity in this adventure.

Her dreams have been haunted by the silver-grey shapes of the airships that she saw, and she wakes sweating as she relives the deadly struggle in the ruins with the masked men from those ships. There are the shadows as well, shadows seen from the corner of her eye that are cast where they should not be, cast by nothing that she can see, and when she turns to look at them, they are gone.

This morning, though, there are other things to concern her. As they sit in the tap room, breaking their fast with dark bread and watered-down ale, the light from the doorway is blocked for a few moments. Lament glances up, taking in the three men who enter. The first is a man of average height and build, but something about him is far from average. He would appear to be in his late thirties. A pointed beard and curling moustache emphasise the sharp angle of his face. Iron grey shoulder-length hair escapes from under the broad-brimmed dark green hat that he grips with a gloved hand and removes with a flourish. It is then that Lament notices the eyes of the man. They are a bright emerald green that, even from a distance, seem to pull her towards them.

Pieter raises his head and swears under his breath. "Van Ijzendoom!" He nods towards the man striding between the tables, who suddenly looks directly at them as if summoned by his whispered name.

"Ah, good Sergeant. Well met, sir!" He walks directly up to their table and gives an extravagant bow, and then those emerald eyes lock onto Lament's. "And this must be the good Captain. You caused quite a stir in Naarden, or should I say your absence did." He laughs at his joke before continuing. "But I am gladdened to see you returned intact. The sergeant was quite concerned for your wellbeing." He speaks to Lament in English, very good English with a trace of an accent.

Lament motions their guest to be seated and takes in the man's companions as he does so. They have stationed themselves on benches near the door. Two large men bearing scars and blue-black markings on their faces, gold rings in their ears. They have an oriental cast about them, and she marks them out as Tartars. She has encountered men like these before. Both men are well-armed, and she catches a glimpse of chain mail under the knee-length, loose-fitting coats that they wear.

"I believe I owe you a debt of thanks, sir, for obtaining the release of my Sergeant at Arms here and for directing him as to where to look for me when he was free." Lament decides that it serves no purpose to be coy.

"Think nothing of it. One must do one's best to aid fellow seekers." He raises his gloved hand and gestures to the serving girl, who hurries over. Lament takes note of the large rings on the gloved fingers. One has an oval stone so black that it seems to absorb all light, and the other is a deep blue shot-through with smoky yellow veins. Both are set in ornate gold mounts. "Bring us a bottle of your finest Rhenish. Oh, and make sure the two gentlemen by the door get a jug of ale." He smiles an unnerving smile at the girl, who blushes and quickly moves away to do his bidding. His men by the door give him a nod of thanks before they return to their taciturn scrutiny of those entering the establishment.

"We have not been properly introduced. I am Count Godard van Ijzendoom, special envoy to the Holy Roman Emperor Rudolph II, and tasked with acquiring certain artefacts for his holiness. He does have a penchant for curiosities!" He sighs as if contemplating a spoiled child. "I am acquainted with your large friend. The good Sergeant and I had a fine conversation before he was released." He smiles at Pieter, who nods his massive head, returning the smile with less enthusiasm. "But I know little of you, Captain Lament Evyngar, other than your wonderful ability to evade the City Watch and obvious disregard for the property of others..." An eyebrow arches as he gives Lament a smile that has something of a challenge in it.

"Count Godard, we were tasked to retrieve something, and this we did. We bear you no malice. One of your men bore the brunt of the enterprise along with the Bishop, of course. But we had no option as a taskmaster commissions us whom we can't disobey without dire consequences to others. If you have come here seeking some compensation for your goods or your honour, then I can only offer you this as satisfaction." Lament places her hand on the black hilt of her sword and sees the two men by the door sit forward, fingering the hilts of their blades.

"Come now, Captain. Would I have helped the Sergeant here if I had meant you ill? What you stole from the collection is of no consequence, and the buffoon who sought to stop you was meddling in things of which he had no right. A little knowledge is a dangerous thing, and it proved to be his undoing."

The serving girl returns with the wine, and the Count makes a show of pouring three glasses before taking a long sup himself. He dabs at his mouth with a square of lace that he produces from his dark maroon doublet. "No, I am intrigued, Captain. I am intrigued by *you* and by what my divinations have revealed about your exploits so far."

Lament eyes him and sits back in her chair, but she does not remove her hand from the sword hilt. She is tired of others watching her actions from afar. "It would seem from what the

Sergeant has told me that you know quite a lot more about me than you admit. Is this not so, Count?"

"My scrying reveals certain things, but it is never laid out clearly. There are things about you that remain cryptic, Captain, things I would have answers to." Count Godard van Ijzendoom once again delicately dabs wine from the corners of his mouth, his smile never faltering.

Lament allows herself to relax and gazes not directly at the man opposite her but slightly off to one side. She has found that this often brings on her witch-sight and the visions of the otherworldly beings that inhabit so many of the players in these games of men. Her vision shifts slightly, and the room around them becomes indistinct while the form of the Count comes into sharp contrast. But there is nothing. Van Ijzendoom has no cosmic horrors using him as a puppet. That does not make Lament feel any easier; perhaps it even makes it worse...

Her attention is drawn back into the room by a hand on her shoulder, gently shaking her. "Are you with us, Lam?" Pieter gives his friend a rueful smile. He is also getting used to Lament's strange trance-like states, but he knows that now is not the time for the Captain to be absent.

Lament shrugs off the hand, not wishing to seem weak in front of this man who already knows too much. "Yes, thank you, Sergeant." She grips her wine perhaps a little too tightly.

Count Godard stares at her intently, that smile frozen on his narrow lips. The emerald eyes search Lament's for clues until Pieter decides to break the spell. "How is it that you managed to evade the Spanish at Naarden? You forewarned me of their impending attack, but you did not leave the city yourself."

A flicker of irritation crosses the startling green eyes but is instantly replaced by that all-encompassing smile. "A good question, my friend, but not really a mystery. As envoy to the Holy Roman Emperor, I have letters of safe passage that are respected by all God-fearing Catholics and all but the most rabid Calvinists. Naarden was a city of liberal views, which is why I chose it. But those views have resulted in its destruction. Fortunately, I am known personally to Fadrique Álvarez de Toledo, and it was nothing to get word to him, thus allowing myself and the remains of the Emperor's collection to be escorted safely from the city by his troops." The Count sips his wine once more as he returns his attention to Lament. "But this is all in the past, good Captain, and I would strike a bargain with you for our mutual benefit."

"Sir, I am beginning to tire of bargains. They seem to always leave me at a disadvantage." Lament drums her fingers on the table in irritation.

"Be that as it may, Captain, I believe that you owe me at least the courtesy of listening to my proposal. After all, you did steal a map from the collection that was under my care, and I did obtain the release of the Seargent and vouch safe information as to where and when he could find you before the Spanish Fury took full hold of the city!" There is a hint of frustration in van Ijzendoom's wheedling voice.

Lament raises her sword-calloused palms, accepting defeat. It is obvious that she can't avoid at least listening to the Count's proposal, even though she has the distinct feeling that no good can come of it.

"Shall we remove ourselves to my lodgings then my friends?

This establishment is beginning to become busy, and what I have to say is not for curious ears." Count Godard flashes that predatory smile at the serving girl, who seems to be taking an inordinate time to clean a nearby table. She reddens and scurries away, dropping an empty trencher in her haste, the skin on the back of her neck crawling.

# Chapter 20

The distant clock in the main square is striking midnight. To-night is a particularly dark one. No moon, and made darker still by the low cloud that seems to have conveniently drifted inland from the Narrow Sea.

This suits them well, the five figures who creep through the black to the base of the square tower. Dark cloaks wrap around them like extensions of the night, and they halt, pressing themselves against the rough stone. But the sound that caused them to halt was only a shutter closing on a building a street away.

Lament stares up at the structure rising above them. There are small windows piercing the walls at irregular intervals. Not a light shows from the tower, so at least they have that to be thankful for. Pieter hugs the wall next to her, a bulky shadow with his own reservations about this endeavour. He does not trust the Count, who has just slipped around the corner ahead of them, and he does not trust the Count's men who follow behind them. He had made his concerns plain to Lament after they had heard the bargain that van Ijzendoom was proposing. But the Captain had shrugged, resigned to a fate that seemed to be in the hands of conjurers and the whims of strange spirits from beyond their world.

The bargain had been straightforward. Count Godard van Ijzendoom would help Lament and Pieter to recover the second of Dr Dee's prizes, and in return, Lament would submit to yet another ritual. They had thanked the Count but insisted that they required no aid, but the Count had correctly identified that they were searching for a necklace and had even given the location where the necklace could be found. He had also given dire prognostications as to what would happen if they went to retrieve it without the help of a mage. He had made it plain that what they would face was not an overzealous apprentice whom they had managed to overcome through luck. No, this time, it would cost them dearly if they were not prepared. And the ritual as payment? Well, that was nothing more than a chance for the Count to see Lament's skin markings at work and perhaps fathom how she was able to seemingly slip in and out of existence. As simple as that...

But Pieter does not know what the Count told Lament when the big sergeant went with the Count's men to obtain rope and grapnels for their upcoming endeavour. Count Godard had asked if Lament had wondered why, since they had landed on the shores of the Low Countries, they had seemingly attracted death wherever they had gone. After all, whole cities in which they had gone to ground had been razed by the Spanish, one after another. Did Lament not think that a strange coincidence? Aware of Lament's witch-sight, he had worked divinings to discover the consequences of its use. Those consequences are that the entities that Lament can see are becoming more and more attracted towards her, even though they are not aware of why. Like a lode stone pointing north, they are increasingly drawn in her direction, and the death and carnage they bring in their wake is the result.

Lament had paled as the Count unfolded this knowledge. *Was she responsible for the deaths of all those caught by the forces of chaos and order as they flowed towards her?* She felt her soul slipping away from her. *Must she be damned for all eternity as the one who brought death to all those innocents?*

Could the Count take this curse from her? Could he undo the sorcery of Dr John Dee? If he could, then this bargain would be worth the hazard. She still needed to return to England with Dee's necklace, or the doctor would make good his promise, and she would see her family go to the stake as heretics. But if she could be free of these blasted incantations… Maybe then there would be a chance for her to redeem her soul.

So now they crouch in the black night at the foot of a bleak, square tower in which lies a bauble they must acquire.

"Count Godard, why can I not see the location of the necklace? When we were above the vaults in Naarden, I could see, like a phosphorescence, the location of the map though it lay beneath the ground." Lament whispers into the Count's ear, noticing once again the smell of rose water with which the Count likes to scent himself.

"I told you, my dear Captain. This tower has been constructed to keep its secrets safe. The vaults from which you stole the map were merely a storeroom with one or two mechanical traps. I was not expecting thieves aided by sorcery to be breaking and entering. Especially not to be stealing something as mundane as a map!" Count Godard does not take his eyes from the windows above, but even in the dark, Lament can sense that strange smile that never seems to be far from his lips.

"Prey tell Count, where is our point of entry? All I see is stone and windows too narrow for us to climb through even if we could reach them." Pieter follows Lament and Count Godard around the corner of the tower, his patience wearing thin.

In answer, the Count steps back away from the wall and into the centre of the narrow alley that runs along this side of the tower. He points a gloved finger upwards towards the face of the tower. There, just visible beyond the gloom of the surrounding buildings, is a darker rectangle approximately the width of two doors. As they stare up at it and their eyes become accustomed, they can make out the frame that runs around the rectangle. Centrally, above that frame, the end of a wooden beam protrudes from the wall, and the shape hanging from it comes into focus as a block and tackle.

"Is this truly the only way to enter?" Lament finds it hard to believe that such a building as this would have no other door.

"There *is* another entrance, Captain. But it can only be accessed from the river, and a massive iron gate seals it. Even if we could somehow get beyond that gate, there are *things* in the passageways leading to this tower that we would do well to avoid. I fear that we will have enough to keep us occupied once we are inside without inviting anything else along with us." Count Godard signals to his men, and they move into position in front of him. Two lengths of knotted rope with grapnels are unwound from their bodies, and after accessing the distance, they begin to whirl the iron hooks. They throw, and even Pieter concedes to their skill as first one hook finds purchase over the winch beam, and then the second bites into the frame at the base of the doors.

The two men throw their weight backwards, testing the grip of the hooks. Satisfied, they turn and nod to the Count, who gestures wordlessly that they should begin to climb. They are not small men, but they move up the ropes with the unexpected ease of side-show acrobats until one sits astride the beam, and the other somehow manages to wedge himself into the tight lip around the doors. He carefully pulls a metal bar with a flattened tip from the canvas bag hanging beside his sword, and he forces the tip into the slight gap where the two doors meet. He is unable to gain much purchase and so must slowly twist and turn the flat end in until he is convinced that it is secure.

Lament watches, fascinated, as the man lowers himself back down his rope a few feet, and then his comrade swings from the top of the beam and hits the side of the metal bar with both feet. His weight and momentum force the doors apart, and he grips the top of one door as it swings open. For a moment, it seems that the bar will fall on top of them, but the first man deftly catches it before hauling himself back up and over the lip.

There is a moment of bated breath as the Count's men disappear inside, then a head reappears, a hand signals for them to follow, and they grasp the trailing ropes.

Shuttered lanterns have been lit, and by their yellow light, they can see the chamber around them. It is longer than would be anticipated, judging by the appearance of the tower from without. The grey stone walls are hung with tapestries depicting hunting scenes. Hounds chase down stags, men in brightly coloured garb from a hundred years ago spear rampaging boar and lords and ladies fly hawks at game birds. There are several stools scattered around, and a storage chest sits against the wall opposite the doors. Other than that, the chamber is empty.

To their right is an arched doorway through which steps can be seen leading both up and down. The Count angles one of the lanterns up through the doorway, and they can see that the steps rise in a narrow spiral to the next floor.

Pieter sniffs at the foul air coming from the void of the descending steps and wrinkles his nose. He looks at Lament, who has noticed the smell, too. It is a mouldy, damp odour. The smell of a river at low tide, but it is mixed with something else. The rank smell of animals kept locked in a confined space. Perhaps dogs?

Count Godard draws them back into the room away from the doorway and speaks in a quiet but urgent voice, reiterating the information he had told them earlier in the day. "What we seek, gentlemen, is two floors above us. When we reach the next level, Captain, what you call your *witch-sight*, should show you its location on the floor above. But again, I caution you to be silent and be wary when we leave this floor. Not everything may be what it seems. Take nothing but that which you have come for."

"You have still not explained how you came to know of the location of the necklace other than through your divination. There seems to be much you know about this tower that you have not vouched safe, and I would have some answers before we put ourselves in further peril." Lament's eyes harden in the yellow lamp glow; she is determined to have an answer from the Count before they continue.

"Good Captain, this is not the time for a comprehensive discourse into my methods!" But the Count can see that he must make some explanation if they are to proceed further. "Very well. There are certain grimoires to which I am privy. Rudolph II may be a generous benefactor, but he has little real knowledge regarding the things that he collects. I, on the other hand, have a great deal of knowledge. One of the grimoires makes mention of this tower and its owner, Duke Carl von Weisner. He lived more than a century ago, a necromancer and one whose tastes were said to run to the perverse. He fell afoul of the church elders after the disappearance of young men and women from the surrounding countryside. He was accused of heresy and sorcery and broken on the wheel, his shattered body cast into the fire, and it is rumoured that he laughed as he died. This tower has remained abandoned since that day. Tales of awaiting horrors kept the people at bay, but then it was as if they forgot. It is speculated that sorcery performed by the Duke before he was captured makes people forget this place almost as soon as they see it. It hides in plain sight."

"Then how is it we are standing within it now?" Pieter sticks out his red-bearded chin belligerently.

"As I said, I have a great deal of knowledge, and once I had read the description of this place, I could be forearmed and, through my workings, make sure that all in this party are immune to the spell that keeps this tower nothing but a cautionary tale to scare children with." He shows his teeth in that smile again, and Pieter has the strongest of urges to knock them out.

"Now, good sirs. Can we please continue? My men will lead the way upwards." He gestures to the Tartars, who grimly begin the ascent, lanterns held aloft and long, curved knives at their sides.

As they reach the next floor, they immediately notice a subtle change in the atmosphere around them. The Count's men have moved into the centre of the chamber, which is much the same as the one below except that the walls hold long, narrow strips of dark glass instead of tapestries. Even when they all enter the space, the light from their lanterns barely manages to illuminate their surroundings. The very air seems to suck in the yellow light making the room somehow darker. Even the dark glass does not reflect the light of the lanterns above the level of a dull gleam. Lament's skin rises in goosebumps as she gets the powerful impression that the strips of glass are, in fact, windows that look out onto *somewhere else*. As she gazes at them, she believes that she can make out faint outlines that could be the black fingers of dead trees.

Pieter touches her lightly on the arm. "I like this not at all, Captain. There seems to be movement in the glass that is not our reflection. I think we are once more in the midst of some damn sorcerer's playhouse." His whispered voice is hoarse with a dread of the supernatural, and Lament can do nothing but nod her agreement.

"Captain now would be an opportune moment to use your witch-sight to alert us to the location of the necklace so that we do not blunder around these chambers for longer than is needed." Count Godard's whisper focuses Lament once more on the purpose of their being in this hateful place. She closes her eyes and forces herself to relax. There is an odd buzzing around her head as if she is next to a hive of bees or perhaps a swarm of flies. Opening her eyes again, she is drawn to a spot on the ceiling above them where there is a pulsing blue incandescence. As with the church in Naarden, she knows that the glow marks the location of their prize. But, as she raises her hand to indicate this to the Count, she sees them, the things in the glass, and before she can cry out, they attack.

The Count's men are the first to be hit. They have strayed from the centre of the room towards one of the walls, and they are suddenly engulfed in amorphous blue-grey shapes that detach from the glass strips surrounding them. Muffled screams come from the two men as if they are distant or perhaps buried under layers of heavy cloth. The others can just make out the thrashing forms of the Tartars through the clinging miasma. For a moment, Lament is plunged back into the memory of that other London and the clouds of gas. She reaches up to check her mask before remembering that this is not that place.

Instinctively, they stand, backs together, drawn weapons facing outwards in three directions. The Count looks desperately at Lament, "They are *Shade Wraiths!*" He grabs frantically at his hands as if to remove his gloves and then is wrapped in the sentient mist.

Pieter lashes out with his falchion, but the heavy blade passes straight through the rearing shadow before him. The unformed shape descends like a wave crashing, and he is engulfed. He feels darkness surround him and press upon him as if it would pass through his skin, and there is a coldness that numbs him to the bone. The tendrils of shadow enter his ears, and then a terrible susurration begins. Perhaps if the souls of the damned could speak, and they all did so together, a million different voices whispering a million different things all at once, then that is what beats against the inside of their skulls as the things from the glass swirl around them and through them.

Only Lament seems untouched. She looks on in confusion as the others claw at their heads and strike out at the mass of writhing nebulous forms. But *she* stands in a circle of calm. The Shade Wraiths rush around her like the edges of a maelstrom, but they do not come nearer than arm's length to this woman whom they see as a lattice of molten fire.

They are ancient these things. Trapped in the dark panes with the sole purpose of guarding the tower. Capable of moving to their own dimension but bound by dark magics to return to this world should the sanctity of this place be broken. They feed on the rational intellect of their victims, and they are hungry.

Lament watches as one of the Tartars, his ears torn and bloody from trying to free himself of the whispering wraiths, runs head-long into a wall. He hits with a sickening thud, his skull cracks, and he falls twitching to the floor. Lament is, for the first time, aware that Pieter and Count Godard are no longer next to her. Somehow, without her realising, they have moved away from her and are sorely beset by the seemingly insubstantial things. Moving quickly, she grabs the prone Count and drags him over to the bulk of the kneeling Dutch giant, and standing over them forces the wraiths to withdraw by virtue of her presence alone.

"Count Godard! It is time for you to act if you have the knowledge that will save us!" Lament shakes the blank-eyed, drooling van Ijzendoom. The man laughs hysterically at her for a moment, and then the green eyes clear, and he frantically claws at the rings on his gloved hand.

"This, this!" He thrusts them at Lament, his eyes rolling and his teeth gnashing. A panicked look, a look of utter desperation, comes over him that Lament does not understand. "Smash them together!" He screams.

Lament grips one ring in each hand and brings them together with all the force she can muster. For a moment, they resist each other, pushing apart like the same poles on two magnets, and then they meet, and the blue and yellow stone enters the black stone as if it is a dark pool. There is a deafening crack and the smell of the air after a lightning strike. A window opens in the air above them, and the Shade Wraiths are sucked, shrieking into it. The window hangs there for a few moments and then flickers out of existence. Lament looks at her hands, but the rings have gone. There is only dust that drifts away as she moves them.

She looks over at her friend and sees the haunted look in his eyes, and she helps him to his feet. She turns to the Count to help him up, but he is already standing, although somewhat unsteadily. "We must move now! Quickly, that will not contain them for long, and I have nothing else to fight them with." The Count drags at the small ruff around his throat, eyes wild. "We must get the necklace and be gone!"

Lament leads the way to the next staircase, and they step over the bodies of the two Tartars. One with his head smashed open like an egg, and the other lying twisted on the floor, strange spiderwebs of broken blood vessels spreading across his face and neck as if something inside has exploded.

# Chapter 21

They stand at the entrance to the next level. It is fair to say that there is more than a little trepidation about stepping across the threshold.

"We must move quickly if we are to cross the lower chamber to the other staircase before those *things* return." The Count has lost his cool composure. A haunted look clouds those startling green eyes.

Lament stares hard at Pieter, who has not spoken since the wraiths departed. She has never seen the big man like this before, and the thought that he may have lost his mind weighs heavy on her. "What terrors can we expect in this room, pray tell? You vouched safe little warning of those things below." Lament does not take her eyes off her friend as she berates van Ijzendoom.

"Captain! You do me wrong! I only knew what I had learned from the grimoire. If I had not obtained those rings, then we would all be lying dead upon that chamber's flags, except perhaps for you." The Count juts out his pointed beard in defiance.

"And how did you chance upon those rings, may I ask?" Lament at last turns to face the Count.

"Once I knew where you were heading and the possible

dangers you would face, I performed certain magics that drew the stones in those rings to me from other realms. Now, please, Captain, if we are to leave here alive, we must act! The grimoire said nothing regarding further guardians at this level, so let us make haste!" Like a small cockerel, the Count puffs himself up, pride masking the fear that has so recently held him in its icy grip.

"After you then, good sir." Lament mockingly bows and waves the Count forward. Turning to Pieter, she touches a massive shoulder and looks into the startled eyes that turn upon her. "Pieter, wait here and guard the stairs. We will be gone from here shortly." She squeezes the muscular bulk, and Pieter nods; he has a task, something he can focus on.

Gingerly, the Count advances into the chamber. He looks over his shoulder to reassure himself that the Captain is indeed following him. Lament signals to a seven-sided block of stone in the centre of the room, a room that is ringed with bookcases, the contents of which have mostly collapsed into mould and dust. Low cabinets are dotted between the bookcases, and they are crowded with large glass jars that are filled with a vile-looking piss-coloured fluid, and in that fluid floats noisome warped things from the depths of a madman's nightmares. Things that can only be described as unholy, desperate, perverse thoughts made flesh and frozen at that moment. Lament feels bile rise in her throat as she looks at them and quickly, for the sake of her sanity, averts her eyes.

At the heptagon, her witch-sight reveals a hair-thin gleam of blue radiance that runs around the top edge of the stone. She places the tip of her dagger into that crack and gives the hilt a firm blow with her palm. There is a moment of nothing, and then a hiss like the exhalation of long-held breath, and the top of the block rises about a thumb's width. Standing on either side of the block, they grip the newly risen section and, between them, lift it clear. There beneath it, in a seven-sided chamber that is lined with black velvet, is the necklace.

The Count gasps, and Lament is dumbstruck. The necklace is a broad, flat chain of some silver metal that neither can identify. But the teardrop-shaped stone, about the size of a large hen's egg, that hangs from it is even more startlingly rare. It is like a miniature sun that blazes a golden-yellow fire which moves within the gem's depths. Undulates and swirls in some vortex that threatens to pull them into it.

Carefully, Lament reaches into the heptagon and gathers up the jewel and its chain in the black velvet cloth. She can't say why, but she is loath to touch it with her bare hands. As she places it into the pouch at her belt, a voice murmurs through the chamber. *"What have you done? This was never meant for her! You will break the web of time. What have you done?"* Accusing, the hissing tones seem to come from everywhere at once, and there, by the wall opposite the stairs, the faint figure of an old man in clothes that were ancient before the time of King Edward points a finger at them and shakes his head in sad despair.

"Let us away from this place!" Lament grabs the Count's arm and drags him back to the steps where Pieter awaits with gritted teeth and cold steel.

The wailing voice follows them as they rush headlong down the narrow stone stairs and burst out onto the floor below.

"Oh, sweet Jesu, no!" Let us pass quickly!" The fear in van

Ijzendoom's voice is palpable as he spies the smoke-like tendrils beginning to search outwards from the glass panes once more. A thought flits through Lament's mind that perhaps, despite the Count's claims to sorcerous powers, he is not as skilled or experienced as he would have them believe. Yet another self-proclaimed *gifted* amateur playing at being the all-powerful thaumaturge. As he himself said, a little knowledge can be dangerous. She laughs, a harsh bark of a sound that startles the Count, making him scowl. As he turns, his vanity peaked, Pieter grips him in a massive paw and rushes him bodily through the next doorway and onto the stairs to their exit.

Lament follows close on their heels but is brought to a sharp halt by the startled grunt of his friend and a cry of despair from the Count. "What ails you..." But Lament's question dies on her lips as she sees exactly what ails the Count.

The doorway to the next chamber and their escape is no longer there. Bare stone with not the slightest sign of the opening is all that faces them, and regardless of Count Godard's pounding fists, no way through appears.

"Can you not use your magics?" Pieter spins the man around, growling in his suddenly pale face.

"If I had time to perform the correct workings, yes, of course. But we don't have that luxury! Now unhand me, you dolt!" The Count's primacy has once more been slighted, and he rages like a spoilt child at the giant before him.

Pieter's grip tightens on the falchion hilt, knuckles growing white. As he is about to respond, Lament's urgent whisper halts him. "They are coming!"

The wraiths begin to slowly leak from the chamber above and

onto the cold stone steps. Their passage is tentative at first, as if this has never been possible before this moment, but they seem to grow in confidence, and there is suddenly a mass of pulsing, living smoke at the top of the staircase.

"Quickly! We must descend!" Lament gestures with her lamp towards the steps that disappear into darkness below.

"No, there are creatures beneath that protect the passages to the river. They will rend us apart!" Count Godard's fevered eyes flit from the stairs above to the darkness beneath and its fetid stink.

"All men must die, sirrah." And Pieter propels the protesting Count before him into the darkness and stench.

* * *

It seems as if much time has passed since they began their descent, but it has barely been one hour.

The Shade Wraiths appear to have given up their pursuit, or perhaps they are merely slow in following, although none of the three trudging through the odorous damp tunnels would willingly go back to check. Whatever might lie in wait for them down here would seem preferable to the mind-sucking terrors of those amorphous denizens of another world. As for the creatures that dwell in these tunnels? Nothing has been sighted thus far except for shards of shattered bone littering the filthy cobbled floor. Those bones have been of undetermined origin so far. They have been picked clean and crushed so that the marrow may be made accessible, and they have been a variety of sizes from what can be ascertained by the remains.

They have all tied lengths of cloth around their lower faces to dimmish the stench, but even so, they must breathe shallowly through their mouths if they are not to gag.

"Hold. What is that?" Lament stands stock still, ears straining for any slight sound.

"I hear nothing. Let us press on." The Count is becoming more petulant. It would seem he is beginning to regret his offer of assistance and the bravado that went with it.

"There!" Lament holds her lamp aloft as if she can illuminate the sound.

"Aye, I hear it. What in God's name can that be?" Pieter has regained a little of his composure, but Lament suspects that he will only be happy when he has managed to kill something in this foul place.

The sound comes again. A loathsome tittering followed by a whooping sound. It is answered by more whooping from a side tunnel that they have just passed. The sounds are some ways away but are getting closer.

"I have heard that sound before. I know that sound! Where have I heard it?" Count Godard glares around him, searching his memory.

"Did your intelligence not provide you with information as to what manner of creatures guard these tunnels?" Lament draws her sword as the sounds intensify and are joined by others.

"I only know what the book told me and what I gained from questioning others who know the legend of this place. The Duke is said to have purchased beasts from far countries and bred them to produce unholy hybrids. Those he kept in these lower passages. How they are still living, I don't know. Perhaps sorcery?

Perhaps they feed upon each other and anything else small enough and foolish enough to stray in from the river." The Count still wracks his brain for the memory of what makes that cry.

The sounds are closer now, and the whooping has become more excited. "Ah, I do know that sound. The Holy Roman Emperor collects exotic animals as well as esoteric objects. That, I fear, is a baboon. We will have a fight on our hands, gentlemen!"

Almost on cue, a gnarled muzzle pushes around the edge of a bend in the tunnel ahead. It certainly has some resemblance to a baboon, but as it reveals itself, it is obviously also dog-like. Its neck is stocky with a ridge of spiky hair, and it sticks out from powerful rounded shoulders while its skinny waist disappears into bowed haunches with a short stub of a tail. On the ends of its forelimbs are deformed paws that resemble human hands, while its rear limbs terminate in splayed hound-like paws. But its head holds their attention. It is a wedge of bony muzzle attached to a skull that slopes back between small, pointed ears. The eyes on either side gleam with amber malice and an intelligence that is shocking in that bestial visage. The tittering sounds again and ends in a gleeful whoop of triumph as the creature focuses its eyes on the humans in its domain.

"By all that is holy! That thing is at least part hyena as well!" The Count has drawn his rapier now and is backing away from the abomination that paces towards them with slathering jaws that reveal long, curved yellow fangs.

"Fuck that! Is the bastard thing mortal?" Pieter does not fear anything that is flesh and blood.

"Yes, yes, I believe it is..." stammers the Count.

Sergeant Pieter Hertgers has had more than he can stomach

of the supernatural. More than enough of feeling helpless in the grip of tenuous, whispering shadow things that would steal his reason. Now he has before him an enemy he can cleave with steel, and the battle lust comes into his eyes, and he roars his war cry and charges. The Count stares open-mouthed as the red-bearded giant cuts the snarling creature from neck to chest.

"Did you imagine we would negotiate with them, sir?" A savage smile crosses Lament's lips, and wild-eyed, she joins the fray, handing the lantern to Count Godard. Her black-hilted sword darting with blinding speed as she thrusts again and again into the beasts emerging from the side passages.

The creatures take wounds well. They are strong, and their hides are resistant. Perhaps because they are on their own territory, they are not inclined to flee. A grasping, clawed paw catches in the folds of the Count's cloak, and he slashes at the fore limb. The edge of his rapier cuts to the bone, but the paw still grips tight, drawing him towards the snarling jaws. He turns his body and thrusts towards an amber eye. The blade misses its intended target and slides across the bony muzzle before entering the thing's cheek and then its brain. It falls, twitching grotesquely, paw still locked in the folds of his cloak. Stumbling forward as the beast collapses, the Count trips on the body and falls against the slime-covered wall of the tunnel. He turns, frantically disengaging himself from the creature's death grip and puts his back against the brickwork. In the yellow light of the lantern, he can see his companions waging war on the vile baboon things. Dead and dying creatures lie around them, but more are coming from a larger passage beyond them. He becomes suddenly aware of a different smell amongst the stench of the beasts. From where he crouches, he can scent the odour of water, dirty water, and the mud flats of the river. There is the faintest glow of light touching the edges of the tunnel ahead. The grey wolf light of dawn.

"Ahead! The exit is ahead!" He shouts above the whooping, gibbering noise of the attacking beasts, and pushing himself upright, he tears free of the claws and runs towards the grey light, slashing right and left as he goes. Lament and Pieter follow. They fight, as always, shoulder to shoulder. Lament's sword and dagger dart while Pieter's falchion rises and falls with a business-like regularity. Both are wearing the blood and gore of the beasts they have slain.

An iron gate stands across the tunnel. It is partially in the water that laps into the tunnel from the river that is now visible at the end of the passage, a mere stone's throw away. A great iron pin that passes through staples on the gate and disappears into the wall holds the gate closed. It would seem that the Duke had no need for locks to keep out trespassers. He must also have trusted that his creatures would not gain intelligence enough to remove the pin themselves.

"I believe that this will need your strength, Sergeant." Count Godard steps back from the iron, defeated by the rust and the weight of the metal. He stands beside Lament and hurls the lantern at the approaching creatures. The lantern shatters, and burning oil spills across the stone, igniting several of them and forming a momentary barrier to the rest, who leap and scream in rage. Those that are alight rush on enraged by the pain and driven to a frenzy by the prospect of flesh. Lament cuts one through the neck and steps aside as it whirls past her and crashes into the brickwork. Then she lunges low, avoiding grabbing talons and thrusts through another's heart. Count Godard is not a fighting man, and his rapier is more of an ornament than of any practical use. Still, he has had enough fencing lessons to be able to skewer a third beast through the throat, although as the thing keeps coming forward, its death throws force him back against the gate. Lament kicks it away before it can set the white-faced Count alight. There is a brief respite as the others avoid the burning oil.

Pieter beats at the pin with the pommel of the falchion, aiming at where it passes through the staples. As the rust flakes off in an orange shower, he pushes in the tip of the blade and levers it to loosen the pin. There is movement. Sheathing the blade, he wraps huge hands around the pin and begins to twist. Forearms used to wielding a mighty zweihander flex, and then with a ferocious wrench, Pieter pulls the pin loose. He slides it through the staples and, putting his shoulder and prodigious weight against the gate, forces it open with a squeal of protesting hinges.

Lament and the Count slip through the gap, and Pieter follows, forcing the gate closed again as the creatures see their prey escaping and leap the flames, some not successfully. Pieter risks putting his hands through the iron lattice to slide the pin back into place and snatches them back just as a burning baboon face slams into the rusted iron. There is panic at the rear of the attacking creatures and the vague impression of insubstantial tendrils slipping around the corner of the tunnel, searching, grasping. Several of the beasts drop to the slime-covered stones and thrash around, wrapped in hungry smoke.

"Will they follow?" Lament asks as she watches their now madly flailing attackers.

"I think not. They seem disinclined to approach the daylight." The Count stares on, fascinated, as they back away from the gate towards the river. Wading through the thigh-deep water, it is now obvious what the creatures have been surviving on. There must be a slaughterhouse upstream, and anything that can't be sold is dumped into the river to find its way into this tunnel entrance by virtue of the river current and, hence, wash up against the gate where the things scavenge it.

Wading through the remains of a butcher's shop is the perfect end to a night of horror.

# Chapter 22

They have scrubbed themselves clean and sent their filthy clothes off with a maid to be washed. Fortunately, Lament and Pieter have been guests of this inn before and have some credit built up with the owner, which guarantees no questions are asked.

"And you felt nothing when those shadows attacked?" Pieter asks the same question again, not convinced that any man or woman could have withstood the intrusion of those dark things.

"Again, no. My friend, it matters not how many times you ask; the answer will still be *no*." Lament breaks off a crust from a loaf of dark bread. She is more concerned at the moment with not breaking her teeth on the grit that seems to have been baked into this bread. But she does look upon the Sergeant with worry. Whatever happened when the shadows entered his mind has rocked his reason and left a haunted look in those normally humorous eyes. "It must be something more to do with Dee's enchantment. Perhaps I should be grateful for this effect. The Lord knows I have been grateful for little else he has bestowed upon me!" She sits back on her stool, and the open front of her shirt reveals the dull grey markings on her flesh. Pieter glances at them and averts his eyes. Lament is convinced she sees her friend shudder.

"Are you sure you would let van Ijzendoom perform yet more sorcery upon you? After his showing in the tower, I would question his abilities..."

"I share your concerns, big man. But I would be free of this." She holds her shirt open to expose more of the markings. "At least the power that they have, even if I am still decorated like a Javan pirate!" She grins, but the smile on Pieter's lips is forced. "When we get to the Count's lodgings, I will leave it to you to see that he plays fair." The grin fades, and Lament's eyes are suddenly hard.

"Aye, you can rely on that Captain. I am fast losing forbearance with sorcery and those who practice it. I fear for our souls. Perhaps it's already too late..."

* * *

There are geometric shapes set in circles drawn upon the wooden floorboards. More cover the wooden panels of Count Godard's bed chamber walls. It is plain to see that he has been very busy since they parted company this morning.

The sun is sinking, casting lurid red shapes through the polished horn of the window casement and onto the arcane symbols. This only adds to the fact that some of them are hard to focus upon, as if they leave the surface upon which they are drawn only to reappear a little further on.

Lament stands self-consciously, near naked in the centre of the room. She is surrounded by the largest of the symbols, her feet planted in the middle of an irregularly pointed star. Strange symbols are scrawled around the periphery of the circle encompassing the star, and in the blaze of the sunset, they appear to writhe and twist as if they are alive.

Count Godard moves around the chamber and fusses with the alignment of dark, nameless objects. He lights thick yellow candles and places them at regular intervals around the room. Pieter watches from a bench at the far side of the room. He is aware of his Captain's discomfort and does his best not to stare. Several candles are placed on either side of the bench. The smell of the candles reminds him of something, something unpleasant that he can't quite put his finger on.

"Are you ready, Captain?" Count Godard sweeps across the chamber in front of her, careful not to cross the circle. A crimson hooded cloak billows around him ominously, like blood in water.

Lament doesn't know if she is ready. This feels to her too much like the ritual performed by Dr Dee, and the Count seems to have a leer on his face, which thankfully was missing from the doctors. But at least this time, she is standing and has scraps of linen wrapped around herself to give her at least some modesty. She nods anyway.

The Count turns away to the bed pushed up against the wall opposite the door. When he turns back, he is holding a large book in front of him that he opens towards Lament. The pages are blank, and Lament frowns as Count Godard begins a rhythmic chant, and something around the edges of the bookbinding begins to move. A question forms on Lament's lips but dies unspoken as long, slender chains tipped with vicious barbs shoot from the edges and strike her.

Pieter looks on horror-struck. He tries to heave his body off the bench, but it is as if he is held down with soft restraints that deny his body movement. His mind suddenly identifies the smell of the candles, and he spits in distaste. He has smelt enough bodies burning to know that this is the reek of melting human fat, and there is something mixed in with it, something sickly and cloying that dulls his senses and seeks to rob him of his agency. *Opium*, the drug of the Turks! Through blurring vision, he can see that the chains snaking out from the book are dragging Lament towards those empty pages. Her skin stretches unnaturally as she tries to pull away, but there are a dozen barbed chains, and it seems plain that they will flay her skin whether she follows them or not.

The Count's eyes have rolled back in his skull and show only white as his litany continues. An ecstatic look is upon his face, the look of the fanatic.

Red marks begin to show up on the blank pages, which turn of their own accord as they become full, and through the pain, Lament realises that the marks on the pages are the marks upon her body. But this does not feel like a release. No, this feels as if the book will take everything. Throwing her head back, Lament screams at the wooden beams above her. There is a vision of whirling constellations, which are blacked out momentarily by impossibly large wings, and then she feels the fire surging through her skin and lighting up the patterns on her body.

Staring back at the book, she sees that the chains now glow as if they are alight, and the pages begin to curl at the edges and char. A look appears on the face of Count Godard van Ijzendoom as his eyes roll back down, a look that is no longer ecstatic. Instead, it is a look of confusion and mounting terror as the leaves of the book begin to burn. Without warning, a hole appears in his forehead, and he falls to the floorboards with the burning book on top of him, its chains withering away.

Pieter drops the smoking pistol as he is finally released from the narcotic spell that held him, and he grabs a sheet and rushes to catch Lament as she collapses, wrapping her in it. For a moment, as he enters the circle, he sees the whirling stars and feels the chill wind from the void. And he hears the voice that freezes his blood with fear, a voice that whispers to Lament, *"You will never be free."* Then Lament is gone.

* * *

*That vertiginous fall once again. For a second, I think I will vomit, but the world stops revolving and comes to a hard stop. The light is bright. It is hot. Have I somehow caught fire from the demon book? No, it's the sun. Judging by its intensity and the humidity, this is not late autumn in the Low Countries.*

*There's a song playing on the radio, although I have no concept of what a radio is. I like it, so I sing along. I somehow know that it's White Room by Cream. The words are strange and haunting, and I mangle them as I join in.*

*I have the oddest feeling that I shouldn't be here. It's as if I have woken up from a dream into another dream, and the dugouts I am walking past are the familiar parts of an alien landscape.*

*How do I know the words to this song? The rhythm and the*

*instruments all seem wrong. But I carry on anyway through the steaming heat. My mind does that flip, and I know where I am...*

Walking past a blast wall, I see the Yards, our indigenous allies, squatting down in the shade and cooking whatever it is they have managed to hunt in the forest edge. They are fierce little bastards and hold a special place in my heart, although, at this moment, I couldn't tell you why.

Their shaman, Bong, is looking at me in that disturbing way he does. As if he sees right through me, sees some other me that is a shadow in the background. This time it is even more intense than usual, like I am wearing some sort of fancy dress that makes me stand out, or maybe a big neon sign that says *Where the fuck am I?*

I hear the whistling and join the shouts of "In coming!" as I dive for cover. The mortar explodes over on the apron, but there are more on the way. This is FOB 4, so we are used to being targets, but it's usually just Chuck throwing the odd mortar to keep us on our toes, their attempt to dissuade us from going out on our kill missions, I guess. This, though, has all the signs of being a full-on attack because the ordinance doesn't stop coming, and there is the bark of automatic weapons.

I look over to my right at the helipad, where a Jolly Green is just coming in for a landing. An RPG hits it through the side door, and it's suddenly a ball of flames with screaming crew members trying to get out. The big beast slews to one side, and the rotors hit the concrete and fly in all directions as the body crumples. I watch as the pilot and copilot melt before my eyes, black carbonised hands clawing at nothing.

Bullets are rattling off the corrugated steel lying across the hootch roofs, and I can see figures advancing from the forest. *Fuck!* They must be battalion strength, and there are more off to the north. We return fire, and I can hear Claymore's detonating. I scramble back to pick up my RPD, the cut-down Soviet bad boy I have recently acquired and begin to lay down some hate.

As I blow holes in the advancing VC, I notice a movement in the treeline. It's like in that King Kong movie where all the trees start bending as the big muther is pushing his way through them. There are plumes of smoke rising through the waving forest, and there they are... Soviet Mk II Mechs! We had heard rumours from the North that the Soviets had gifted Ho Chi Minh with some of their battlefield mechs. Not the brand-new Mk III good stuff, but not quite the original WW2 iron that they threw at Berlin in the last days of that conflict. Iron that crushed its way into that already broken city and paved the way for the Red Army to go on the rampage – payback is a mother fucker. We had seen them in action a few times during raids but never in a full-on assault against our bases. These are heavily armoured cockpits mounted in a sort of rotating drum-shaped turret. They move on bipedal legs that make them look a little like headless chickens or maybe a mechanical Baba Yaga Hut. On either side of the cockpit are some combination of machine guns, cannons, flame throwers, and rocket launchers. The plumes of smoke are from the high exhausts that sit on their backs.

The heavy machine guns begin to chew up our cover quick time. The Mechs are hard to bring down unless you can get a straight shot at the chicken legs. This means we must wait for them to exit the tree line and start coming at us before we can hit them effectively. In the meantime, we scramble for cover and try to return fire from Charlie sappers, who are intent on over-running us before the Mechs claim the glory.

There is screaming in the sky above, and an F1 flashes past. I can hear Jimmy on the coms calling in the air support, and suddenly, there are more. Silver pods drop away, and the edge of the forest is angry red and orange flames. I can feel the heat from here. Outstanding!

The stands of bamboo go up like torches, incinerating anyone unlucky enough to be hiding in them. A couple of the Mechs are caught, and the great Soviet iron beasts turn in shambolic circles as their drivers attempt to get them clear. Too late for that! The furnace heat from the bamboo, and the napalm begins to twist and warp the metal. Munitions explode, and then so do the fuel tanks. Even though we can't see at this distance, it is easy to imagine the two-man crews roasting to death in their iron strait jackets the way our chopper pilots did.

The stink of burning and the sharp smell of kerosene drift across us as we get back to the work of driving away the VC. They seem to have lost some heart now that two of their Mechs have gone down, but a third stomps out of the inferno behind them, seemingly untouched, and once more, we are ducking for cover as .50 rounds eat our defences.

Charlie sappers come through the wire, and it is all confusion and death as it becomes hand-to-hand fighting.

The RPD jams, and I use it to club the first enemy that comes within range. He goes down hard but immediately scrambles back to his knees, AK trying to get a bead on me. They are tough little bastards! But we have our own tough little bastards, and Bong comes out of nowhere and cuts the VC down with his big jungle knife. Not to be outdone, I stick my K-Bar into an exposed armpit and then fumble with the ammo drum, and the gods of war smile on me as the RPD kicks back into life with a satisfying roar.

We find ourselves fighting side by side as more VC cross the wire, and we stand a very good chance of being overrun, especially as the Mech has made it about halfway between the burning forest and our lines. It spits out anti-aircraft shells from one side of the turret and a mix of armour piercing and tracer from the other side, its jointed metal feet splaying out as it stomps closer.

Explosions begin to tear up the earth outside the compound. Those dashingly disturbed flyboys have joined the party with a vengeance, and somewhere up there, Puff, The Magic Dragon, is raining hellfire on our attackers from its 40mm Bofors and miniguns.

At last, they begin to withdraw, zig-zagging across the erupting earth as they try to find some safety back in the forest. But the Mech doesn't make it. A hit on one of its chicken legs causes it to come to a stumbling halt just beyond the compound. Looking up, I can see into the cockpit and the bloody ragdoll of a human that hangs in the harness. Soviet *advisor* by what is left of the uniform. There will be another one in there somewhere, and already, the engineers are trying to dig him out. It appears that the hit on the leg sent shards of steel up into the body of the Mech, and they signal that there are no survivors. So, they kill the engine and the exhausts cough and then stop belching out oily smoke. The Mech just sort of slumps like a tired, fat man and is still, as if it had a life of its own to give up.

In other places on this fucked up planet, normal folk are watching men walk on the moon, but in this sweltering South-east Asian hell, we are killing each other over the idea that our political dogma is better than yours and maybe the right to drink Coca-Cola. And, of course, there is the unsubstantiated story that Russian scientists have reanimated the frozen corpse of Rasputin, who now aids them with some weird sorcery – could it get any fucking stranger?

Bong is looking at me again, really, really close. "You separate, Number One. You not here." I spread my hands in a *What?* gesture, and he makes odd passes with his hand through the air in front of me, and suddenly everything is spinning.

* * *

Lament is on her hands and knees, retching violently. The world around her has ceased to whirl, but she digs her fingers into the soil beneath her in an attempt to arrest any further motion by sheer physical effort.

The world, this world, gradually comes back to her, and as she draws ragged breaths into her lungs, the sounds around her fill her ears. There is cannon and musket fire and hoarse shouts. People push past her with a sense of urgency, some with more than a little panic. Strong hands grip her arms and haul her to her feet.

"What is the matter with you, woman? Are ye drunk? This is no time to be in your cups... or maybe it is!" The stocky soldier is English. A solid, square face on top of a solid, square body. The high-crowned hat partially shades a face that sports a thick black beard and a burn scar on the right cheek. Lament knows instinctively that it is a powder burn from a matchlock.

"Get yourself to your home and dress yourself. The Dons are at the walls, and it would not be fitting to die with your arse hanging out!" Eyeing her, as much for the marks upon her skin as for her partial nudity, the man laughs and hands Lament an old cloak. For a moment, Lament looks bemused, but then she stares down at herself and realises she is naked except for two lengths of linen and a badly arrayed sheet.

Once more, the cogs of her mind mesh together, and she nods thanks and looks around to orientate herself before moving off to where she knows her lodgings to be, cloak wrapped around her. The black-bearded man shakes his head and laughs as he watches Lament disappear through the press of people. Then he shoulders his musket and heads towards the barricades.

Back at the inn, Lament dresses rapidly. Her clothes and weapons are neatly piled on the bed, along with her pouch containing the necklace. There is also a note from Pieter.

*Lam, I pray you get this message. You have been gone four days as of this writing, and the Spanish are mustering beyond the walls for an attack. I will join the militia in the hopes that we can keep them at bay. At least it will be a clean fight against mortal foes. If you return and get this, then look for me at the barricades at the eastern gate. If I live, I will be there, and if you live, it would be good to see you. Seargent Hertgers.*

"Well, you mad bastard, I can't let you die alone." A rueful smile plays upon her lips as she ties back her dark hair, settles her hat, and adjusts her sword. As she leaves the room, she unconsciously whistles a tune from another time.

# Chapter 23

It doesn't take her long to find Pieter. His giant frame, topped with the ostrich-plumed barett, fills the space behind the upturned carts, barrels, and crates that block the entrance to the east gate.

Wooden spikes have been mounted onto the carts to discourage a cavalry charge, and large wicker baskets have been filled with earth to give some shelter from musket balls and crossbow bolts. The huge iron-bound gates that should seal the gatehouse stand half open, one almost off its hinges. There is a frenzy of activity as carpenters work to repair the gate.

Beyond the barricade on the raised road that leads to the gate can be seen the standards of the Spanish, billowing flags of yellow and red emblazoned with the royal coat of arms. Dotted amongst these are the colours of the regiments of Catholic Dutch who have arrived from Amsterdam and gathered for the destruction of Haarlem. A line of pike and musket straddle the road, and now and then, a shot tears earth or stone or wood and sometimes flesh. But the range is long, and only the foolhardy put themselves completely out in the open.

Lament squeezes through the press of bodies and claps Pieter on the back. The big man turns, annoyed at the familiarity, until he sees who it is. A broad grin splits the red beard, and he clasps Lament by the shoulders. "Merciful heavens, Lam! I began to wonder if I should see you again. You found my note then?"

"Aye, Pieter. I found myself naked in the street and not without a few slaps on my bare arse to send me on my way back to the inn. Your note was well received; thank you, my friend." She grips the huge arms, glad to see Pieter's broad, smiling countenance. "So, what came to pass here? It would seem an odd time to renew the city gates when there are Spaniards who should be denied entry. Is this some misplaced confidence?"

"Ha! No, Spanish agents within the city rolled a barrel of powder to the gate in the dawn. They were spied and shot for their troubles before they could get it into place. But the barrel made it close enough and was detonated. It blew the gate over yonder from its bottom hinge, and so we fill the gap with our bodies and what we can find until it is repaired. William the Silent has commanded that we hold the gate, and so hold the gate we shall! Besides, I had nothing better to do, and Utricia needs some exercise." He wraps his massive fingers lovingly around the hilt of the great zweihander sword.

Lament cocks an eyebrow and laughs. "When can we expect an assault?"

"The roadway is narrow and falls off to deep water on either side and around the walls. This is the only true weakness, so I think they will come at us here before the morning is done." He gestures to those around them. "We are in good company, Captain. There are English, French, and Germans here, as well as the Dutch. But it is Toledo again who we face, and he has Catholic

Dutch from Amsterdam in his force." He spits, a dark scowl clouding his face before he smiles a savage smile. "Fuck them! There will be plenty of death to go around, so let them all come!" Those closest to them raise a cheer in response to Pieter's bravado. But Lament is not listening. She is gazing out at the forces arranged against them. Involuntarily, her mind has shifted, and the witch-sight reveals to her the shape of their enemy.

A billowing cloud of bruised purple floats above and around them. It is shot through with red, the colour of congealing blood, and a putrescent greenish blue underlies it all. The whole pulsating mass has the look of a vile festering wound, and she feels bile rise in her throat as she looks at it. There are huge, more tangible shapes within the clouds. Vivid flashes of colour suddenly illuminate dark, capering, malformed silhouettes before they merge back into the chaos. All this somehow sits atop the human soldiers who form rank upon rank of bristling pike and straining cavalry.

So, this is the nature of their enemy writ large. This is the thing that plagues humankind. Some hellish sideshow in which the players are mere meat puppets operated by the otherworldly things representing two opposing dynamics, wearing their hosts like disposable costumes for their own entertainment. Lament knows that if she turns the witch-sight onto those that surround her, her own side, she will see something similar, and so she chooses not to. Instead, she closes her eyes tightly and pushes the visions back into the dark places of her mind, and when she opens them again, it is just the vainglory of man that meets her gaze.

"Have I brought destruction upon this city, Pieter? Was van

Ijzendoom correct that it is I who draw these forces towards me like a magnet to iron, like some carrion upon which the crows come to feast?"

Pieter looks upon his friend, his Captain, and sadly shakes his head. There is a note of pity in his deep voice as he answers. "I know not, Lam. I only know that you have been dealt a bad hand, and you must seek to play it as best you can. There is more of the unnatural about you now than either of us would care to admit, I think. You have more in common now with these forces that seek to manipulate us than links you with the rest of us. I have noticed the shadows that seem to accumulate in your vicinity, my friend, as if you are watched by beings, not of this world... Whatever happens here, it was never in your gift to prevent, but you may make a difference to the outcome."

Those close by look on, not sure what to make of the strange dialogue. They avert their eyes as Lament looks around at them, suddenly aware that there is an audience for this scene of the play she finds herself forced to act in.

"I hear trumpets. This may be over for us all before the day is done." She realises that she is glad of the impending fight. It is a thing that requires action rather than thought, and she would lose herself in that violence rather than dwell upon Pieter's words.

The lines of Tercios begin to advance along the roadway. Drums beat, and trumpets blare as the sound of marching feet grows louder.

Two heavy guns have been dragged into place behind the barricade by teams of horses, and now the artificers make their calculations and adjust the angles of the weapons. Sections of the defences are pulled aside as the guns are primed and loaded. Heavy cannon balls are manhandled into the gaping black barrels along with the charge that will project them towards the enemy. There is a moment of tense silence, of anticipation, and then the matches touch the powder, and the roar is deafening.

Two gaps appear in the advancing lines, scarlet gaps. Pikes topple like saplings felled in a forest, and the scream of mangled men can be heard even from this distance. The guns are reloaded, and they roar their righteous anger once more. Down go the Spaniards and Dutch forces from Amsterdam, but still, they advance, stepping over what is left of the dead and wounded.

Musketeers on the walls above the barricade have found their range, and now a hail of lead joins the cannon's mighty hammer. The Tercios return fire. Their discipline is astonishing, but there is enough cover to make it a futile, one-sided duel, at least for the moment.

It is obvious that they aim to force the breach by main assault. They have the numbers to achieve this, but there seems to be a miscalculation on the part of their commanders. They must advance along a narrow path into the teeth of a determined defence. Even though the Dons are known to be careless with their losses, especially those of allied troops, surely even they can't think that this will be such a rapid victory that they can afford to lose a battalion or two just to make a point. But Lament knows the reality of what drives the advancing men. It is not loyalty or thirst for glory. No, the strange things that choose to play out their wargames upon this Earth infect their hosts with a kind of madness that sits well with their savage desires, and there can be no concern for loss.

Looking over her shoulder, Lament shudders as she watches the guns loaded for the next salvo. This time, the iron maws are fed with a vicious mix of chain shot, nails, stones, and anything that will maim or kill. She remembers only too well being on the receiving end of similar when they had fought in Flanders what seems like a lifetime ago. The recollection is all too vivid of the field surgeon digging shrapnel from her thigh and hip. She had been lucky that day; the front two ranks had borne the brunt of that exchange, evaporating in front of her, and she had limped away with only slight wounds.

She looks back towards the advancing Tercios. Uniforms of red and yellow. Sunlight reflecting from breastplates and helmets. Off to their left are the blue uniforms of the Dutch. Then she hears the order to fire, and the crackle of burning powder followed almost instantly by the cannon's roar. The first ranks disappear in a pink mist. It looks like a slaughteryard in which mewling, screaming things that bear little resemblance to humans flop around in their gore.

The next ranks have taken heavy wounds, and they clutch at themselves and fall or stagger in aimless circles while those behind push past them, trampling dead and wounded alike. They know they must close the gap and silence the guns if they are to survive. Savage desperation drives them on as they charge, prayers turning to battle cries.

"Brace! Hold them at bay!" The major who gives the order is English. He stands astride the wicker earthworks, waving his sword. There is a mad gleam in his eye, and for a moment, Lament's witch-sight shows his true form. A skeletal wraith clad in bright plate armour of some unearthly design, a cloak of white and sea green stripes floating out behind him on the winds of another plane of existence. The skeletal head turns and looks in Lament's direction for an instant, and there is momentarily a look of confusion and surprise as if the thing is suddenly aware that it is visible to some human. A volley of shots hits the earthworks around it, and it returns its attention to the advancing enemy.

Lament shakes her head, and the vision is gone. Once more, the major is a potbellied, bow-legged gentlemen adventurer, wearing doublet and hose that cost more than most of those manning the barricade will see in a year.

Now, the enemy is here, and they are thirsty for revenge as they storm the barricades. Pikes are thrust from both sides as axes seek an opening to cut through the wood of the carts. Shorter polearms with hooked blades are employed to snag and pull down the timbers. The defenders respond with pistols fired at point-blank range and swords thrust through the gaps into Spaniards and Dutch, who are jammed hard against the barricade by the press of men behind them.

It becomes a work of grim slaughter. Lament and Pieter stand side by side, sword and zweihander fully engaged in the bloody task. There is no skill in this. It is simply a battle of wills, and the forces of Toledo must not be allowed to prevail. So, blades thrust, and chop, and slash and men struggle and die.

It appears sheer numbers will prevail as the troops beyond the gatehouse grow denser in number. But the artillery officer has no intention of giving the day away so easily. He rams chain shot and any debris that he can grab into his cannon, and as his men grapple with their Catholic countrymen, he lowers the barrel of the gun. There is an awful moment of realisation from all of those in front of it, some of whom are his own men. Then he fires the cannon. The effect at close range is devastating. Everyone within the cone of fire is vaporised, and suddenly, half of the road beyond the gatehouse is clear, at least of living things.

Lament looks up, her ears ringing from the blast, and she sees a figure on a grey horse standing amid the ruin that is scattered across the bridge. The figure stares directly at her with a strange intensity, and Lament is aware that she has seen this *man* before. The brightly coloured clothing, the hat with its vast brim and cockade of what look like peacock feathers, and that long narrow face that seems to be half covered by a continually changing mask. Shot whistles past him, but he does not move. Even the great grey stallion seems frozen to the spot. Lament blinks to stop the witch-sight, and with a shock, she realises that this creature before her is indeed fully present in this world. There is no parasitic jester form sitting upon a human host. No, this *is* its true form.

The rider gives a small nod of the pale head, a slight smile playing upon narrow lips as he draws the great curved blade, and then he kicks the stallion forward, scattering the remaining soldiers on that part of the bridge before him. El Arlequín is coming.

The hooves of the grey send sparks flying from the cobbled road surface, and anyone unfortunate enough not to get clear is ridden down by the grey with the burning coals for eyes. Lament shouts to Pieter without taking her eyes from the advancing apparition, "Sergeant! We have a problem!"

Pieter eyes El Arlequín and utters a stream of obscenity. "He may turn the battle if we can't repel these bastards!" He slices down with Utricia, the blade shuddering through the flesh and bone of a Spaniard. Then he thrusts forward without withdrawing the blade, hitting the next attacker on the breastplate and forcing him from the cart he has just climbed, the sundered Spaniard falling on top of him. Gleefully, the militia spears him as he struggles to get out from underneath the tangle of limbs.

Lament uses the growing piles of the dead as steps and then leaps to the top of the wicker earthworks. She hears Pieter's shouted exclamation, but there is no time now to respond. Kicking an enemy musketeer in the teeth, she leaps from the relative safety of the barricade. Her black-hilted sword skewers the staggering musketeer as she lands and walks out onto the road surface of a bridge that is awash with the stinking, crimson pride of the Spanish and Dutch. She draws her dagger with her left hand and walks toward the charging entity of chaos, arms spread wide, inviting this thing to its death. There is a tingling across her skin, and she imagines that the geometric patterns tattooed into her flesh by vast, cold, angelic beings are glowing again like molten metal.

As the stallion reaches her, Lament angles off to her right, forcing El Arlequín to strike down across his own body. The blow is fast, and the blade heavy but spoiled by the sudden elusiveness of his quarry. The dagger that Lament thrusts into the motley-covered thigh as he passes suffers no such problems, but the jolt that passes up her arm and into her body sends her staggering backwards. It is as if she has been struck by lightning. The withdrawn dagger drips a blue-black gore that evanesces into nothing before Lament's startled eyes.

As he wheels the gnashing stallion round to face Lament, the hellish rider speaks through gritted teeth, wild eyes still laughing. "Ha! A woman with skill. You are not like these others." He waves the curved blade to indicate the soldiers who stagger past. El Arlequín's voice is deep, like the echo of ocean waves breaking in a cave. He speaks in English but with an accent that Lament can't place; it certainly isn't Spanish. He walks the grey forward, but instead of attacking Lament, he swings himself from the saddle and stretches his wounded leg. There is a look of vague irritation that seems to be concerned more with the damage to his brightly coloured breeks than the wound beneath them.

A blur of motion, Lament barely manages to dodge the blade that suddenly flashes through the space she occupied mere moments before. She is gasping still from the blast of energy that knocked her backwards, but a life of swordplay has left her reflexes operating at a level beyond thought. She parries an upward diagonal slash with her sword, and a lesser jolt of energy surges through her again, causing her to grit her teeth.

As Lament lunges, her dagger held high to intercept the curved blade and her sword thrusting forward at the brightly coloured chest before her, the witch-sight comes on in a wave. She is taken by surprise as the ground beneath her feet becomes boiling vapour that erupts in great gouts of evil-coloured steam and almost misses as El Arlequín twists his torso to avoid the thrust and whirls his blade down and around to make an uppercut. Lament rolls to her right even though she does not trust the seemingly insubstantial ground around her and finds that it is solid enough as her shoulder jars on unseen cobblestones. She springs back to her feet, expecting a rush of whirling steel, one that she knows she may not be able to withstand. This entity has a skill and strength that is not reliant upon a human host's ability, and in this contest, he is more than capable. But the rush does not come. Instead, the extravagantly bedecked man thing places the tip of the curved blade on the billowing ground, leaning upon it with both hands. Then he cocks his head to one side, the shifting mask taking on the form of a white moth, his black eyes looking through holes in the wings.

"How came you by those *markings*?" He gestures towards Lament's chest, where the shirt has parted, revealing glowing patterns. Lament tenses, ready for an attack, poised upon the balls of her feet, suspecting a ruse, a distraction. But as the seconds pass, it is obvious that El Arlequín is not going to strike. Taking a pace back to move out of range, Lament finds herself curiously wishing to converse with this chaos creature.

"They were a gift that I would not have accepted had I a choice, for the consequences of wearing them, I think, outweigh their value to me." Lament gazes at this harlequin opposite her, who knowingly nods his head, a sigh passing through him.

"We are all pawns, my friend. I am placed here from another time as a weapon by masters who dream small, feeble-minded dreams. And you? You seem set upon a course that will alter that future, driven by masters of a different calling. I think that maybe you have already witnessed something of that future..." The mask morphs once again into a mirror in which Lament can clearly see herself reflected, and El Arlequín cranes his neck forward to stare even more intently with those black eyes. His inhuman lips part in a small gasp. "Tell me your name, swordswoman."

"I am Captain Lament Evyngar, sir. May I ask what business that is of yours?"

El Arlequín reacts as if he has been slapped. The mask flickers, and for a moment, a pale, aquiline face is revealed before it changes to a pattern of geometric lines that mimic Lament's own and hides the features once more. "I did not suspect that it was *this now*. Ah, they play cruel tricks upon us!" He shakes his head violently, dark hair drifting around him.

"Sir, of what do you speak? What do you mean by *this now*?" Lament finds there is a tightness in her chest as she asks the question.

A wild laugh escapes from behind the mask. He sweeps the curved sword up and returns it to its sheath in a well-practised move. "I fear you would not understand, but then again, perhaps you would... The streams of time and reality are not fixed, Captain. I go where I am sent by forces that I have no control over – yet, and I have the sense that it may be the same for you, although you are very much at the beginning of your journey. And we have common ground, you and I, Captain, more than just the vagaries and whims of fate." El Arlequín turns and begins to walk back to the patiently waiting grey.

"Hold, sir! What common ground?"

As he mounts, he looks back at Lament, a strange light in the black orbs that reveal gold flecks scattered across them like stars in the heavens. "My mother." Then he removes his hat, bowing low in the saddle, and wheels his mount before galloping back along the roadway, that wild laughter trailing behind him.

A trumpet blares, and suddenly, the Spanish and their allies are in flight. A small unit led by a large captain with a dark, swarthy complexion attempts to make an orderly retreat. It is a brave attempt, but the gunners are re-loading the cannon, and it is too much for the Tercios, so they turn and run. The captain stands his ground for a moment, shouting insults at the fleeing men, but then his eyes grow wide, and he looks down at his chest from which has sprouted an axe. He feebly grips the haft and then, with a look of sad despair, sinks to his knees before toppling forwards, never to rise again.

Lament watches, dazed, as they run past along the far side of the bridge. Her mind whirls at the suggestion that has been planted in it, that the motley creature may be her offspring, *that* part of the blasphemous, insane bargain with Beatris that should not have been physically possible. She stoops to retrieve a peacock feather that has fallen from the hat of El Arlequín. She briefly stares into the blue-green eye of the feather before placing it into her belt pouch. A great cheer goes up from the defenders. Some still send missiles at the backs of the retreating Dons, but most slump back against the barricade as exhaustion takes hold, and Lament walks slowly back to the earthworks and accepts the reaching hands that help her over.

The defenders drag the dead and wounded back into the city, at least their own dead and wounded. Any of Toledo's men still breathing are dispatched without mercy by the women folk who wait in the safety of the walls. The bodies are stripped, and then all are thrown without ceremony into the moat that surrounds the city. It is not what Lament would have done. There will be disease from those rotting corpses. But it is not her city.

# Chapter 24

Pieter pulls off his boots and flops back onto the bed. "That was a close-run affair, me thinks!" It is early evening, and they are finally back at the inn after helping the engineers re-fit the gate and then dismantle most of the barricade. The earthworks will remain as a second line of defence, but the carts, or what is left of them, have been reclaimed by their owners.

Lament laughs, shaking her head at her huge friend's talent for understatement. "That it was big man, that it was." She places her baldrick and sword on the chest beneath the window and stretches. She has noticed a reticence in Pieter; he has not asked what occurred this time when Lament disappeared, and he has pointedly refused to talk about what happened on the bridge with El Arlequín other than to congratulate Lament on gaining them enough time to repel the attacking forces that were left. The defenders at the barricades had all refused to make eye contact with her, and all that Pieter would say was that there was a *look of the unnatural about it.* Lament had chosen not to elaborate even to her friend.

For all his formidable strength and ferocity, it is obvious that Pieter can't cope with any more of this unholy pact into which

Lament is locked. She opens her mouth to speak, but Pieter beats her to it. "Lam, I fear I can no longer be a part of this. What happens when you disappear? I know not. But I do know that I can't be of aid, and I begin to have grave doubts about the safety of my sanity, if not my soul. I feel both have been sorely ill-used." He pushes himself back up to a sitting position and holds up his hand to prevent Lament from interrupting. "Do you remember when we were at Mechelen? There was a girl there called Sophia."

Lament nods, not quite sure where this conversation is going.

"I thought she must surely perish in the Spanish Fury. It did not sit well with me to leave her, even though her husband had returned. But she escaped though her good Catholic husband was butchered and, by some miracle, has arrived here. She has been in the city for a week, and our paths crossed two days ago." There is a quirky smile on Pieter's scarred visage, a look that Lament thinks must have been his natural state when he was a child before war, and the occult had left their marks.

"And...?"

The smile disappears, and Pieter looks awkwardly guilty. "There will be a siege, that much is certain, and I will not run and leave her again." He holds up his big hands, something like despair clouding his eyes. "I know you must leave. You must play out this game of Dee's; you have no option if you are to keep your family from the scaffold and flames. But I must stay here and help to fight against the forces of the Duke of Alba and what they represent. These are my countrymen, Lam, and I may have found a woman that I love!" The look of guilt is almost comical on such a great bear of a man, and Lament steps in and grips a massive paw.

"My friend! This is not how we foresaw our futures. But I am happy for you. I think that whatever the fates have in store for me, you can no longer play a part in it. Come, let us drink and celebrate today's victory and try to forget death for a little while."

* * *

Today, they stand on the dock, heads still muggy from the drink and revelry of last night. Pieter has a massive arm around the shoulders of Sophia, and she looks up at him adoringly from just below his equally huge chest. Lament can see her friend is smitten with this pretty young woman, and she is glad for him. There is also sadness and a longing for what she feels she may never have.

She shrugs off the melancholy; there will be time enough for that sort of pondering when she has discharged her commission for Dr Dee. At this moment, she must secure her escape from Haarlem before the siege takes full hold. There are ships willing to run the risk of Spanish gunfire, but their captains wish to leave as a matter of urgency. It will take some time before the forces of Don Fadrique Álvarez de Toledo can surround the city. Still, Lament has enough experience with Spanish scouts to know that they will take any opportunity to disrupt the escape plans of those who cross their path.

So, Lament has secured passage on a trading vessel along with a contingent of English and French mercenaries who see no profit in being trapped within a besieged city. The ship will sail the waterways inland before turning towards the Narrow Sea.

"You could still come with me, the both of you." Lament looks at the couple and knows the answer even before she finishes speaking.

"Nay, Lam. Our courses are set differently now. I will run no more. Maybe I can make amends here for all that has gone before, and at least I will have this woman by my side." He grins down at the blushing face that beams back up at him. Lament can scarcely believe that it is the same man. They say love can tame even the most savage beast...

"Then, Seargent, I wish you and your lady well. I pray that the Spanish lose interest before they ever come within reach of Utricia!"

"My Captain, I hope that you can find some release from the demons that plague you, and if you have the opportunity, give that devil crow, Dr Dee, some hard knocks from me!" They embrace, and in that moment, both know that they may never meet again on this side of heaven. Lament steps away, and without another glance, she walks up the gangplank of the ship.

* * *

The journey thus far seems to be charmed. The ship has made it through the narrower winding channels and out onto the wider waterway that runs to the sea. Other ships have not been so lucky. Black smoke rises in the distance behind them. Several of the vessels have been caught in the narrows and fired. Talk on board is of the Dutch Catholic forces loyal to Phillip II, who are moving to block traffic on the waterways. It is only speculation, but it will prove to be correct.

Lament watches the smoke rise from her place in the stern of the Gelderland. The wind has caught the sails and pushes the merchant vessel on at a quick pace, along with a dozen more that were fortunate enough to be at the vanguard of the small fleet.

A figure moves to the rail next to Lament, and a voice that she recognises speaks. "So, Captain, you found your clothes, I see."

Lament turns to regard the square, black-bearded face that sports the powder burn. "Indeed, sir. I offer my thanks for your assistance yesterday, although I am unable to return your cloak."

"Ha! In truth, I *borrowed* it from a German pikeman who was otherwise engaged. It seemed you were in greater need. And I apologise for not recognising an officer, although, in my defence, you were in a slightly compromised state." A lopsided grin splits the square face. "Lieutenant Nathanial Carrow at your service, Captain. I saw you and your large compatriot at work on the barricades. You ply your trade with a fearsome efficiency."

Lament ignores the rather clumsy compliment and instead chooses to introduce herself for the second time in as many days. "Captain Lament Evyngar at your service, Lieutenant Carrow."

"Did your large friend not wish to leave? It will be an unpleasant place to be trapped if the Dons have their way."

"No. The Sergeant has his reasons for staying. After all is said, this is his country, and he felt it time to take a stand." Lament's eyes give away her sorrow and guilt at having to leave her friend, and Carrow reads the look and nods sadly.

"I fear we all leave something behind us here. But come, share a drink with me and my men. I think that we are beyond the grip of Alba's forces for the moment."

Lament accepts the invitation willingly and joins Lieutenant Carrow and his band of musketeers. But she looks one last time at the fingers of black smoke from the burning ships and can't help but feel that, somehow, they are an ill omen.

# Chapter 25

The storm is relentless. A sky the colour of old pewter presses down upon the Gelderland. They lost sight of the other ships a day ago behind a wall of mountainous waves and a storm that stung like wind-driven needles. Men lash themselves to whatever will not wash overboard as they vomit up bile and pray for Christ to save them, even though some wish that they were dead.

Lament has tied herself to the main mast alongside Carrow. The black-bearded soldier has lost his colour and his good humour. There is a look of abject terror in his eyes and perhaps resignation. A cross spar crashes to the deck, crushing two unlucky souls in its fall. It slides across the deck, dragging rigging in its wake and breaking more limbs. The screams of injured men mix with the howl of the storm, and Lament begins to wonder if this is what hell is like. She closes her eyes as a wave strikes to starboard and dashes icy brine across them, and when she opens them again, face running with water, she sees the expression upon Carrow's face. This is something more than the storm.

"By God's mercy, Captain, what is happening to you?" As Carrow watches, Lament begins to evaporate like morning mist in the sunlight. There is a moment when their eyes meet, and then Lament is swept away, gone in a swirling vortex in the air. Lieutenant Carrow throws his head back and laughs, and the laugh becomes a scream, and his sanity departs with the furious wind.

* * *

*What am I doing shuffling towards the edge of this precipice? The wind is screaming beyond the gaping opening in front of me. Is it the storm tearing the ship apart? What ship is that? What mad fantasy plays through my brain thirty seconds to jump?*

*There is loud, loud music blasting out of the speakers behind me. I can hear it above the roar of the C130's engines. I feel the rush of adrenaline that I always feel in these seconds before that leap into nothing, and the visions of storm-wrecked ships are swept away in the wind...*

The men around me are ready to go. We are all wearing oxygen masks strapped tight around our faces and goggles sealed tight against the tearing gale. There is a moment when I remember staring through the round glass eyepieces of another mask, but that memory is lost, a dream that never was. What we are about to do is a HALO jump; that is why I am almost at the edge of a ramp high above the Afghan desert, and right now, nothing else matters.

Guitars crash stridently, and we stare fixedly at the red bulbs on either side of the ramp. We each check the man in front, and I run through the routine of ensuring that all is fitted correctly before we give ourselves up to gravity.

"YOU OKAY CAPTAIN?" Sergeant *Tricky* Davis bellows at me above the mounting heavy metal and the clamour of the engines. Through his mask, I can see a look of concern. Of course, I am okay! What the fuck is wrong with me tonight? I give him the thumbs up, and he slaps me on the shoulder. I have been doing this shit for the past three years; of course I am alright!

We shuffle tighter together so that we will all fall together, and the speakers scream THUNDERSTRUCK. The lights turn to green, and the parachute dispatcher yells GO! GO! GO! We go, and I remember that I fucking love this stuff!

Everything is black as I hurtle headfirst downwards. The altimeter on my wrist ticks down, and I look left and right, catching glimpses of the others around me. They fall with me, falling from heaven. Avenging angels cast out of paradise, sent where no one else will go to exact some vengeance that no one will remember in a hundred years.

Five thousand feet, and I pull my chute. The open canopy drags me violently upwards as it arrests my fall. I hang here, floating. This is the worst part. I can steer the chute, but until I hit the ground, I am a sitting target for anyone from the local militia to bored goatherders. Everyone here has a gun, and no one likes the *infidel*.

Why are we doing this? Because the Russians aren't supposed to still be in Afghanistan. We have done everything we can except declare war on them. We have trained and funded the warlords and the Taliban, and for a time, it looked as if it was working. But the hill tribes and their warlords have begun to fight with the Taliban over ideological differences, and now a charismatic religious leader has come down from the mountains and aligned himself with the Russians. He preaches an ancient Sumerian end-of-the-world religion that seems to gel with Islam, and many of the tribes and even the ultra-conservative Taliban have begun to follow him and have gone over to the Russians. Reported sightings of this *prophet* have him wearing multi-coloured robes and riding a grey horse, his face masked.

Intel has come in that the Soviets have set up some sort of silo in one of the many cave systems in the mountains, and the analysts are concerned that they are preparing to use tactical battlefield nukes to finish the mujahideen once and for all. There is also some weird intel about giant scorpions summoned from deep underground that do the bidding of this prophet... At this point, we can't ignore anything; the world just keeps getting weirder.

One thousand four hundred feet, and I release my bergen so that it can hit first and then steer after the others towards the IP, the Impact Point. The ground comes up fast, and I bend my knees almost too late. I roll and then scramble back to my feet, wrestling the canopy to prevent being dragged across the desert.

Stripping off the oxygen mask, I get on comms, and after a few seconds, I hear the voices of my team coming back to me. The wind has been our friend tonight, and we have not been scattered far and wide. I home in on them, and then we head off into the darkness towards our rendezvous point.

A local warlord who is still loyal to the coalition forces has sent his men to meet us, and we reach them just before dawn. We have a possible location for the Russian silo and the nukes, and these crazy-looking bastards are going to take us there. They wear a random collection of fatigues, chapan coats, and, of course, pakol hats and Ray-Bans. Most of them have tactical vests with as many ammo clips and grenades as they can fit adorning them. Plus, the ubiquitous Khyber knife – never leave home without one! There are some wild eyes staring at us when they lift their sunglasses, and I know from previous experience that some of these nut jobs will be high on the meth that they cook up from one of their local plants. Ah, joy!

Our job is to access the veracity of the claims made about the silos and give coordinates for an air strike. Or, if it comes to the worst-case scenario, attempt to blow them up ourselves. Not a great chance for a happy ending, but you take what you are given.

No surprise that we are travelling in their *technicals*. The converted Toyotas and Nissans sport .50 cals mounted on the open-backs, and they delight in showing them to us as if we have never seen guns before. The engines growl into life, and we set off across the red rock and sand wasteland towards a ridge about twelve klicks distant. The wind picks up with a vengeance, and we all cover our faces with shemaghs to keep the stinging sand at bay.

We are now seven klicks out from the target, and white rocket trails stab suddenly into the sky from our approximate destination. "Tell me that's not a launch!" Corporal Haynes voices what we all fear. There is an endless pause as we continue to bounce across the desert, and then a soundless white flash lights the horizon with an evil glow. I can hear brief exclamations over comms, and then it goes dead as the technicals slew to a halt. There is just static. I stare in awe at the rising dome of the mushroom clouds. Another pause and the sound hits, shotgun blasts followed by a continuous roar that seems to come from the very centre of the earth.

We are too late. The nukes have been deployed, and as far as I can tell, they have exploded south towards Kandahar and east towards Kabul. We all look at each other with a sense of resignation. There is nowhere to go from here except forward. If there are more warheads in the hidden silos, then we must give JATAC the coordinates to bury them forever. The technicals start moving again, but ahead, the surface of the desert comes alive. Giant arachnid forms with pincers and long forward curving tails are shaking themselves free of the sand. My stomach lurches as if I am back in freefall... Spinning. Spinning.

* * *

Lament's eyes snap open. She draws in a huge, ragged breath as if she has been without air for a very long time. Pushing against the wet ground, she manages to sit up, a wild look in her eyes as she stares around, expecting to see vast burning clouds and monstrous creatures. But the clouds are not here, nor the beasts. Instead of desert sand, she is surrounded by cold, grey fog and the skeletal fingers of reeds. Wildfowl panic and fly heedlessly from cover, their cries bleak in the chill dawn.

Gasping for breath, she realises that she is soaked through and shivering, shivering as much from what she has witnessed as from the cold. Part of her would try to make some sense of the visions of destruction, but another part of her wishes only to shut the visions away, to pretend that they are not real. Perhaps it is an instinct for survival that wins, and the explosions and everything that went with them fade like a nightmare in the cold light of day.

She clambers slowly to her feet, untangling the short cloak from her limbs. Her sword is miraculously still at her side, as is her dagger. There is a moment of dread as she searches her belt. If the necklace is lost, then so is she. But probing fingers locate the pouch and the prize within it. Her breathing slows, and she gradually takes stock of her surroundings. Fenland, saltwater marshes. There is no sign of the Gelderland. *Ah, the storm!* Now, she begins to remember.

Doubling over all of a sudden, she grips her knees and vomits into the reeds. The taste of salt is strong in her mouth, mixed with bile. As she wipes her lips and chin on her sleeve, she hears voices behind her and the splash of oars.

"Halloo! Over here. Are you well?"

Lament raises a hand to signify all is well, but the small boat still holds its distance from the tiny island on which she stands. "Yes, yes, I am well. I would be grateful for your aid, my friends." The boat edges closer, and Lament can see two men dressed in rough smocks. There are woven fish traps stacked at the back of the craft and coils of well-used rope.

"You are not ill, are you? There is plague about, and though we do not wish to be un-Christian, we can't risk helping one who may be sick." The man at the bow is as thin as the reeds and looks at her through drooping, moist eyes. His bare arms are knotted with stringy muscles and streaked with mud from laying the traps in the shallows.

"I assure you I do not have the sickness. I was shipwrecked and have somehow washed ashore here. It would aid me greatly if you could set me down on solid ground and, even better, should you be able to get me to a fire to dry off."

The two men look at each other. The second man, older and stockier, nods, and they swing the boat in close to the peat bank that makes up Lament's island. She climbs on board and instinctively goes to sit at the stern on the ropes. It doesn't do to trust men too easily, especially in a wild place such as this. So, Lament wraps her cloak about her and keeps her hand on the hilt of her dagger.

"They were pulling wreckage from the sea about three or four mile up the coast. But that were days ago. You would have the devil's own luck to survive that long. We haven't heard tell of any other ships being lost." The stocky man is suspicious, and Lament decides to take a chance. She knows that many of the folk who live outside of the view of the authorities still follow the Catholic faith, and she knows that Catholic priests and their supporters are often smuggled into the country along less inhabited coastal areas.

"I had the misfortune to be on a smaller vessel that went down when the captain attempted to navigate one of the inlets during a sudden storm. I was the only survivor, I believe. May the Blessed Virgin show them mercy." She crosses himself, and the stocky man nods and touches the crucifix that lies on his chest beneath his smock.

# Chapter 26

Crows sit on the tree branches, watching her as she rides on by. Most of the leaves have fallen, and the fat, black birds infest the treetops like some sentient growth. Lament would rather not think about why they are so well-fed. Not when she has seen the villages with the white crosses painted on the nailed-shut doors and the pits into which the plague victims have been thrown.

She skirts places where there might be people. The pox is no respecter of a woman's needs; it takes high and low with equal relish, and it can't be bargained with. Even the gates of Norwich were barred to her, the Watch at the gatehouse warning her off before she could barely get within shouting distance. So, she rides on. The palfrey she managed to purchase is not the best horse she has ever ridden, but it will do. She dismounts at intervals and walks with the horse to give it some rest. There is still a day's ride before she will get to London, and a lame horse will not aid in her cause.

As night begins to fall, she leads the horse off the road and into a thicket. There, she tethers it to a fallen tree in a small clearing, and it grazes contentedly on the thick grass. Less contentedly, she unwraps the bread and thick rind cheese that has served as her sustenance since she parted from the fisher folk who aided her. She can't risk a fire. There are bands of desperate people wandering the countryside, and to draw attention will doubtless result in death or injury to all concerned. But at least the locally brewed mead in the grey stone bottle has enough fire to help keep her warm.

Wrapped in her cloak and with a felt hat acquired from the man who sold her the horse pulled low against the drizzle, she settles herself against a large oak on the edge of the clearing. Sword across her lap, she chews on the stale bread. There will not be much sleep tonight, but at least she can stretch her legs in relative peace.

Jerking awake from the dream that had crept up on her, she darts a look around, but all is quiet. The palfrey dozes where it stands. Everything is still; even the drizzle has halted for the moment.

Leaning her head back against the trunk of the oak, she tries to picture again her dream. Beatris had been there. Two tall standing stones, carved with pagan runes, had framed a path into the forest, and Beatris had walked out of the darkness to the trees and between the stones as if they were a doorway to another world.

She had smiled at her with lips as red as blood and then walked past her, and she could not turn to follow her. Another figure appeared between the stones, an old man, insubstantial as if made of smoke.

Lament had the strange sensation that she had seen the man before. The costume he wore was of a bygone century. Then La-ment's skin had crawled as she realised that it was the apparition from which they had fled in that dark tower in Haarlem. The old man opened his mouth to speak, but all that came out was blackness and roaring wind. But in her mind, Lament could hear the words. "*It is not meant for her!*"

She shudders without knowing why and grips the hilt of her sword. This is the feeling of someone walking over her grave, and she longs for the gruff voice of Pieter, laughing at the terrors of the night and singing songs of women and life. But that is no more, and Lament has a premonition that she will never know peace again.

* * *

Horsemen are waiting for her as she approaches the crossroads. In the distance, she can see Finsbury Field, beyond that, The Moor, and as a faint smudge beyond those, she can just make out the outline of the city, church towers against the grey gloom and the darker line of the city wall.

She reins in before the waiting men. She has already decided that she can't outrun them on her tired palfrey, and they show no sign of threat... at the moment.

"Good afternoon to you, gentlemen. Am I to be allowed to pass?" There are three of them, and they have a business-like demeanour. She takes note of the pistols, the swords, and the garb, which, to her, all say *swords for hire.*

"Captain Evyngar, welcome home!" A fourth figure emerges from behind the others, leading his horse, who had been drinking from the stone trough at the side of the road. Lament recognises the voice, although the man himself presents a rather different aspect from when they had last parted.

"Ah, Master Blexham. I feel that, at this point, I should not be surprised to see you. I would guess then that you are here to escort me to Dr Dee." Garrat Blexham has indeed seen his fortunes rise since he parted company with Lament and Pieter in the Low Countries. He now wears cloth of a finer cut, even if it is still predominantly grey, which is his preferred colour. But now the grey is broken by designs of a lighter, almost silver shade, and instead of a hood, he sports a fine charcoal grey hat with a yellow feather and a short red cloak.

He observes Lament's appraisal of him and makes a mocking bow. "The good doctor is most generous to those who provide him with exceptional service. He was overjoyed with the map and rewarded me handsomely." Garrat nods to the others as he remounts, and they part to allow Lament to ride between them. Another rider awaits further along the road, and Lament narrows her eyes as she sees something familiar about him. The man turns his horse away to lead them at a distance, but something in the way he sits his mount and the set of his shoulders reminds Lament of a captain that they met when first they reached the Low Countries on this mission of Dee's. The name escapes her, but she makes a note to watch this man.

Garrat is speaking, although Lament barely listens. "You are correct, of course. We are here to welcome you back and see you safely through the city to Dr Dee. He vouched safe the knowledge that you would be here at this hour."

Lament gives a harsh laugh. "So, his fortune-telling still

works, then! It would have been fortuitous had he been able to send help at other times during this adventure."

"So you say, Captain. But he has been most vexed by your continual disappearances while abroad. He believed on several occasions that you were dead. That would not have been a pleasant result for your family. Their continued safety was always dependent upon the successful completion of your mission. Dr Dee is a man of his word when it comes to promises of that ilk." Garrat gives Lament the smile of a man who believes that he has risen to be in a position of power and to be in the confidence of his employer. "You no longer travel with Sergeant Hertgers? A shame. I had almost grown to like the big lump."

"No, the sergeant and I have parted company. He has decided that his destiny is now linked to the future of his country and the defeat of the Spanish." That is all the information that Lament is prepared to share regarding Pieter.

As they ride on, Lament watches her escort in her peripheral vision. They cast calculating glances at her, and if they do look at Garrat, it is with contempt. She knows men like these of old. They have been paid to do a job and told to follow the orders of a youth for whom they have no respect. Now, they are wondering if there is more profit to be had in killing and robbing their charge. The light will be failing soon, and Lament knows that if it were her doing the planning, then she would wait until they were crossing The Moor as the sun goes down.

The low winter sun begins to sink, colouring the west. Skeins of dirty cloud catch the last of its light and, for a short while, turn to the red mauve that can be seen on the breast of a wood pigeon.

*It might be a pleasant day tomorrow if I can survive this night,* Lament muses to herself. She knows the odds are not in her favour. Garrat wears a sword, which Lament would wager is just for show. He also has a brace of pistols in holsters upon his saddle, but Lament knows that they will not be primed. So, she can't rely upon the young fool to be of any assistance.

As they begin to pass Mallow Field and The Moor Lament readies herself. She will have to attack first and hope to kill or wound as many of the escorts as possible before they have a chance to round upon her. She is certain that their pistols will be primed, and if she can grab one, it may make a difference.

Then, suddenly, the threat is gone. From both sides ride more men with lanterns, and from the way they are attired, they would seem to be part of the City Watch. They outnumber the hired swords who have been escorting Lament, and those men immediately begin to drop back, black looks on their surly faces. The man who has been riding ahead of them looks over his shoulder and then spurs away as if he has nothing to do with them. For a moment, as he turns, the scarf pulled up over his lower face slips, and Lament recognises him. Captain Bowcer, the very same captain of Sir Humphrey's force who felt so slighted in the port of Brielle that he threatened retribution, and as he rides away, there is the faintest hint of the creature that wears him before Lament blinks back to the reality around her.

The Watch sergeant, a big man astride a big horse, moves in close to Garrat and Lament. "God's mercy and a good evening to you, Master Garrat. Dr Dee requested that we ride out to greet you and the captain and give you a proper escort to Somerset House." He nods at Lament and then glances at the other escort, his eyes suddenly fierce under bushy dark blond brows. "You gentlemen are no longer required. I understand you have received some payment, so find yourselves a tavern and enjoy the evening in front of the fire. Goodnight to you, sirrahs." Turning back to Garrat, he grins a gap-toothed grin from within a thicket of a beard that is the same colour as his eyebrows except for a streak of white from an old wound.

All the Watch are heavily armed and wear some form of armour. They look on as the hired swords halt behind them before heading back the way they have come. With the fatalism of their trade, they know when to cut and run, and as the Watch sergeant said, at least they have been paid.

"I do not understand, Sergeant. I recruited those men for this task. Why did the doctor see fit to send you to replace them?" Garrat asks peevishly, his pride not a little hurt.

"Those men would like as not have cut your throats and left you in a ditch. I know not how the doctor knew that you were in danger, and I care not to guess at his methods but send us he did. So, be glad, young master." The sergeant winks knowingly at Lament, who smiles back in return.

Perhaps tomorrow will be a pleasant day after all... Lament does not see the dark look that Garrat casts in her direction.

They ride west past the Barbican and on to Smithfield Marketplace. The slaughtermen are clearing up for the day, and the smell of blood and livestock is pungent.

The sergeant would like to talk, just to pass the time, and Lament finds him amiable company. Garrat has fallen into a sulk and refuses to engage, and so finds himself the butt of jokes. He stares ahead into the lamp-lit gloom and quietly seethes.

Leaving the marketplace behind, they pass on to Holbourne and then turn south on Flete Strete. Off to her left now, Lament can see the mass of St Paul rising above the other buildings. She keeps half an ear on the sergeant's conversation as she watches the shadows of the side streets.

The men of the Watch who ride behind them are relaxed and confident of their superiority. But Lament has enough experience of conflict to not relax before she is sure it is safe to do so. Although she does not believe that the hired swords would be foolish enough to attack a force of the Watch, especially this close to the city, she is not convinced that the shadows are empty of threat. Now and then, from the corner of her eye, she thinks that she sees dark shapes moving. She relaxes her vision and allows the witch-sight to take over, and there, in the blackness between the buildings, are dark silver-grey forms changing from mist to solid as they move. Pale yellow orbs stare from elongated heads, and exaggeratedly long limbs drag equally long fingers along the walls as they pass, and there is the impression of black, folded wings lying against their backs. She can't imagine what these things want, but she doesn't believe that they are a threat. They just seem to be observing... watching. So, she allows the witch-sight to pass and goes back to discussing the merits of German wine with the garrulous sergeant.

Passing through Temple Bar and onto the Strande, they can at last see the shape of Somerset House lit by the braziers that provide some light in the larger thoroughfares. Candles illuminate many of the windows, and silhouettes pass across them. There would seem to be a party in progress, although Lament doesn't imagine that she is invited.

The sergeant bids them farewell at a large side gate that leads into the grounds. It is near time for the city gates to be locked for the evening, and he must be off to his post. Lament and Garrat dismount, and their horses are led away to the stables by grooms. Armed men are patrolling the grounds, and Garrat leans in close to take Lament into his confidence.

"There is a gathering of several members of the Privy Council here this evening. They have brought their wives or mistresses and undoubtedly an army of hangers-on." Lament detects a note of jealousy in the young man's voice. It seems that just performing good service to Dr Dee is not enough to get him accepted into the social mix of the great and good. Again, Garrat's naivety shows itself. Lament wonders whether Garrat will ever realise that his humble beginnings have guaranteed that he will never find favour with the people he seeks so earnestly to impress.

"Is Dr Dee awaiting us in the house, or are we to brave his labyrinth once more?"

"Dr Dee has no time for entertainment!" Garrat scoffs at the idea and once more seems overly bitter. He points towards a gated entrance set into the side of a folly at the edge of the garden. "No, Captain. My master will greet you in his chambers. I believe you will remember them." Lament raises an eyebrow at the element of spite in that last comment.

Garrat takes a large iron key from the purse at his belt and opens the gate in the folly. He takes one of the lanterns that hang on either side and leads Lament down a steep flight of steps and into the Stygian gloom. The last time that they did similar together, they ended by fighting demons in a church vault. Lament silently prays that, on this occasion, there is nothing so dramatic.

# Chapter 27

An unaccustomed and perhaps a little unnerving smile greets Lament.

"Well, met Captain! Welcome back, welcome back!" The tall, black-robed figure of Dr Dee steps aside from the door and ushers Lament into his study like a long-lost friend. Garrat attempts to follow, but Dee holds up a hand to halt him. "I think not, Master Blexham. That will be all." With that, he closes the door in Garrat's open-mouthed face. There is a sense of finality.

The doctor is very animated, his movements rapid and jerky. Lament can feel the anticipation in the room as a palpable thing. So, it is no surprise when Dee cuts straight to the chase. "The necklace, show it to me!"

Lament is tired, tired of the games that she has been forced to play, so handing over the necklace and discharging her debt seems to her a fine conclusion to this tale. She digs into her belt pouch and draws forth the black velvet cloth, slightly the worse for wear after its dip in the Narrow Sea, in which the necklace is wrapped. The cloth falls open, and she holds it out on the palm of her hand, the chain curled serpent-like beneath the jewel that looks like nothing less than a fragment of the sun.

Dr Dee reaches out a thin, long-fingered hand and tentatively touches the jewel. He snatches the hand back as if he has been scalded, his eyes wide with a look of startled terror.

*Ah, the thing has the chill of the void!* The words rush through Dee's mind. *How can the Captain bear to hold it?* Then he sees the truth of it. The faint marks on the skin of Lament's wrist, put there by Dee's ritual, are glowing slightly, and he realises that they have become more than he ever imagined they would.

"Will you not take this infernal thing, sir? You desire it enough to send me on a quest, but now you will not take it from me!" Lament steps forward to press the necklace into Dee's hands, but Dee backs away, scuttling out of reach like a great black spider.

"Nay, Captain! I cannot hold the jewel. I suspect that not many mortals can now I have seen it. You are unique. The rite I performed upon you has done far more than I had imagined it would. There is only one for whom this jewel is destined, and I believe that you must be the one to present it to her." The doctor's eyes shine with a light that now has awe mixed with the terror.

Lament has a sinking feeling in the pit of her stomach. A small voice in her head tells her that her part in this is far from over. "And to whom, pray tell, is this bauble to be given as a gift?" She believes she knows the answer already, but a vain hope remains that she is wrong.

Dr Dee seems to become infused with rapture, and before she even hears the words, Lament's heart sinks. "It is for Her Majesty, Queen Elizabeth."

* * *

Morning comes, and Lament feels somewhat more rested. A servant brings her a platter of bread and dried fruit and a jug of breakfast beer, so she takes her time to eat and relax a little.

Once Dee had realised that it would perforce need to be Lament who handed the necklace to Her Majesty, he had gone into a frenzy of activity. Her Highness would be expecting to receive the jewel, after all, had not the doctor told her the exact day and time. But taking Lament into court could prove problematic. Security has increased dramatically of late due to the threat of Catholic assassins. The Jesuits have become more daring and more desperate. But then, despite all, she is a woman...

Dee has disappeared off into Somerset House to attempt to use his influence with certain Privy Council members who were invited to the party. He has by no means the confidence of all of them; many think him a mere conjurer, and so he must make his enteritis as he can.

Before leaving, he called for a servant to show Lament to a sleeping chamber, and just before he left, Lament had managed to ask him two questions. "Do you know of a Count Godard van Ijzendoom?"

Dee gave her a sidelong glance and hesitatingly answered, "Yes, what of him?"

"The Count aided us in the appropriation of the necklace. He was also the custodian of the artefacts from which we took the map. He said that he was in the employ of the Holy Roman Emperor." Lament watched the twitch that passed across Dee's narrow face. Professional jealousy, perhaps.

"That would explain why I was unable to see the exact location of the map and why it was constantly hidden in transit. The Count is an annoyance, one who is not without a certain level of skill when it comes to the occult sciences, although more of a dabbler than a true magus. Why would he aid you in obtaining the necklace?" Dee's eyes narrowed with suspicion as if he expected Count Godard to suddenly materialise out of thin air.

"That was between me and him, and let us just say that it didn't end well for him." Lament's tight smile negated any further explanation.

Dr Dee raised his eyebrows, "Ah, so the Count is no longer with us. Interesting... I will have to send my condolences to the Emperor and offer my services in his alchemical experiments. He will need someone to take over when I have some time..." A smug smile cut the long beard.

"Would that not be contrary to your work with Her Majesty?"

"No, Captain. There are ways that all needs can be satisfied. Her Majesty knows that I have worked with others in the perfection of my art, and if it furthers the aims of her realm, she will not object. There are members of the Privy Council who may be less than open-minded, but when all is said and done, they will toe the Royal line." He almost rubbed his hands together with glee. "You have another question?"

"Yes. What might the things in the shadows be?" She explained that she had caught sight of their shadow forms before during her journeys and that they had followed them far more openly through much of the city. And, unlike other entities she had seen, these needed no human host.

This had caused the doctor to halt in his tracks. He gripped the back of a chair as if to support himself and seemed more than a little ecstatic when he responded. "I vouched safe to you, Captain, before you left on your commission that the witch-sight would show you the true nature of many things. I also told you that because of the ritual I performed and the actions you were to undertake, the very nature of our reality would change. You are helping to bring something great and wonderful into being, and celestial creatures are beginning to manifest upon this Earthly plane as a result. Praise be to God, Captain! The dawn of a new world is at hand, and we shall return mankind to his rightful place in the Garden!" Dee had squeezed Lament's shoulder in proud, almost fatherly fashion for a moment and then had bid her God's good rest and rushed off into the night. Lament was not reassured.

The servants had taken Lament's filthy clothes away last night, and now they bring her fine, new garments, although they are of a female persuasion. After seeing the look in Lament's eyes, they hurry away to find something more to her taste.

The doublet and breeks they return with are a deep midnight blue marked with a faint pattern of tiny black diamonds. The slashed sleeves have a contrasting lining of deep yellow, and the short black cloak has a lining to match. She nods her acceptance, although she rejects the ruff and instead makes them bring her an undershirt with a high collar. The ensemble is topped off with a deep ochre, wide-brimmed hat sporting a cockade of blue and bright yellow feathers. She feels that is enough prettying. She pulls on her boots, which have been dried and cleaned and is just preparing to don her baldric and sword hanger when Dee appears in the doorway.

"Good morrow to you, Captain." He observes the clothes and, with a small sigh, decides not to fight this battle. "You will not be needing your sword. No weapons are allowed in Her Majesty's presence save for those carried by her personal guard." Dee looks her up and down, not necessarily pleased with the change of appearance, but it will be adequate.

Lament cocks an eyebrow and reluctantly places her sword back on the bed. "I feel, sir, as if I am being fattened up for the feast."

The doctor ignores the lack of pleasantries; this is a momentous day, and he will not have it marred by churlishness. "Will you attend me in my study, Captain?" It is not really a question, and he turns and walks away without waiting for a response.

They sit in the high-backed chairs that Dee favours. The low table between them bears a tray of wine and a glass bowl of hazelnuts.

Dr Dee has many questions that he would ask of Lament, but today is not the day for those. He reaches for his wine, and before he can speak, Lament begins with a question of her own. "Doctor, you say that you can't handle the necklace, and yet you intend for me to hand it to the Queen. How is it that she will be immune to whatever force it is that you claim for the thing?"

Dee raises his eyebrows and takes a sip of wine as he observes the woman opposite him. "Her Royal Highness rules by divine right. She is the emissary of God's power on Earth, and therefore, she is not a mere mortal. The jewel will magnify her greatness, and she will become Empress of a new age. It is her destiny to rule over this world and the new world yet to come, and I shall, with your aid, make all this possible!"

A shiver runs down her spine. There are many descriptions of Dee rushing through her mind, but one seems more apt than the others – *fanatic*. Lament looks away to mask her distaste. "This was never written into our contract, sir. My commission was to locate the two objects you desired and to get them back safely to you. Your lackey returned with the map, and I have brought you the necklace. That should be the close of our dealings!" Lament would extract herself from the manipulations of lunatics.

"I say nay, Captain. If you would see your recusant's confession destroyed and be released from my service, then you must complete this act to my satisfaction." The doctor gestures grandly with his glass, spilling wine. "Her Majesty will receive us at Westminster Palace at noon. I persuaded Sir William Cecil that it was in the interests of England that we be granted a private audience. The Queen would often visit me at my library at Mortlake, but given recent attempts upon her life, she is less prone to leave the security of the palace when she is in London. At least *her advisors* are less prone to allow her. For you, an unknown, to be granted a private audience, I needed to persuade certain Privy Council members of the import of the meeting." He sits back in the chair, revelling for a moment in his ability to manipulate those around him.

"I am quite close to Sir William, so once he was convinced, the others gave their agreement. The map that you secured for me has gone a long way towards buying me good favours with him. It has opened trade routes to the East Indies via the Northwest Passage and shown the location of new lands in the southern oceans that were previously unknown. Already, our ships are at sea exploiting this knowledge. Soon, our empire will stretch around the globe!"

Inwardly, Lament sighs. She was correct – *fanatic.*

* * *

Gilded doors stand closed before them. On either side are men armed with pikes who stare stonily straight ahead. The guard captain in polished armour oversees the process of searching Lament. Even Dr Dee must face the indignity of being searched. However, his does seem to be more cursory.

Dr Dee is carrying a pouch containing the necklace, and he explains to the captain that it is a rare gift for Her Majesty and must on no account be handled by anyone but her. Lament had warned him against this as it could be seen as suspicious. Perhaps the necklace is coated with poison? But Dee has already made sure that Sir William Cecil would brief the guard captain, and the pouch remains unmolested.

Now, convinced that the two are not concealing Jesuit assassins about their persons, the guards swing open the ornate portal.

Shafts of sunlight stream through the leaded panes at the far end of the throne room. They are dazzling. Even this weak winter sun can offer surprises, and there, outlined against the windows, is a figure to rival the glory of the sun. She turns towards them. Lament knows that this is all done for effect, but it works, and they sweep off their hats and bow deeply, almost against their will.

For a moment, Lament sees the golden dress studded with

pearls. A collar of lace rises from her shoulders to frame her head, and it glitters with what can only be tiny diamonds. Her white face, the red hair piled up above it in an outrageous display, looks down at them with cool amusement that only comes from a sense of power and maybe a little interest in the fact that the woman before her is dressed as a man and bows instead of curtsies.

Then, unbidden, the witch-sight takes her, and Lament must steady herself so as not to stagger backwards. Unlike the entities that usually present themselves, what she sees makes her gasp. For there, behind, maybe even passing through the Queen, is a single shard of crystal. It is perfect. It glows with a pale silver radiance, and it vibrates so that the air around it seems to pulse outward in waves that make Lament want to cringe away from them.

Whatever it is, it is alive in some alien way that is very wrong. Its total perfection is an abomination that would threaten Lament's sanity, and she asks herself, *Is this what it is to look upon the face of God?* She looks down and closes her eyes, willing herself to stop the witch-sight, but to no avail. This vision cannot be unseen.

Dee glances over at her nervously and, taking the initiative, grips her by the arm and helps her to stand once more. He is aware that something is amiss with Lament, but he chooses to believe that it is tiredness from her journey combined with being overawed by the presence of Her Majesty. He bows again to the Queen as she glides towards them.

"Good doctor, it has been too long since we have had the pleasure of your company. We do miss our visits to your library and our discussions. These assassination attempts are such a bore. One is forced to forgo many of our usual delights." Her voice cuts through the air with all the control of a master swordsman.

"Your Majesty does me great honour." Yet another bow before continuing. "May I present Captain Lament Evyngar to your Royal Highness. This is the Captain whom I dispatched to secure the jewel which we discussed almost twelve months past when you last visited me." He makes a sweeping gesture towards Lament, who is suddenly the centre of unwanted attention.

Lament can still see the perfect crystal form rising, and now, carried forward on one of the pulsing waves, the white face with its red hair rushes towards her. She bows again, as much to delay looking upon that face as through courtesy, and when she straightens, the cold eyes are fully focused upon her.

"Captain, you are most welcome. We have heard something of your exploits. A swordswoman is, after all, something of a novelty in our realm. We trust that your quest upon our behalf went well and was not too arduous?" Crimson-painted lips move, but the words seem to come from the air all around her.

There is a pause while Lament gathers her wits, then. "There were dangers, your Majesty. The Low Countries are awash with the forces of Phillip of Spain." She answers almost by reflex. She does not believe that the Queen has any real interest in her hardships, let alone the thing that inhabits her.

"Indeed Captain. The papists would invade these shores given the chance." The eyes seem to burrow into her.

"Perhaps you could present Her Majesty with the jewel,

Captain? It would be fit to see it in its rightful place." Dee is sweating slightly. He is full of the nervous excitement of a child.

Lament looks down as Dr Dee hands her the pouch, grateful to break eye contact. She opens the drawstring and produces the velvet cloth. It is as if the very universe holds its breath as she opens it. A strange, disquieting sigh comes from the Queen as she gazes upon the jewel that glows with liquid fire in Lament's hands. She reaches out a pale, long-fingered hand from amidst the glowing crystal radiance, and she strokes the jewel with her index finger. A wave of cool yellow light washes through the pulsing silver that surrounds her, and the sigh turns into a moan of pleasure.

"Captain, be so good as to fasten it around our neck." It is not a request, at least not one that can be ignored.

Lament allows the chain to slip through her fingers, being careful not to handle the jewel more than she needs to until she holds the clasp, which she unhooks. The Queen's high lace collar means that she must reach around her neck, placing her hands into that crystal shard. There is a moment when her nerve almost breaks, her face too close to this otherworldly thing that is and is not her monarch. Then it is done, and Elizabeth holds the jewel in both hands, staring at it before lowering it to lie between her alabaster white breasts.

Lament steps back, and as she does so, the pale yellow light of the jewel suffuses the Queen. It mixes with the glow of the crystal like a drop of blood spreads through water, and then a beam of light shoots up from her. It is as if the roof of the palace does not exist, and the beam blasts a hole in the billowing clouds.

Light spreads outwards like some enormous thunderstorm and races off into infinity.

Dee gazes on in rapture. He does not see what Lament sees. To his eyes, Her Royal Highness places the jewel upon her chest, and the rays of the sun illuminate her, making the jewel flare with majestic radiance.

He sees the future, the plans he has schemed to bring about, not for himself but for the Empire. For the good of all men, and his Queen will reign over it, and God's Kingdom will return to this corrupted Earth.

"We are pleased, Dr Dee. It is everything that you promised it would be. We must gather the council together and make a beginning upon this *Great Work*." The Queen's eyes glow with the reflected light from the jewel, and for just an instant, the doctor knows fear. But he forces it away. After all, is this not what he has dreamed of?

He takes Lament's arm and backs away down the length of the throne room, bowing as he goes. There seems to be something wrong with the Captain; her limbs are stiff, and she still stares as if moonstruck at Her Royal Highness. But that matters little, and they are quickly through the gilded doors, which swing shut on the view of the Queen staring raptly at the blazing jewel.

Ushering the captain away, he mutters excitedly to himself. "It is done, it is done. Now the work can begin!"

Lament stumbles forward as if waking from a dream, nay, a nightmare. *What has she done? What has she become part of?* A premonition of a doom greater than that of just one woman washes over her. She feels a tugging at the edges of her mind and would be away from this madman who leads her through the palace, babbling of things Lament does not understand.

A voice echoes in her befuddled brain. An ancient voice that calls to her from dark places with a strange urgency, as if there is more at stake than meets the eye. One phrase repeats itself, one phrase she has heard before, *"It is not meant for her!"*

# Chapter 28

Sleep does not come easily, and when it does, it is full of visions of a monstrous creature that strides across the Earth, bringing sorrow in its wake. It is the sun and moon. It is life and death. It is the beginning and the end.

She awakes, the sheet cast onto the floor, but she is wet with sweat. Her eyes leap to the window that looks out over rooftops, searching for the shadows that flit suddenly out of view. The shadows of creatures from another realm of existence cast somehow into our world, and she believes that they watch the acts of feeble, greedy, savage mankind, and they pity them even as they spin their webs to snare them all.

It has been almost a week since the audience with the Queen, although Lament has lost count of the days. She excused himself from Dr Dee's company as soon as she had secured the confessions that had forced her on this damnable enterprise. She had perhaps expected some complaint from the doctor who had expressed the wish to question her about her otherworldly experiences in retrieving the map and necklace and, more importantly, the effects of the marks upon her skin. But Dee had waived her away with a heavy purse of coin, saying that there would be time for reminiscing once he had worked with the Queen and her Privy Council on the first stage of the Great Work.

Lament had departed with no small sense of relief, burning the confessions in a brazier by the exit to the underground passages. Then she had boarded a wherry at Bridewell and crossed downriver to Bankside, and there attempted to lose herself in the stews of Southwark.

Almost a week of drinking, gambling, brawling, and doxies. Still, she can find no peace because something eats at her, something that tells her with an awful certainty that handing the jewel to that woman will result in untold misery and death for millions for centuries to come. So, now she sits on the edge of her bed in a Southwark garret, wrapped in a damp sheet, and full of the cold realisation that she must either retrieve the jewel or kill the woman who now wears it. Perhaps both.

She holds her head in her hands, and then, suddenly, she is laughing. What mad cause must she now champion? Whatever, it will like as not be her last.

* * *

To gain access to the Queen is no mean feat. She no longer travels as openly as she once did, not since papist assassins made attempts upon her life as she rode through the city. Missed pistol shots on both occasions. No, it will need to be done at a palace, and at this moment, she resides in Richmond, the palace built by her grandfather. It will need to be done quickly before she moves her vast retinue to some lucky lord's house for the Yuletide festivities, which will remove her for at least two months.

The thought does come to her that perhaps she should enlist the help of one of the many Catholic cells seeking to end the Queen's life. She muses upon this as she walks through Paris Garden towards the Globe Theatre and the bear pit beyond. By the time she has purchased a pasty from a woman carrying a basket of them balanced on her hip and eaten it as she walks on towards London Bridge, she has discarded that notion. The Jesuits who run the cells and support the overthrow of what they describe as that heretic whore Elizabeth are fervent in their cause but have always seemed to Lament a little incompetent. From what she understands, hired assassins made the last two attempts, ex-military men from the war in the Low Countries and Ireland, and yet they still failed dismally.

Could it perchance be that whatever possesses the Queen has some ability to see the future, or perhaps the intent of those around her, maybe even the ability to deflect danger? Or mayhap she is indeed divine and protected by God himself.

No, Lament decides, just as she passes beneath the rotting heads on the spikes above the south gate, that she must act alone and that it must be done with no thought of escape. Only full commitment to the deed will give her a chance of success.

And what of the shadow things that seem to watch her? Will they warn the Queen or directly try to prevent the act? For some reason she can't define, Lament has the feeling that these *celestial beings*, as Dee calls them, are not entirely what the good doctor imagines them to be. But whatever their purpose, she will have to take her chances with them.

* * *

Lost in thought, she almost misses the two men who detach themselves from the crowd and follow her. Almost...

How long have they followed her? She suspects that they have been there since she left her lodgings, and she is correct. The men were indeed waiting as she left her rooms, and if she had not been so distracted and hungover, she would have spotted them sooner. She may even have noticed the third man who went ahead in some haste.

But no matter, she has seen them now, and they look familiar. As she weaves through the crowds of traders, shoppers and the usual mix of cutpurses and other villains looking for a mark, she contrives to glance at them. Yes, they are two of the hired swords that Master Garrat had brought with him when they met on the road. Has Dr Dee once again tasked Garrat with keeping an eye on Lament?

She passes a cloth merchant. Bolts of fabric of many hues are stacked in the racks behind the garrulous-looking shopkeeper. Soon, Lament will be at the warehouse that Thomas, their would-be business partner, had owned. Ah, it seems like another lifetime since she had dispatched Thomas' murderers and then been arrested for her trouble. Perhaps it would be apt to confront her followers in the yard of the warehouse? But the option is taken from her as a grinning Garrat approaches from the doorway of an alehouse, the third man trailing behind him.

"Oh, Captain, you do look the worse for wear. Come and stroll with me a while." Garrat turns, and Lament feels the other two men close in behind her.

"As we appear to be travelling in the same direction, I will accompany you for the moment."

Garrat gives a short, harsh laugh. "You never cease to amaze me, Captain. You seem capable of cheating fate no matter what hand you are dealt."

"What is it that you want, Master Garrat? Has the doctor sent you to keep a watch on me? I would have thought him more than capable of doing that with his magics as we are in the same city."

A sneer curls the younger man's lips. "You are correct; he did charge me with keeping you under watch. It seems that he is now too busy with the Queen and his *Great Work* to bother using his sorcery to keep watch upon you himself. It would appear you have played your part and are no longer of any great import." Garrat's eyes narrow into ugly slits. "He has returned me to menial tasks since your arrival. He promises much but is fickle with his favours once he has the things that he needs. My choice of an escort for you was not to his liking, and perhaps he was correct. I had planned to take the jewel from you and return with it myself to secure his patronage once and for all. You would, of course, have met with an unfortunate accident, perhaps died of wounds received upon your journey... But it seems he had some precognition of those events." He spits, maybe to shed himself of the very memory of his failed scheme.

Lament notes that Garrat's clothes seem somewhat less fine than when they had met on the road. In the daylight, she can see that they are threadbare in areas and none too clean. "So, where are we *strolling* to sirrah? Does the doctor require to see me?"

Lament feels the two men behind them move in, still closer, while the one now in front clears a path for them.

"No, the doctor is in meetings with the Privy Council. It is I who wanted to see you. I spent all my money to hire these gentlemen." He gestures to the hirelings. "And I require compensation for beggaring myself. I have promised them a share of what you have returned with!"

Lament sees the truth of it. Garrat has all along plotted to make himself foremost amongst Dee's men. He sees himself as more than his actual worth, believing himself entitled to status and riches. He also believes that Lament has brought back other valuables that he can use to secure his position.

"You are a moonstruck fool! I barely made it back with the necklace for your master, and that has now gone to the Queen. I have a purse of coin that Dee gave to me, but that is all."

They have reached an alleyway between the buildings that line the bridge sides. This space leads to the parapet overlooking a waterwheel that spins in the racing current below. The noise of the river is loud here; it is dark, and there are no onlookers in evidence. "Oh, do not be shy, Captain; it does not become you." Garrat turns and leans against the parapet while his hired men range around their intended prey. "I overheard Dr Dee during one of his scrying sessions when he converses with his spirits. He oftentimes talks out loud to himself. He said that you had obtained something that you always carried with you, something priceless that defied death itself. I know he intends to wrest it from you when time allows, but I would have it. I will find a rich buyer, maybe even a King over the sea, and it will lift me up and out of his service. It will make me a prince!" A lunatic light shines in his eyes, and Lament knows that there will be no reasoning with him and the men to whom he has obviously promised great riches.

The sole of Lament's boot connects with Garrat's breastbone and sends him over the parapet. For a moment, the long-fingered hands try to grip the stone as a look of desperate horror replaces the look of avarice. Then he is tumbling through space, a long, terrible wail escaping his lips, to smash upon the remorseless waterwheel. The shattered body is sucked under and swept away in the rushing waters of the Thames. There is a moment of utter shock amongst the three henchmen, but only a moment. They are, after all, professionals. But it is a heartbeat that Lament can use to her advantage, and she does.

The black-hilted sword clears the scabbard and pierces the first man as he attempts to draw his blade. The dagger, which is suddenly in Lament's left hand, stabs low, finding the second man's thigh. Bright blood sprays across the cobblestones as she steps diagonally right, ripping the dagger clear and leaving a massive wound. She pivots, sweeping back the sword and catches the third man's lunging thrust.

This one is not unskilled and uses the folds of his short cloak to turn aside the riposte. He slashes to gain some space and then steps forward again, his blade darting back and forth. Lament lets the attack continue, circling away to her left. She moves fluidly; it is what she has trained half her life to do. She slips past a thrust at her face and feints with the dagger. Her assailant throws himself sideways, rapier slashing down at an angle, and Lament rises onto the balls of her feet and places the tip of her sword against the man's throat. Perfect precision. The blade slips through unresisting flesh, and the man gurgles and dies. It is over in moments.

Lament surveys the scene. The first man is drowning in his blood, his lung punctured. The second is bleeding out against the parapet. He is very grey and trying futilely to hold his gaping thigh together. The third lies face down and, save a few twitches, is already dead.

As Lament wipes her blades clean on the man's cloak, she glances towards the street. The shape of another man detaches itself from the shadows cast by the overhangs that almost meet above the alleyway. She moves back a step onto clearer ground, and as she does so, this newcomer advances towards her, wheel-lock pistol pointed at her and drawn sword in his left hand. Captain Bowcer smiles a savage, predatory smile. "Ah, you are good Captain Evyngar. Your reputation with a blade is most justified based upon that little demonstration."

"Captain Bowcer, I was wondering when you would make an appearance. Do you not care to test your skill?" That ghastly maypole of floating grey ribbons, like flesh flayed from a victim of the Inquisition, drifts around the elongated form. Lament forces the witch-sight away and gauges the distance between them. She will never reach Bowcer before the pistol discharges, and at this range, it would be difficult to miss.

"I think not, you whore bitch. I have some skill in swordplay, but I fear not to the degree that you exhibit. I am, on the other hand, a very fine shot."

"Pray, before you dispatch me, tell me why you aligned yourself with Master Garrat. It would seem an odd coincidence that we meet under these circumstances." Lament does not rise to the insult; all she can do is play for time and maybe cause Bowcer to make an error.

"It's a happy coincidence, at least for me. I realised that my fortune did not lie with the Company of Sir Humphrey and its adventure in the Low Countries, and so I excused myself and made my way back here. Master Garrat, God rest his soul, was one of a number of commissions that I undertook for a reasonable purse. But when I discovered that this latest one was to be you, dear Captain, I was overjoyed at the chance to see you brought low and make redress for my honour." The pistol does not waver.

"Is this then about the slight that you perceive was made upon you at our last encounter? I must say that you have very little else to consume your time if it has preyed so heavily upon your mind. I would suggest that you venture out more often. I am sure that there are plenty of others who would be only too willing to make mockery of you!"

Bowcer snarls, "I may just wound you bitch and have my way with you before you die. But if not, then goodbye, Captain." But before he can pull the trigger, a shadow drops from above him, obscuring him from view. Lament throws herself to one side, and the pistol shot goes wide, flying out across the river. As she rolls back to her feet, Lament sees the strange, winged shadow dissipate back amongst the true shadows of the alleyway. There is a panicked look upon Bowcer's not unhandsome face as he stares about himself wildly for whatever it was that had caused the night to descend upon him so suddenly. And then he sees Lament, and his guts are gripped with a more immediate fear.

He throws the pistol, which Lament dodges, and swaps his

sword to his right hand. He, like the other men, carries a rapier, a more civilised weapon for London society, and he makes a passable lunge with it as Lament recovers from the dodge. Lament parries and thrusts low, but Bowcer dances back and avoids the blade entering his groin. He twists sideways and thrusts high. Once again, his blade is parried, but this time, he attempts to slide the blade along Lament's and turn it towards her throat, but Lament's sword pushes the lighter blade away.

For a moment, there is a space between them, a silence broken only by panting breath. Bowcer changes to a hanging guard, sword point down. He can see Lament's feet are almost in the spreading pool of blood from the hired sword who received the throat wound. If he can drive Lament onto it and cause her to slip... He drops low, lunging fast with his left hand on the ground, sword aiming at her gut. But Lament is not there. Dancing swiftly to her left, she comes down from a high ward and makes a horizontal backhand cut that removes part of the top of Bowcer's head. It is one of the benefits of her heavier sword that it will cut formidably. A strange, uncomprehending look comes into Bowcer's eyes, and he crumples to the cobbles still stretched out in his lunge.

It is done, and there are no gawkers, no witnesses to raise the alarm, at least none who would be seen. After all, what deeds men perform in the shadows are their business, and sometimes, it would seem those shadows come to life.

Without a backward glance, she leaves the alley with its sound of deafening water and copper stink of blood. *Farewell, Master Garrat*, she thinks, *you were never the brightest of fellows.*

* * *

Early afternoon and Lament has composed a letter to her father and dispatched it with a messenger. She has had no contact with her family for many years, but she feels she must warn them of what is to come. For she has saved them from the charges of recusancy but will now cause them to possibly be implicated by association with regicide.

She warns them to flee north where there are still lords who are staunch Catholics who will shelter them. Maybe even to her mother's family in Northumberland.

Ah, the wayward daughter, always the bringer of glad tidings…

# Chapter 29

A heavy blanket of clouds hides the moon and makes the night darker still. It reminds Lament of a night not so long past when they had used the pitch dark to gain entry into a square tower in Haarlem. She deeply feels the absence of Pieter, and even though she knows that the big Dutchman would have followed her in this madness without hesitation, she is glad that maybe he will get a chance at some other life and not die here for something that he could never truly understand. Lament puts those thoughts out of her head and concentrates on moving silently between the topiary hedges of the palace gardens.

She wears once again her favoured clothing, a little faded but cleaned and mended by Dee's servants. The blackness of it serves her well in the darkness, as does the well-used softness of the material that does not rustle in the way that fine, decorous cloth would. Her only concession to new attire is the broad-brimmed black hat that replaces the one she lost when shipwrecked. The black-hilted sword is in her gloved hand, and a short, powerful crossbow hangs across her side. She has made the decision not to use her pistols until the need is dire. Silence must be her greatest ally for now.

Dropping into a crouch, she watches a guard armed with a halberd patrol along the edge of the flower beds. They are devoid of greenery in this season, and the guard, although watchful, seems more intent on keeping himself warm. Lament has some sympathy with that, having added a padded jerkin as an extra layer beneath her well-used arming doublet.

The guard's breath shows in a cloud of white as he passes one of the torches that line the paths. He reaches the corner of a decorative wall and turns left, disappearing from view. Lament moves quickly. She runs to the corner of an ornate building and is at once struck by a strong animal stench. Gilded bars line an open section of the wall she presses herself against, and from the edge of her vision, she sees a shape beyond the bars moving along with her. She raises the sword to thrust, but the eyes she sees glowing in the darkness are not human. A low growl comes from the dark, and she lowers her blade. This is one of Her Majesty's pets. She has become, like so many of her fellow monarchs, something of a collector of exotic beasts. Lament moves quickly on, and the leopard goes back to its pacing.

Beyond the menagerie, a broad avenue leads to a terrace at the palace's edge. Two guards are stationed, one on either side, at the top of the stone steps which lead up to it. There are torches set all along the balustrade of the terrace, and there will be no shadows to hide in.

For a moment, Lament considers the idea of releasing the leopard from its cage. But she does not. She knows that the beast is far more likely to savage her or just run off into the gardens than to attack the guards. Even as a distraction, it would result in the alarm being raised and armed men converging upon her location. Pieter would have enjoyed the irony.

It is often chance combined with basic human needs that can shift the balance, and in this case, it is no different.

As Lament watches, one of the guards turns and says something to his comrade. The other man laughs, and the first guard heads into the bushes around the side of the terrace. He is going to relieve himself and needs to be out of view of the palace windows. He would find himself on the end of a whipping or worse if Her Highness observed him.

Lament wastes no time. She swings the crossbow around in front of her. It is already cocked, and she just needs to nock a quarrel onto the thick string. She takes a dozen fast strides from the shelter of the menagerie and drops to one knee before the remaining guard is aware that something is moving in the garden beyond the torchlight. The crossbow is already raised, and she breathes out, calming herself and pulls the trigger. The quarrel is as thick as her index finger, and the bow is very powerful over short range. The guard cranes his head forward to see better, opening his mouth to alert his pissing companion, and the heavy four-sided bolt punches through his face between nose and eye.

He is dead before his body sags over the balustrade. His halberd leans for a moment against the carved stone before it tilts to one side and begins a leisurely slide that will make enough noise when it lands to alert the other guard. So, Lament begins to sprint, swinging the crossbow back behind her.

The halberd clatters to the stone slabs that floor the terrace. There is an exclamation from the bushes, and the absent guard appears, lacing the front of his breeks. He is met by Lament at full tilt, who clamps a hand over the man's mouth to stifle any cries for help, and they barrel backwards into the bushes. Her dagger seeks an armpit, but the guard grabs at her and the point slides across the breastplate and misses.

This guard is a wrestler; he has won prizes at county fairs, and he is strong. Lament finds her wrist pinned under the guard's arm, and the man tries to sink his teeth into the hand covering his mouth while his right fist batters at his attacker's head. Using her momentum, Lament continues to push the guard backwards, but powerful legs dig in, and the man seeks to grab his attacker and throw them. As his hands reach for a better hold, there is a moment when Lament's wrist has the freedom to move, and in that instant, the blade slices up as it is withdrawn, severing through the biceps and artery.

The guard's eyes go wide. He knows he is dead, but he would take his attacker with him or at least sound the alarm so others can exact vengeance for him. Lament forces her gloved hand further into the guard's mouth and, with a savage ferocity, thrusts the dagger again and again into the unprotected groin. A sob escapes from around the glove, and the eyes glaze. There will be no posthumous glory for this guard.

Kneeling on the body, Lament tries to regain her breath while listening for the sound of other guards approaching. For the moment, all is quiet save for the pounding of blood in her ears.

* * *

Inside the palace, it is silent. She makes her way through empty corridors as she searches for the Queen's chambers. She quickly realises that there are too many rooms for her to search at random. And then, berating herself for being a fool, she remembers the witch-sight and how it led her to the necklace once before.

Closing her eyes and slowing her breathing, she lets her mind slip once again into that waking trance state. Opening her eyes, there is a vague shimmer to the surrounding dark, and there, over to her right, is the blue glow that reveals objects of power. It is several rooms away, but now she knows where to look, for she senses that now she has it, the Queen will not easily be parted from the jewel.

Another glowing shape moves behind the jewel, darker and larger. This, she surmises, must be the Queen or whatever it is that possesses her – if indeed she is possessed. Lament suspects that, just like El Arlequín, she is something else entirely.

The glow leads her to the throne room by way of an inconspicuous side door. There are no guards. In fact, she has not laid eyes upon a single guard since entering the palace. That doesn't *feel* right, but she is now committed come what may.

Slipping soundlessly along the length of the throne room, she follows the glow which seems to be coming from a room at the far end. A tapestry of some Arthurian scene and lions rampant conceals a door. She halts, and using a cocking rope, she re cocks the crossbow and fits another quarrel. She knows that speed will be her best advantage, and although she has not imagined surviving this endeavour, the lack of guards gives her faint hope.

Lament reaches out and touches the gilded door handle, giving it an exploratory twist. Her breath stops; it is not locked. She stares at the wall and door in front of her, her witch-sight showing her the position in the room of the jewel and its dark wearer. Nightmares from her childhood rise in her unbidden, and for the first time in many years, she crosses herself unconsciously. She almost laughs at her sudden thought that she is a heretic - she is way beyond that now. The thick door opens silently on well-greased hinges, although the sounds that greet her would drown out any creaks. She enters the Queen's chamber and a scene of pure insanity.

The Queen lounges upon a fur-strewn couch. She is naked save for a diaphanous robe of gold that falls away on either side, doing nothing to hide her. Before her are naked men and women, courtiers perhaps, and they are writhing on the rug-covered floor in delirious orgy, though they do not look as if it is pleasurable. Their faces are fixed masks, teeth bared, and the noises they make are more the sounds of pain and terror. They remind Lament of the nest of adders that she saw as a child, twisting and coiling in some desperate dance. The blazing crystal shard that is alive with its own otherworldly intelligence rises through and around the Queen, throbbing with malevolence at the scene before it. The jewel that sits between her naked breasts seems to have become part of her, and the liquid yellow light it emits seeps into her skin and her veins are flushed with it.

Lament sees all of this in an instant, but it is an instant too long. She begins to raise the crossbow as the Queen's eyes lock with hers, and she knows she has missed her chance. Perhaps she never truly had one...

She is suddenly there before Lament, seemingly without having moved. The transparent golden robe floats around her for a moment as if caught in the breeze of a rapid motion before settling once again. Her bone white face is inches from Lament's, and those lips that are too crimson part in a strange rapacious smile revealing pointed teeth. Red hair that is still piled high weaves itself around her head as if she were Medusa, and that totally alien geometric crystal form that suffuses her has moved with her, singing its disturbing pulsating song.

The crossbow points at the Queen's heart, but Lament cannot fire it. A pale hand that is unnaturally strong grips hers, and it is as if she has been plunged into a snow drift. A freezing numbness spreads through her, a paralysis of her body and mind, and she loses the ability to act. Still, the lips smile as the crossbow is drawn away from her. The cord it is slung from disintegrates as if it suddenly becomes ancient, rotting away, and the weapon is discarded. Those pale eyes search Lament's face.

"What are you?" The Queen's voice is a whisper that insinuates its way into Lament's mind.

"What am *I*!" Lament doesn't understand the question, coming as it does from a creature obviously not of this sphere.

The pale, slender hands grip her shoulders and spin her around, propelling her forward between the writhing bodies on the floor. There, standing on a raised area against the wall, is a tall shape draped in a sumptuous cloth of deep violet velvet trimmed with gold cord. The Queen halts Lament before it and steps to one side so that she can take hold of the cloth. As she begins to pull it from the object it hides, Lament is filled with a nameless dread that rises within her, and at that moment, she would rather be anywhere else but here. But, even though she squeezes her eyes shut, it is too late, much too late...

"Open your eyes, swordswoman!" It is a command, whispered,

but a command nonetheless, and Lament can do nothing but obey.

Before her is a full-length mirror set in a frame of dark wood carved in a way that makes it appear to be naturally growing from the floor itself. All this she registers in an instant before her eyes are drawn inexorably to the reflection in the glass. She convulses, her hands flying to her mouth, perhaps in an attempt to muffle the groan of despair that escapes from her.

This is the first time that Lament has seen herself through her witch-sight, the first time that she has seen what she has become, and she feels her mind attempt to crawl away and hide in some dark corner.

In the mirror, the air around her is a glowing net that is the twin of her body markings, as if they have expanded from her flesh to take on their own physical presence in the air. Within that net is the shape of a human figure so dark that it seems to pull all light into its form. It is like staring into the void. And there, somehow overlaid but separate, is the form of a gigantic naked creature, to all intents human but with a body that is both male and female and is dotted about with glowing eyes that never blink. From behind, it spreads vast wings that wrap around the light-sucking silhouette and its gleaming web of arcane designs.

"You did not know…" The Queen's voice contains unexpected pity. "This has been with you for many years, mayhap not in this shape, but I would guess since your first kill. That was when you opened the door and let the *other* in."

Lament is numb; small sobs escape from her. She is more lost than she ever imagined. She is no better than the things she has learned to despise since she first caught sight of them. The Queen mercifully covers the mirror and, placing an arm across Lament's shoulders, turns her away again.

In the periphery of her vision, Lament can see the naked figures on the floor around her, but now they appear to be gasping for life, withering, dying as she watches. A thin grey vapour leaves them and is sucked into the crystal form. The Queen is feeding, and the realisation causes her to finally jerk away in revulsion.

Lament would reach for her sword if only her limbs would obey her commands, but alas, guards are coming from the throne room behind her, somehow summoned by this thing that is Elizabeth. The struggle is brief, and she is rapidly overwhelmed. Arms pinned, she takes blows to the head, and she can feel her consciousness slipping away. As it does, the witch-sight goes with it, and her last sight is of Her Royal Highness, a woman like any other mortal woman, in a golden dress, while around her courtiers dance and musicians play.

*What fresh madness is this?* Lament surrenders to the dark.

# Chapter 30

Dr Dee slumps in his high-backed chair. The candle flames gutter in some source-less breeze, sending freakish shadows dancing around the study. He takes a drink of his wine and wipes a hand across his troubled brow. On his lap is the confession of Captain Lament Evyngar, carried from her cell in the Tower after hearing it from her lips. Reread with agitated haste, and now almost at an end.

Dee steels himself; what he has read troubles him deeply. It is heretical treason, and he is implicated. If it were not for the Queen's new faith in him and his plans for a British Empire, then he may well be sharing a cell with the unfortunate Captain.

Clearly, the magics that have been at play have unhinged the poor woman. At least that is the tale that Dee will tell the Privy Council, although it will be the adventure itself that has produced the madness in her weak female brain – no need to mention the occult, at least his part in it. He replaces his glass on the side table and turns to the remaining pages.

* * *

"You know the rest of my sorry tale. I awake in the Tower where I have resided for these past... eighteen months? Put to the hard press by Master Topham, I have been under duress to implicate others in my plan to kill the Queen. But there are none to be drawn into my fate. I understand that my family, who are wholly innocent of this deed, have fled to Ireland and are safe from the clutches of the Privy Council. I acted alone and for the good of mankind. I can't even say that I acted in the service of God as I no longer know what that means given the things I have seen."

"This began with your desire for an empire that spans the globe, Dr Dee, your summoning of angels, or whatever they may be, and your fervent hope to hear the sounding of the trumpets of Revelation. But through your sorcery, I have witnessed the truth of what lies beyond the ken of human understanding, and I warn you, sir, that this road that you take will not bring God's Kingdom back to Earth. It will not bring a return to man's state before the Fall. It can only usher in a future that will crush all who cannot or will not bow before it."

"The shadows that have followed me from the day of your ritual have a form, a form that is not that of the creatures of order and chaos that I have witnessed wearing men as costumes, and neither is it that of your *Angels* that gifted me with these markings and this witch-sight. They are something altogether *different*, something that has indirectly aided me all along but have not the power in this world to influence events themselves. They have spoken to me. Since my incarceration, they have visited me and told me of things to come, some of which I have already seen, things which I have inadvertently caused to be by my successful completion of your commission. I am *responsible*, Dr

Dee, as responsible as you for what is to come to pass. And now I await my fate. Those leaps to distant times and places appear to have ceased, even when they would have been most convenient! And, if I ever had any power to summon or control them, then that, along with my good fortune, seems to have fled."

"The vaguely remembered words of a song I heard in a place separated from here by thousands of miles and hundreds of years come back to me as I write this. They seem apt..."

*"Thus, I will wait in this place, where the sun doth never shine.*
*Wait in this place, where the shadows they run from themselves."*

* * *

Dr Dee stares at these last words, a strange emotion that he can't describe filling him. He knows that he can never show this document to anyone else for fear that it will bring him and his plans down. No, this must be hidden away. He can't bring himself to destroy it - not yet, and he had the Queen's express permission to gather this confession, so he needs only to answer to her. So, he will hide it away...

* * *

He has not slept well. The things he has read continue to trouble him, and perhaps there is more than a touch of guilt at what will become of the Captain. Despite her rank and service, she will be burnt at the stake because she is a woman. Although he doesn't see the option of being drawn and quartered as a mercy, it may at least be quicker... perhaps. He shakes his head as a servant helps him to dress in his usual black robes. His reflection in the mirror, dark rings under his eyes, looks even more crow-like than usual.

Damn the Captain! She has brought this upon herself. If only she could have seen the Great Work for what it truly is, the dawn of Revelation and the chance to start again. If only she had not been touched with madness and made an attempt upon the Queen. Almost anything else might have been forgiven.

They will be placing her in the cart shortly for the journey to the scaffold, and as Dee leaves Somerset House to witness the final act, he remembers Lament's parting words to him.

"We will meet again before the end, Dr Dee."

"No, Captain. You are to be executed on the morrow, and although I will be present, we will not meet."

"I do not mean *this* end, doctor..."

A shudder passes through him, and he pulls his robes about him more tightly as he descends the steps to the waiting wherry and the morning mist that rises from the river like the ghosts of failed dreams.

# Epilogue

Smithfield is crowded. It seems as if all of London is here. But then folks do enjoy an execution, especially the execution of a heretic who has attempted to murder the Queen.

As usual, the pyre has been erected in the centre of the marketplace, and the almost festive mood changes to one of righteous fury as the cart carrying the condemned draws near. A fat, red-faced cooper curses and shuffles in his position as he tries to see around the human mountain that has chosen to stand in front of him. He loudly grumbles to no one in particular and then indignantly pulls at the giant's sleeve.

A broad, scarred face turns towards him, half hidden by a bristling red beard. A bushy red eyebrow arches questioningly, and the cooper suddenly has other places to be.

Pieter watches as the cart moves slowly towards the stacked cords of kindling. Soldiers keep the rabble at bay, but they still manage to throw rotten food and the odd cobble at the figure tied there.

It had only been when the siege of Haarlem had at last broken that he had received news of other events. The attempt upon the life of Elizabeth, By the Grace of God, Queen of England, France and Ireland, Defender of the Faith, by one Captain Lament Evyngar had featured prominently in that news delivered by English merchants.

The siege had been hard, but he and Sophia had survived to see the Dons and their Dutch allies slink away, defeated by disease and further troubles in other provinces. They had celebrated as best they could in a city starved and on its knees, but upon hearing the news about Lament and the impending execution, he had shipped a now pregnant Sophia off north to his family and had vowed to do what he could to aid his friend.

So now he stands and looks on with sorrow as his oldest friend and comrade is dragged to a savage death. He knows that he can't rescue Lament; the odds are beyond even his abilities and optimism. But, with the pistols hidden beneath his cloak, he can give the Captain a merciful end before the flames scorch her.

The cart stops at the foot of the scaffold, and two soldiers drag Lament from it. She is a sad, broken sight in her dirty white shift. She looks in some pain, and Pieter can only guess that they have been less than kind to her. The soldiers partially carry her up the steps, and at the top, she is turned to face the baying mob.

A worthy of some sort steps beside Lament and begins to read aloud the charges and sentence. Pieter does not listen. He has seen on the raised seating area off to the left a figure he recognises. There amongst the members of the Privy Council and well-to-do is a lean figure robed in black, with a long tapering face and beard. *It is a good thing I brought two pistols,* he thinks.

The reading of the sentence comes to an end, and Pieter looks back at Lament. Their eyes meet. Pieter is not the sort of man who can hide easily in a crowd, especially wearing his feathered barett. Lament smiles, the first real smile in a long time, and the great bear of a man smiles back, although it breaks his heart. Lament frowns then. It is as if she can read Pieter's thoughts, and she shakes her head slowly from side to side, mouthing one word, "*No*".

They strip her of the ragged shift she is wearing, and instead of the usual crude and mocking shouts, the crowd grow silent at the sight of the markings on her body that seem in some way to move slightly, unnaturally. There is a hushed whisper, and many ask for protection from Jesus against the woman who is so obviously a witch. She is pushed back to the post that will hold her in place, and a rope is tied around her neck as her hands are pulled behind her. Pieter looks at her pleadingly, but again, Lament mouths, "*No*".

As they begin to stack the cords of wood around her, Pieter reaches for a pistol, determined to do one last thing for his Captain, but the executioners in their black hoods move in front of her and obscure his shot. A blazing torch is passed up to them from a brazier at the foot of the steps, and it is touched to the kindling with almost a flourish.

As the men step away from her, lighting the farther edges of the pyre as they go, it can be seen that they have not even given her the mercy of a small bag of gunpowder tied around her neck. They want this to be a spectacle. There have been burnings where the victim took half an hour or more to die – this cannot be allowed.

Pieter raises his pistol as the flames begin to touch Lament's flesh. The crowd are oblivious to the actions of the giant in their midst; they are focused solely on the impending torment. But as Pieter takes aim, the space around Lament fills with swirling shadows that drive her executioners further back. A pulsing in the very air itself makes the area surrounding Lament bulge and distort as if she is seen through a glass lens. The markings on her body begin to glow, brighter even than the flames that would scorch her, and her racked, emaciated form returns suddenly to its youthful state.

All around her, the air is torn asunder, and through this rip in space, the silent crowd sees what lies beyond. Giant, obscenely malformed figures stride across desolate wastelands of boiling glass. Cities rise and fall like the waves of the ocean, each one more elaborate than the last. A vast, tentacled thing embraces the Earth with its love, a love that is terrible like the coldness between the stars and will grind all it touches to dust.

There is a collective gasp from the mob that quickly becomes hysterical shouts, and Lament spreads her arms wide, snapping the bonds. A winged form grows behind her, casting its shadow across the marketplace and the panicking throng, and then everything around her shimmers and Captain Lament Evyngar, along with the shadows and visions of lunacy and hell, disappears, leaving no trace.

There is uproar. The crowd stampedes as women and some men faint away to be crushed by the trampling feet. They cry out for God's mercy, and still others rave like lunatics. On the raised platform, among the confusion, Dr Dee sits, his mouth open and eyes wide. As the others flee, he tries to regain his composure, attempting to make sense of what he has witnessed before joining the other dignitaries in leaving. Partway down the steps, he spots the red-bearded giant in the crowd who looks at him without blinking, pistol still held in a massive fist, and the doctor pushes past his peers into the safety of the soldiers who will escort the dignitaries away, a cold sweat on the back of his neck.

Pieter stands still as a statue in the sea of panic around him as the crowd surges away from the blazing pyre. A grin splits that thicket of a beard, and he feels his spirit lift. He closes the pan on the pistol and hides it once more, then, turning away, he strides after the fleeing mob and heads towards the docks and a ship that will take him home.

# Coda

The people on foot move out of the way of the group of riders heading towards the bridge. They are a strange band in their finery and ornate armour, and some on the road whisper that they are *The Spanish*.

On a huge prancing grey sits the one they call *El Arlequín*. Phillip II of Spain is dead, and his son Phillip III has inherited an empire beggared through constant warfare and the seemingly unstoppable rise of this new upstart empire of Elizabeth. He loses sleep over the success of English ships and English armies and seeks a treaty. El Arlequín has been sent as an envoy to broker peace and obtain whatever concessions he can.

As they pass beneath the south gate, El Arlequín looks up at the heads of traitors that decorate its spikes. He reins in his mount and stares, hand pushing back the brim of his hat. To him, the severed heads are not just rotting pieces of meat. He sees the ghosts of soulless eyes rolling in now empty sockets and hears the lipless mouths howling in damnation and whispering secrets that only the dead can tell. He ignores the shadows that watch from the high frontages that line the bridge. After all, they aren't his problem.

He squeezes, and his horse begins to move again. Smiling to himself, the harbinger of chaos, the physical manifestation of a fate-doomed union, the son of Captain Lament Evyngar laughs. "I think that I will like it here."

THE END

Andy is a lifelong fantasy/sword & sorcery/weird tales fan and also has a bit of an obsession with historical fiction. He started writing around ten years ago as an experiment in having the discipline to write something every day during a period when he was travelling extensively for work. He wrote on a phone and iPad during train journeys, flights, backstage at events, 2 am in hotel rooms, and even during stops at motorway service stations. The result was his first novel, the darkly funny ME AND THE MONKEY: CHRONICLES OF THE MONKEY GOD VOL 1. He has since written VOL 2 and a novella, THE PADDINGTON INCIDENT. He has studied shamanism and the Western occult tradition and trained in and taught martial arts. When he is not pouring thoughts onto paper he creates motion graphics. He lives in Cornwall in the UK.